What readers are saying about the PJ Sugar series

"Warren does it again with an excellent blend of humor, romance, [and] mystery. . . ."
—*Romantic Times*, Top Pick

"With an enchanting heroine, witty dialogue, and a puzzling mystery, *Nothing but Trouble* is a satisfying start to the PJ Sugar series."
—Rel Mollet at Titletrakk.com

"I had the pleasure of reading this gem, and PJ is a kick. I think a lot of us out there could relate to her more than we want to admit."
—Julie at The Surrendered Scribe

"If you like fiction that is fun, stories that are full of mystery, and characters that remind you of yourself, you'll LOVE this book."
—Heather at Mumblings of a Mommy Monk

"PJ is such an interesting character, and I guarantee you will see yourself just a little bit in PJ."
—Amy at Amy's Random Thoughts

"The characters were fantastic, fully developed, and authentic. . . . I'm already looking forward to the next book in this series."
—Tanya at In the Dailies

a PJ Sugar novel

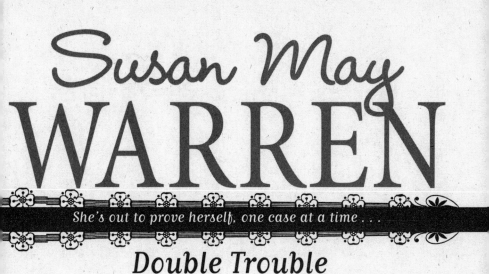

Susan May
WARREN

She's out to prove herself, one case at a time . . .

Double Trouble

Tyndale House Publishers, Inc.
Carol Stream, Illinois

Visit Tyndale's exciting Web site at www.tyndale.com.

Visit Susan May Warren's Web site at www.susanmaywarren.com.

TYNDALE and Tyndale's quill logo are registered trademarks of Tyndale House Publishers, Inc.

Double Trouble

Designed by Jacqueline L. Nuñez

Edited by Sarah Mason

Library of Congress Cataloging-in-Publication Data

Warren, Susan May, date.
    Double trouble / Susan May Warren.
        p. cm.
    ISBN 978-1-4143-1313-9 (pbk.)
1. Women private investigators—Fiction.   2. Minnesota—Fiction.   I. Title.
    PS3623.A865D68 2010
    813'.6—dc22   2009031580

Printed in the United States of America

16   15   14   13   12   11   10
7   6   5   4   3   2   1

For Your glory, Lord

Acknowledgments

God is always so generous to me! A book is never written alone, and I am so grateful for the following people who assisted me on this project.

Rachel Hauck—I am now unable to write a book without calling Rachel every day and hashing out a scene with her. Thank you, friend, for being on the other end of the telephone and feeding my crazy addiction. You're such a talented storyteller—thank you for listening, guiding, and encouraging (and praying!). You rock!

Jennifer Speck—who makes me look good, especially when I come in all shaggy headed, needing an overhaul. She knows when I've been stuck at home writing for too long! Thank you for all the insights into PJ's undercover work.

Cindy Kalinin—my Russian in-law connection. Thank you for sharing your stories. Have I mentioned you should write a book?

Ellen Tarver—my secret weapon for overhauling a book. I give her a mess; she untangles it. Thank you for your friendship, your grace to me, and for partnering with me. God truly blessed me when he sent us both to Russia!

Sarah Mason—the polish. Thank you for making me sound so smooth! I am blessed to work with you and so, so thankful for your talents.

Karen Watson—the visionary! Thank you for believing in this series, in me, and for fighting to make it all it can be! I count my blessings to work with you and am so grateful for your wisdom and encouragement.

Steve Laube—my champion. Thank you for always being on the other end of the line with sage wisdom, a listening ear, and the belief that it'll all work out. What would I do without you? (I don't want to know!)

Andrew and Kids—you know what it's like to live with an author. Thank you for forgiving me when there is no food on the table (or in the house), for rising off the sofa when I get into my postbook cleaning frenzies, for knowing when you need to snap your fingers to get my attention, and for doing your own laundry. I am so blessed to have such an amazing family—thank you for putting up with and even laughing at my mistakes, shortcomings, and foibles. Thank you especially for being my biggest cheerleaders. I'd be lost without you.

Chapter *ONE*

PJ Sugar had been born to sneak up on people. She clearly possessed the instincts of a panther, with the ability to find her prey and slink up to them in the shadows, pouncing only when they least suspected.

Alleged adulterer Rudy Bagwell didn't have a prayer of escaping.

"I'm telling you, Jeremy, we're going to nail him this time." She wasn't sure why she felt the need to keep her voice to a hoarse whisper into the pay phone—or even to press herself closer to the wall of the ancient one-story motel. It wasn't like Rudy or his cohort in crime, Geri Fitz, would hear her. Still, what a time for her cell phone company to cut off service. Just because a gal happened to be short on funds . . .

PJ glanced at her watch—2:14 a.m., a resounding gavel bang to Rudy's guilt. After all, who would be sneaking around after midnight?

Without, er, a good reason. Like a *stakeout*.

"I followed him to the Windy Oaks Motel off Highway 12," PJ continued. She glanced toward the soot-dark picture window next to the peeling door of Rudy's room. A brass number 8, slanted at a corrupt angle, glared against the parking lot lights as if spotlighting the sin behind the closed doors.

If she were picking a location to have a tryst with her old high school sweetheart, she might have aimed higher than a graying yellow motel edged with weeds, a broken swing set, a muddy sandbox, and a Dumpster stuffed with a ripped prison-striped mattress. Oh, the romance.

Just standing in the greasy parking lot made her itch, as if she might be the one engaging in the skulduggery.

Now that she was a PI in training, she got to use words like that. She had even highlighted this one in the *Basics of Private Investigation* manual Jeremy had assigned her to read as part of her apprenticeship. She had read the "Stakeout" chapter three times. And, if she did say so herself, had the "Tailing Your Suspect" techniques down to a science.

Nope, Rudy wasn't getting away with cheating on his wife. Not with PJ Sugar on the job.

"Are you sure it's him?" Jeremy spoke through the gravel in his voice, obviously dredged from a deep sleep.

She heard a faint siren on the other end of the line and did the math. "Are you sleeping at the office again?"

"I worked late. Are you *sure* it's Rudy?"

"Of course it's Rudy. He's exactly the same dirtbag he was in high school—pockmarked face, a permanent scowl. He was even wearing his leather jacket, which seems suspicious given that it's August and about seventy degrees out. . . ."

"PJ . . ."

She heard him sigh, could imagine Jeremy running his wide hand over his face, through the dark grizzle of his late-night shadow and over his curly, thinning hair. "I'm not sure that I'm up to your PI prowess tonight. Have I ever told you that you're hard to handle?"

"Every day. Now, get out of bed and bring your camera equipment. Oh, Cynthie is going to be thrilled! I promised her we were going to take down her cheatin' husband."

And Cynthie wasn't the only one to whom she'd promised results. She'd also made a plethora of private promises to herself. A brand-new job, a brand-new life . . . this time she wasn't going to quit or take the fastest route out of town. She was getting this done, no matter what the cost.

"See, this is your problem, PJ. You make promises you can't keep. Two weeks, and Rudy hasn't been seen doing anything more notorious than ordering extra whip on his macchiato. I'm thinking Cynthie is dreaming his affair. And speaking of dreaming, that's what I should be doing. And you too. Get home. Go to bed."

"I'm on the case, Jeremy. A great PI follows her instincts, and I know Rudy's hooked back up with Geri. You should have seen those two in high school—in the halls, wrapped in each other's arms, making out by the lockers—"

"I don't want to hear this."

"I'm just saying, they were an item, and sparks like that never die."

Silence throbbed on the other end of the phone.

PJ closed her eyes.

"Really." The word from Jeremy came out small, without

much emotion, but PJ felt it like a jab to her heart, even put a hand to her chest.

In some cases, she wanted to add. *But not always. Or maybe, yes, always.* She wasn't sure, not with her return to her hometown of Kellogg, Minnesota, right into the bull's-eye of her high school heartthrob, Daniel "Boone" Buckam, bad boy—turned—detective, who had decided their old flames might be worth stirring up.

PJ had spent too many years roaming the country with his name still simmering in her heart to ignore the fire there.

But Jeremy Kane, PI, had given her a job, even though so far, two months into her gig, Jeremy still hadn't let her run with her instincts, hadn't let her handle her own cases. She knew she could be his right-hand gal if he'd just give her a chance.

So she couldn't find the right reply for him now, as she stood in the darkness, alone, knowing she'd been driven out of her bed and from a sound night's sleep by the stirring desire to prove herself. And maybe something else . . . something she didn't especially want to talk about. At least not with Jeremy, her boss.

Boss. She needed to write that word on her hand or something. Jeremy was her *boss.*

"We got 'em, Jeremy. And if we can get pictures, then we'll have done our job. So get over here."

"PJ, sometimes . . ." But she heard silence on the other end before she had a chance to tell him that she would surely appreciate some Cheetos and a Diet Coke. Investigative work made a person hungry.

Thirty minutes later Jeremy tapped on the window of her VW Bug, looking bedraggled and annoyed.

But because he could read her mind, he held in his hand two cold sodas.

"Scoot over," he snarled as he climbed in beside her, handing her a soda. His scowl only enhanced his hard-edged former Navy SEAL persona, all dark eyes; wide, ropy-muscled shoulders; trim waist; and long legs. He wore a black T-shirt, a pair of dark jeans, and black Converse shoes that made him melt into the night.

In fact, he sort of matched her.

"Is this Sneaky PJ? Black from head to toe? Where are your Superman pants?"

"Hey, a girl has to dress the part. You taught me that."

Only, in her black leggings and oversize black sweatshirt, she looked more sloppy than dangerous. Apparently only Jeremy could pull that off. She'd first discovered the black ops side of Jeremy Kane the night he'd cajoled her into sneaking into the Kellogg Country Club. She'd nearly been caught when she froze in the bright lights of near discovery.

On the spot, Jeremy, the person she'd believed to be a pizza delivery guy, had morphed into GI Joe, scooping her into his arms and hiding her behind boxes of golf shirts, gripping his flashlight like a lethal weapon.

The memory still sent a forbidden thrill through her, one she didn't know how to interpret.

And she still, on occasion, called him Pizza Man.

Jeremy didn't smile, just opened his own soda with a hush, took a swig, and wiped his mouth with his hand. "So, any changes?"

"Rudy hasn't ordered out for pizza, if that's what you mean. Did you bring the camera?"

He shrugged a strap off his shoulder and dumped a bag onto her lap, then levered his seat back and closed his eyes. "I've created a monster."

PJ opened the bag and began fitting the long-range digital camera together.

Three hours later, she nudged Jeremy awake. She'd quietly sung through the score of *The Phantom of the Opera* as well as her complete knowledge of the Beatles and ABBA repertoires, then played "I'm going to the beach and I'm bringing . . ." from A to Z twice and tried to read the chapter titled "How to Find Missing Persons" with the neon blue light attached to her key chain.

She'd even rummaged through her canvas purse that Jeremy referred to as "the abyss," found a bottle of pink polish, and refreshed her pedicure.

Still, a gal could sit in silence for only so long.

"Smile, this is for posterity." PJ held the digital camera out as far as her arm would reach, leaned her head in toward his, and depressed the button.

Light flashed like a bullet, shooting her vision with dots against the gray pallor of morning.

"What are you doing?" Jeremy whipped out his arm and snatched the camera from her hand. "Are you trying to get us made?"

"Oh yes, I'm sure they're glued to the window as we speak."

He scrolled through the previous shots. "What is this—pictures of your toes?"

"I have cute toes. And I was bored. Delete them if you want."

Outside, dew glistened on the car hood. She'd rolled up her window, wishing she'd brought along a jacket when she tip-toed out of her sister's house in the wee hours of the morning, and now shivered. She clamped her hand over a yawn. "I hope they're not late sleepers."

"I can't believe he hasn't snuck out back to Cynthie yet." Jeremy popped his seat up and reached for his now-warm soda. PJ said nothing when he noted it was nearly gone.

"Is that what the cheaters usually do—sneak out for their trysts and then back to their wives before dawn?"

"Sometimes. Depends. The ones who work downtown usually disappear at lunchtime."

"Is PI work always so . . . slimy? I feel a little dirty, like I need a shower or something."

"I have news for you, PJ. You *do* need a shower."

"Seriously, don't we get to solve a real crime? like a murder or something?"

In the receding shadows, Jeremy looked less menacing, although she'd once seen him shoot a man. "Be thankful for the boring ones. They don't hurt."

She didn't respond. But she had thought that being a PI—or rather a PI's assistant—might be more, well, fun. Instead, she'd spent two tedious months parked behind a desk, filing reports, answering Jeremy's calls. Only recently had he invited her to keep him company on his stakeouts.

She longed for high action. Undercover ops and maybe even some karate. In fact . . . "Maybe I should sign up for one of Sergei's tae kwon do classes. I think it would help."

"What—in understanding Korean? or maybe Russian so you can help Connie with the in-laws?"

"Very funny. No, in taking down criminals."

Jeremy ran a finger and thumb against his eyes. Sighed. "Why don't I send you on a mission?"

"A mission? I'd love to—"

"Get us some donuts." He glanced in the rearview mirror. "Good Mornin' Donuts' light just went on."

"Is that all I am to you—a delivery girl?"

The minute the words left her mouth, PJ knew she was asking for trouble. Jeremy wore the inklings of a very devilish smile. "Oh, don't get me started."

Perhaps Boone wasn't the only one trying to kindle a flame.

Jeremy held her gaze and shook his head. "Maybe stakeouts aren't such a great idea."

"I'll get the donuts."

Since she'd parked next to a wall deep in the shadows of the Chinese takeout place, she had to wait for Jeremy to climb out of the Bug before she piled over the driver's seat. He held open the door for her and she scrambled out without looking at him.

"I'll take a bismark."

"What is that—the battleship of all donuts?" She laughed at her own joke.

Jeremy rolled his eyes. "A donut covered in chocolate and filled with custard." He shook his head as he climbed back into the Bug and closed the door.

Sounded like a long john to her. If they were going to work together, they'd need to nail down their donut terminology.

The cool air raised gooseflesh on her skin as she jogged across the parking lot toward the donut shop. The sun, just a sparkle of hope on the horizon, edged into the metal gray sky, and she smelled summer in the tang of grass freshened by the morning dew. Her Converse slapped against the concrete as she hustled to the doors.

The reception area inside remained dark in the early morning shadows. Lifeless. Void of donuts. She cupped her hand over her eyes and peered through the glass, her stomach clenching in dismay. "Hello in there!"

No one. She knocked on the glass door and then spied someone inside wearing a white apron, moving around in the baking area.

"Hello! We need donuts!"

From the back, a body appeared—a teenager with dyed black hair, a lip ring, and darty black eyes, his apron strings wrapped twice around his noodle-thin body (the boy needed to consume his own product). PJ banged on the window, and he jumped as if she might be wielding a rocket launcher.

Good grief, she just wanted a donut. "Are you open?"

The boy drifted toward the front of the store almost surreptitiously, as if he might be letting in the Mongol horde through the gates of the castle.

He unlocked the door, cracking it just wide enough for his lips to fit through. "We're not open yet."

PJ wrapped her arms around herself and tried to appear as waiflike as possible. "Oh, please, please, I'm starved."

He eyed her warily.

"I spent the night in my car." She added a little shiver. Looked pitiful. Smiled.

He might have believed her—and now her less-than-dangerous attire might have actually worked in her favor—because he opened the door. "Quick. In the back."

PJ slunk in, the ever-present danger of a raid hovering over the moment. But never let it be said that when Jeremy sent her on a mission, she returned empty-handed.

She scampered into the back room, where she discovered trays of glistening amber donut holes, freshly glazed. The entire room smelled of baking bread, sugar glaze, and the heady indulgence of chocolate. "I'll take a dozen holes and a bismark—" she glanced at his name tag—"Phillip." She held out a ten-dollar bill, intimating that he keep the change.

After all, that's what PIs did . . . paid for information. Or donuts.

Whatever it took to complete the mission.

Phillip boxed up the holes and the bismark, took the ten, and honest Abe that he was, headed to the front to make change. He stopped short at the threshold to the front parlor. "It's my boss," he whispered. He turned and, for a guy already sorta pasty, went even whiter. "Hurry, please . . . go out the back."

She'd never been kicked out of a bakery before. But to save her new hero . . . she turned and pushed on the metal door, letting it swish shut behind her.

PJ was standing in the back alley next to a Dumpster, a beat-up red Honda, and a pile of old, broken pallets, holding the donut box and giving serious contemplation to digging in right there, when she spied him—Rudy Bagwell, sneaking out a back window of the Windy Oaks Motel.

Oh, she was good at this job.

From this angle she watched Rudy hit the ground and skirt along the back of the motel unit, on the way to freedom.

Sneaky. But not too sneaky for her, the Panther.

PJ hiked the box under her arm and crossed the road, hoping Jeremy saw her angle toward her quarry. Even if he couldn't spot Rudy from his angle, a guy with an eye out for his donuts should know to wake up and grab his camera.

Rudy had stopped at the edge of the motel, leaning away from the wind to light a cigarette.

She slowed her pace and strolled up to him as if she'd just been out early for a donut run. "Hey there."

He glanced at her, and for a second she wondered if he would recognize her—after all, she did have one vivid recollection of a wild high school beach party when he'd passed out and she and Boone had buried him to his waist in sand.

He grunted at her and blew out a long stream of smoke.

"Beautiful morning."

He grunted again, rolling the cigarette between two fingers. He didn't look like a man who'd spent the night in the arms of his beloved high school sweetheart. In fact, he had a rather ugly welt on his chin, and also, if she looked closely—although she didn't make it obvious—a splatter of blood down his white shirt, maybe from a bloody nose. Or his lip—it looked a little puffy.

She took a step back, glancing toward Jeremy. Movement in the VW parked in the shadows across the lot was too difficult to discern from here. But Rudy would have to cross in front of the motel to retrieve his Camaro. Jeremy could get the shot then.

So why had Rudy come this way—around the back, away from his wheels?

"Is there something you want, babe?" Rudy cocked his head at her. "Don't I know you?"

She shook her head. "No, I—"

His eyes widened. "PJ Sugar." He said it slowly, with a hint of a snarl—maybe he did remember the beach party—and pushed himself away from the building. "I'd heard you were back in town. Cynthie said she saw your picture in the paper. You solved Hoffman's murder . . ." His gaze went from her to the parking lot.

"Want a donut?" She shoved the box toward him.

Rudy turned back to her, his smile now gone. "What are you doing here?"

"Getting donuts." Only it came out more like a question. Oops, she'd have to work on her lying.

He took a step toward her . . . and that's when she saw it. Right above the waist of his jeans, small and black, hidden by the leather jacket that, despite the chill in the air, didn't belong in an August wardrobe.

A gun. As if it had claws, it tore at her gaze and PJ couldn't wrench it away.

A gun.

Blood on his shirt. A bloodied lip. A crime of passion? She added up the facts as quickly as it took Rudy to move another step toward her and snake out his hand to grab her.

But he wasn't the only one with a weapon. She shoved her hand into the box just as Rudy's grip closed around her elbow.

With everything inside her, PJ slammed the bismark into his face. Pudding squished between her fingers as she crammed it into his eyes. Then, clutching the box to her chest, she yanked her arm from his grasp and ran.

"Jeremy!"

Footsteps slapping the pavement behind her made her dig into the box again. Her hand closed around a donut hole, and she pitched it behind her as she raced across the parking lot. "Jeremy!"

Another hole, followed by an expletive from behind her.

Thankfully, Jeremy had finally come alive, because he emerged from the Bug, staring at her as if she'd lost her mind.

"He's got a gun! He killed her! He killed Geri!"

Another naughty word from Rudy and the footsteps changed direction. She turned to see Rudy flinging himself toward his Camaro. He Bo Duke'd across the hood and climbed in the window, turning the engine over even as PJ threw another hole at him.

It landed with a splotch of sugary goo on his windshield.

He gunned the hot rod across the parking lot.

PJ dropped the box, her breath wheezing out of her even as she watched him escape.

Or maybe not. As Rudy mowed over a parked Kawasaki and smacked against a Ford Fiesta, she heard another car gunning to roadblock him.

She turned too quickly, wishing she had more time to brace herself.

No.

No!

She nearly flung her body in front of Jeremy as he screeched past her in the VW, a laser streak of lime green on course to intersect with its target.

"Jeremy, stop!"

But Jeremy didn't know that, one, she hadn't paid her insurance for over a month, and two, the brakes on the Bug were a little on the spongy side, because he didn't even slow as he T-boned Rudy's Camaro and pinned it against the metal pole hosting the Windy Oaks sign.

The sound of metal ripping and the dying whine of her beloved Bug buckled PJ's knees. She went down hard in the gravel, gulping a breath, watching Jeremy leap from the car, dive over her hood, and rip the gun out of Rudy's grip before he could even clear his head.

Pinned, he screamed at the top of his lungs.

PJ slumped in the gravel of the lot. Not the Bug. Her Bug. The one remaining possession big enough to hide inside. She reached into the box and pulled out her remaining donut hole, considering it for a long moment as her mind faintly registered the wailing police sirens in the distance. Or maybe the noise came from her, from the keening inside.

Jeremy sauntered toward her, a smug smile in his evil eyes, shaking his head. "I don't suppose there's a bismark in that mess, is there?"

PJ leaned back, cupped her hand over her eyes, and hurled the donut hole at his arrogant smile.

Chapter *TWO*

"Looking for trouble again, huh, PJ?"

Not at all. In fact, for the first time in her life, as far back as she could remember, she'd thought she'd shaken free of trouble and might be headed toward something shiny and new, a different kind of PJ, one who slid out of trouble's clutches.

She refrained from glancing at her tangled, green, hissing and dripping former vehicle and continued to lick sugary glaze from her fingers as she sat on the back of Jeremy's Harley. Her stomach growled, as if she'd only awakened the beast inside. She desperately needed a large latte with double shots of vanilla if the cosmos expected her to face Detective Boone Buckam and his pale blue, call-her-trouble eyes.

It wasn't enough that her successful stakeout had skidded to a loud, earsplitting crunch. Now she had to face the one man who'd sent her out of her warm bed and into all this chaos in the first place.

"Marry me . . ."

"PJ?" Boone's voice turned to concern when she didn't look at him. When he touched her shoulder, the heat of his hand seeped through her.

She sighed, indicated her mangled Bug, and shrugged.

He offered a long, reverent moment of silence. "Please tell me you weren't in that when—"

"Jeremy was driving. It was his brilliant idea to run Rudy down with my beautiful but rather-wimpy tin can."

The sun had given a valiant effort to burning away the gloom of the morning, but dark cumulus clouds over nearby Kellogg Lake suggested defeat. The wind rustled the poplars around the Windy Oaks Motel—she had to wonder where the oaks had gone—and she smelled rain hovering in the air.

A good thunderstorm just might be the perfect accompaniment to this day.

PJ shivered despite her warm sweatshirt.

Boone pulled off his suit jacket and draped it around her shoulders, and for the first time, she turned to him.

Boone Buckam, the boy most likely to drive his motorcycle down the halls of Kellogg High, had turned into Mr. All-American—his bronze hair cut short, his white oxford shirt and black suit pants pressed even at this early hour, his shoulder holster and broad, thick shoulders the only hint that he might be a police detective rather than a Wall Street investor. But he still possessed the one-sided smile that drew up slowly, like the sun on a clear day. He'd been her first love, and that fire had never been truly banked.

Nope, as evidenced by Rudy and Geri and the drama at the Windy Oaks, one never forgot a first love.

She looked away from Boone, catching sight of the skinny, aproned form of her early morning donut hero heading out to bring breakfast to the men in blue. Jeremy waited eagerly as Phillip approached. Evidently, her boss had a singular thought on his mind today—shortly after the police turned in to the gravel lot and the VW's motor had shuddered to a pitiful death, Jeremy had quietly pressed an Andrew Jackson into her palm and suggested she treat herself to another bismark.

She'd pocketed the twenty. She'd need bus money.

"Babe, what are you doing out this early in the morning? What happened here?" Boone knelt on one knee beside her, his blue eyes an ocean, deep and dangerous, with sudden swells that could sweep her off her feet and carry her away.

Right back to last night.

And just like that, she was in the silky darkness, his arms pulling her into the pocket of his embrace as they'd parked along the beach, the sun long gone, the velvet sky above them, a lazy moon dragging a finger of light through the inky water. The radio crooned something romantic from one of his personal mix CDs while Boone closed in on her with his husky, summer air smell. *"Hey Jude . . ."*

"Peej," he'd whispered into her ear, his lips brushing against her neck. It still took her breath away that while she'd wandered the world for the past decade, he'd pined for her in their little hometown hamlet of Kellogg, just west of Minneapolis, a suburb time forgot. But Boone never forgot. He'd kept a weather eye on the horizon—his words—waiting for her and her VW Bug to sail back into town.

Last night, he'd run his thumb over the tattoo high on her shoulder—the one that inscribed his name into her flesh. He had a matching identifier on his arm, although most of the time he kept it concealed.

Hers, however, seemed destined to remind the world every time she wore a tank top, every time she donned a sundress, and especially when she, on occasion, wriggled into her bikini, whom she belonged to.

Or rather, to whom she'd given her heart.

"Marry me."

The words seemed more of a breath than a voice, a heart-beat of desire against her neck, where Boone followed it with the press of his lips. "Marry me, Peej."

At his words, she'd turned in his arms, stared at the starry sky, humming to the music, and pretended she hadn't heard him, even as the question deafened her.

He hadn't asked again.

Still, the question burned inside her, so much so that it had chased her out of her bed, down the stairs of her sister Connie's house in Chapel Hills, and over two posh neighborhoods to stake out Rudy Bagwell, finally following him to the seedy side of town.

Across the street now, in the motel parking lot, overnight guests ogled the sticky, somewhat-bloody, definitely spittin' mad Rudy Bagwell loudly defending his actions, among which included running after PJ with a 9mm Glock.

Boone and his pals had found Rudy's girlfriend, Geri, in her motel room, sporting a black eye and split lip. She was currently airing *her* grievances at full volume, accessorized with colorful language, from inside crooked room number eight.

It made for a loud morning. PJ would bet another donut

hole that these two would be together again as soon as Rudy made bail. She recognized a destructive love-hate relationship when she saw it. Geri apparently thrived on drama. And Rudy obligingly provided it.

PJ would have appreciated not having her Bug be a casualty, however.

Boone still knelt in front of her. "Did Jeremy send you out on this job in the middle of the night?" It seemed he didn't even try to keep the edge from his voice. "Did he tell you to tail Rudy?" He even shot a look at Jeremy, one that should have emitted the smell of gunpowder.

"No. I overheard Geri at the nail salon, and I'd made Cynthie a promise . . ."

"You gotta stop promising people things that just might get you killed, PJ."

"I wasn't in danger, Boone. . . . I followed my instincts."

His skeptical smile had already started sliding up on one side, and she covered it with her hand. "I have them, you know. I'm very sneaky."

He took her hand away. "Oh, I know. How well I know. And I can see that you blend into the night. . . ." He gave a nod toward her outfit as he stood and surveyed the scene across the street a long while. "But how did you know that Rudy had beat up Geri?"

"Instincts. And he had blood on his shirt."

Boone said nothing, then sighed. "I still don't like the fact that you were out here, knowing what he did to Geri, what he could have done to you. I don't like fearing that one of these times, I could get a call and find—"

"Uh, sorry to interrupt, but they need a statement, Princess."

Jeremy shot Boone a look, then turned as though she should follow him.

"Is he still calling you that?" Boone's mouth tightened in a lethal line.

"It's just a nickname." One she should probably tell Jeremy not to use, given that she worked for him.

She got up, starting to slip off Boone's jacket, but he draped it back over her shoulders and touched her lightly on the arm as they crossed the street.

Jeremy turned away from his klatch of officers and watched them, his smile slowly dimming. His gaze landed on Boone, fixing there.

PJ suddenly had the sense of standing between two pit bulls eyeing one juicy steak—her.

But Jeremy was her boss. *Boss.* Besides, he and Boone were colleagues of a sort—or at least had been as of two months ago. She must be dreaming the tension.

She didn't imagine the tone of Boone's voice, however. "Please tell me you didn't let her stake out Rudy alone."

Jeremy's dark eyes jabbed at her, then landed on Boone. His voice came out strikingly cool. "She's a big girl."

Yes, she was! *Thank you, Jer—*

"Besides, she was the one who jumped to conclusions. She came running across the parking lot, screaming murder and throwing rocks—"

Wait . . . *hey!* "They were donut holes, and I was *not* screaming."

Boone cut her a look. "You went after Rudy with pastry?"

PJ glanced at Jeremy and tried to turn him into a pile of ash with her eyes. "I can take care of myself, Boone."

"With what—donut holes?"

She had no comment for that, mostly because he was right. If she hoped to be a super PI, she'd have to get serious about self-defense.

See, she'd been right about the tae kwon do class.

"I should have let him get away, but she acted like he'd taken a knife to her, if not the entire neighborhood, and I just reacted."

"And my Bug paid the price, thank you." PJ clutched Boone's coat tighter around her.

Jeremy's gaze settled on her hands fisted into the lapels. His jaw tightened. "I couldn't think of anything else, Princess. But Boone is right. Someday your so-called instincts are going to get you in over your head, and then even your donut aim won't be able to save you."

PJ narrowed her eyes at him. "Don't call me Princess." She brushed past Jeremy and stalked up to one of Boone's investigators. She recognized him from her previous run-in with crime, a recruit fresh off the streets, holding a voice recorder and a clipboard. "Are you going to take my statement or what?"

He glanced at Boone over her shoulder, and he must have given the all clear, because the junior detective nodded and gestured for her to follow him away from the huddle.

She gave him the rundown of the events, leaving out a few of her desperate sugary lobs, focusing instead on the blood on Rudy's shirt, the welt on his chin, the swollen lip.

Geri had moved from the motel and now leaned against the hood of a cruiser, smoking a cigarette, eyes crawling over PJ as if she wasn't sure whether to hug her or go after her with her fresh manicure.

Which, incidentally, she'd gotten from Turbo Nails, right next to the pedicure chair where PJ got a double coat of Fuchsia Passion. Thanks to Geri's less-than-covert chat with her manicurist, PJ had been alerted to where this clandestine tryst might take place.

Nail doctors were a society woman's bartender.

"So, you didn't think of just letting him walk away, maybe letting the police handle it?"

She eyed Junior. "You're new, right?"

Junior shifted his weight and gave a crisp nod.

"Here's the score, pal: I'm hungry; I smell like two-day-old gym socks; I live with my newlywed sister and her Russian in-laws, a goat, and my nephew, Davy, who wakes me every morning with a mind-jolting jig on my bed. My bedroom is located next door to the newlyweds, I have all of twenty dollars to my name, and I've just sacrificed my favorite uninsured car for the cause of justice. So do you, perhaps, want to rephrase that question?"

"Peej, I think you're done." Boone's hand landed on the small of her back, and he gave a quick, precise nod to Junior, who slinked away. "How about I buy you breakfast?"

She ran a hand through her hair, now tangled and greasy, and it reminded her that her bag still sat in the snarled mess of her only valuable possession.

"I think she needs a nap more than breakfast." Jeremy had retrieved his motorcycle and now rolled up beside them. "I'll drive you home, uh . . ."

She knew a "Princess" dangled at the end of that sentence and gave him a glower.

". . . Fast-Pitch."

She raised an eyebrow.

"Seems appropriate." He gestured to Rudy, now being tucked into a police cruiser. Yellow custard dribbled down his shirt.

"She doesn't need a ride," Boone said, his hand still on her back. "I'll make sure she gets home. Without more drama and sirens."

Oh, but she'd become so accustomed to the entourage.

Jeremy stared at her as if waiting for her response.

"I, uh . . ."

Jeremy's cell phone rang and he dug it out of his pocket. Parking the bike, he strolled out of earshot. PJ watched the dark line of his shoulders, remembered suddenly the stricken look on his face as she'd fled across the parking lot to him, screaming his name.

Boone's voice pitched low, carrying an edge of exasperation as she watched Jeremy nod, glance back at her, and speak into the phone. "You know, the fact is, PJ, you don't have to do this anymore."

"Boone . . ." How many times over the past two months had he lodged his formal complaint over her newly chosen profession? If he only knew her résumé over the past ten years included such things as large-animal feeder for the San Diego Zoo and part-time stunt girl. She risked very little but her reputation sitting outside a motel singing "All You Need Is Love."

Well, her reputation and her own hopes that she'd actually get the job done right. Yet, despite the automotive casualties, she knew she could do this job, maybe even eventually impress Jeremy enough for him to help her become a full-time, licensed PI.

Judging by Boone's expression, he didn't agree. "I just know that someday you're going to end up . . ." As if he couldn't finish his sentence, he shook his head, looked away, ran a hand behind his neck. "I don't want to lose you again."

She couldn't find an answer for that. Instead, she pulled off his jacket. He refused to take it.

"Boone, I'm not going anywhere." She indicated her Bug.

"I hope not." He looked down, shifted, and she knew him well enough to brace herself. "I don't suppose you've thought at all about my . . . proposal."

His proposal. So it hadn't just been impulse, hadn't been the sultry night air, the feeling of yesterday in the sway of the stars, the way she fit into his embrace. "I . . . need more time."

She read his disappointment in the tight press of his lips, the way his shoulders rose and fell with his sigh. She still held his coat, and he finally reached out for it.

"Say yes, PJ. You know we belong together. Just . . . say yes."

"Say yes to what?" Jeremy stood beside his bike, cutting his gaze between them.

Boone didn't speak, his scowl shouting volumes.

Jeremy climbed on his bike. "C'mon, PJ, I'll give you a ride home."

PJ weighed her options, feeling like if she breathed wrong, the entire place might go up in flames.

"No," she said, "I think I'll stay with the deceased." She went over and sat on the fender of her wounded Bug.

Jeremy didn't move. Finally he jumped the clutch and the bike roared to life. "Last chance, Fast-Pitch. I'll buy you a bismark."

She narrowed her eyes at him a moment before she folded her arms and sank her head into her knees. She didn't want a bismark . . . she just wanted to rewind the morning, stop herself before she turned talent into trouble. What was her problem that her good intentions always ended up a snarled mess of broken hopes?

Maybe Boone was right—maybe unconsciously she went looking for trouble.

Two long heartbeats passed.

"I'll call you later. Try not to cause any more blood and screaming between now and then," Jeremy said right before she heard him roar out of the parking lot.

Clearly she couldn't make any promises.

Chapter *THREE*

If PJ could own any house in the world, it would be her sister Connie's 1920s three-story Craftsman situated on a half acre of lush Kentucky bluegrass in the middle of the Chapel Hills neighborhood of Kellogg.

Okay, maybe she'd move it to some milky beach, but she'd keep the elegance abundant in the restored historical master-piece, with its sweeping porch, complete with two rockers, the wide front steps flanked by purple viburnum and lilacs and wild roses bulky with summer flowers. Inside, the oak floors gleamed with a honeyed polish, and the stairs leading up to the second-floor bedrooms creaked appropriately, as if sighing in contentment. The dark coffee leathers of the family room, the stainless steel and blue-veined gray granite of the kitchen, the fragrant breezes collected on the screened porch . . . it all conspired to put a visual to heaven on earth.

Except, it didn't exactly belong to her. PJ was only a

tenant—a freeloading tenant at that. Not that Connie even breathed the suggestion she move out. No, she left that to their mother, who nudged the topic around during the occasional family dinner or via the blunt, red-circled rental ads left folded on PJ's bed.

Elizabeth Sugar obviously believed Connie needed privacy during her newlywed year with Sergei. That Connie even registered PJ's presence, however, might be in question—the woman virtually sparkled, as brilliant as the two-carat marquise on her elegant finger. And why not? When she returned from her law office every night, Sergei, her Russian-born fitness instructor and new husband, lit up, his voice dropping to husky levels. And with little Davy, Connie's four-year-old son, learning to leap into his new father's arms, perhaps Elizabeth was right. PJ needed her own digs.

But short of joining the Kellogg hobo—a rather grizzly-faced former seafarer who spent his days collecting debris and the picnic scraps from the beach—in his home under the Maximilian Bay Bridge, she didn't have a clue where she might transfer herself and the contents of her duffel bag. Especially now that her beloved Bug lay crumpled at Cooters Metal and Scraps.

Maybe Jeremy would let her take over the sofa in his office.

She stood at the entrance to the house, closing the door with a soft click behind her. Through the side-panel window she saw Boone pull away in his cruiser. Thankfully, he hadn't rekindled their conversation or his proposal, just let her ride home in miserable silence.

"Mornin', Auntie PJ!" Davy's cheery voice accomplished some rescue of her spirit as the four-year-old bounced down the stairs. He wore his blue polyester Fellows Early

Education Academy uniform, clothes pressed and curly dark hair combed. In June, PJ had waged a valiant attempt to liberate the preschooler from the prep school, but Connie had reenrolled her future stockbroker the moment she returned from her two-week honeymoon. And she did it without recriminations or even comment about his truancy. PJ had tried to return the favor.

Still, she snatched every available opportunity to flee with him to the beach or into the backyard to climb on his million-dollar yard equipment or even chase the goat—a gift to Davy from his new Russian family—around the yard. She could hardly believe that only two months ago Connie had left her with the care of her beloved son. In truth, PJ probably deserved the bruises he'd inflicted on her shins during their early days together.

But they'd lived. And she'd found her footing back in her hometown and, for now, intended to stick around.

Besides, she was fresh out of wheels.

She scooped Davy up in her arms and hugged him, inhaling his sugar-cookie sweetness as she meandered to the kitchen. Her stomach roared, and she desperately hoped Connie had stocked the freezer with Moose Tracks. At this point, she'd even settle for frozen yogurt.

"Where did you go?" Davy asked, disentangling himself from her grip and hitting the floor before he hustled over to the cereal cabinet.

Sadly, Connie had cleared out all remains of the Cap'n Crunch. Oh, the deprivation.

"I had to check on something," she said. "A friend needed me."

She wondered if Jeremy had called Cynthie yet and informed her that she'd been right. How she loved the sound of that. Right. Correctamundo. On the money. Speaking of, she also had high hopes of a payday in the near future.

She pushed around a package of frozen organic burritos, a couple shiny bags of coffee, and a frozen whole-wheat pasta dinner before conceding defeat and closing the freezer door.

Davy had found some Shredded Wheat and poured it out on the counter, dividing the hay bales into piles. She stole one and he stuck out his tongue at her. She answered in kind.

"Oh, that's nice, PJ. Keep it up and I'll stick you in a uniform and send you to face Director Nicholson." Connie arrived in the kitchen looking like a junior version of their mother— dark hair neatly cinched in the back, subtle pearl earrings, the smell of culture and power radiating from her in her linen suit and some expensive fragrance.

PJ threw a hay bale at her. "Has she forgiven me yet for my 'insolence'?"

"I'm pretty sure your three tardies, coupled with a view of the Superman pants, have relegated you to the untouchables." Connie propped her Coach briefcase on the counter. "Were you out all night?" She finally met PJ's eyes with something that looked half-curious, half-concern.

"No. I . . . sorta had to get to work early."

"Midnight early?"

So Connie had heard her escape from the house.

"I couldn't sleep." She turned to the fridge, hunting for anything with real sugar. "The good news is that I caught the bad guy."

"Auntie PJ is a superhero!" Davy crowed, climbing onto

the counter and springing at her, arms wide. PJ turned just in time to catch him. He wrapped his legs and arms around her. "Aren't ya?"

Apparently he remembered a very different version of their near miss with an international assassin. However . . . "You got it, little man." She kissed his pudgy cheek and set him back on the counter.

Connie frowned and helped him down. "Please go get your shoes on, Davy." Then she turned to PJ, her voice lowered a notch. "Did your late-night escape have anything to do with Boone?"

PJ's eyes widened. "No! Connie, I told you, I'm not that girl anymore."

"I'm seeing you spend a lot of time together, and frankly, he has a 'settle down' look in his eyes."

Gulp.

"Is he getting serious with you?"

PJ managed a wry smile.

"You are still dating, right?"

"Yes—of course. But I'm not sure about, uh . . . getting serious. Maybe it's too soon. Just a couple months ago, I was in Florida wondering if he even remembered I existed."

Connie shook her head. "It's this new job, isn't it? You're under some delusion that you're going to become a hotshot PI—"

"No. I'm . . . well, maybe. But that has nothing to do with Boone."

"Doesn't it?" Connie sighed. "I'm with Boone on this. I don't like your new job, PJ. I especially don't like the idea of not knowing if you're going to come home beat up, or worse, how about with a bad guy on your heels, invading our house, putting my child in danger—"

PJ held up her hand. "Okay, I got it. I agree. I would die if anything happened to Davy." For a heartbeat, her thoughts went back to a showdown that could have easily caught Davy in a deadly cross fire. "I promise you, Connie, I'll be careful. I'll keep my personal and professional life separate. Just like you do."

Connie drew in a breath. As a prosecutor, she might also be on a few bad-guy lists. "Are you sure you won't consider the receptionist position at my firm? It's still open . . ."

PJ turned back to the fridge, found the juice, and poured herself a glass. "I like my job." Even if she had yet to get paid. "It's . . ."

"Exciting?"

PJ lifted a shoulder. "Unique. And I'm good at it."

"Good at suspecting people?"

"Good at spotting trouble."

Connie looked at her with a wry smile and grabbed the juice carton. "Yes, you are remarkably adept at that."

In the pause that followed, earthy snorts crept into the kitchen from the maid's quarters–turned–guest room. Connie's father-in-law Boris's snoring could awaken the dead.

Connie took a sip of her juice, then met PJ's eyes. "I'm just praying that isn't Sergei in twenty years." She made a face.

PJ tapped her glass against Connie's. "I'll drink to that."

They stood in silence for a long moment, trying not to laugh.

Finally Connie set her glass on the granite countertop. "I understand about Boone. Maybe it's too soon, too fast. Maybe you need other options."

Other options. PJ refused to let herself even consider that list. She took a drink. "How's Boris's job hunt going?"

"He doesn't want to work at Walmart, and so far, the applications are killing him—mostly because they're in English."

As if driven from the bedroom, Sergei's mother, Vera, suddenly cracked open the door and slipped into the kitchen wearing an orange bathrobe, her hair tied back in a white handkerchief. She looked at them in surprise. *"Dobra ootra."*

PJ translated for Connie. "Good morning."

"I can figure out what *dobra ootra* means, Peej. It's everything else I can't understand." Connie grimaced as Vera moseyed past them, pulled out a cast-iron pot from under the stainless cooktop, and slapped it on the stove. She reached for the sunflower oil.

"This is where I check out," PJ said, bypassing the coffeepot. Maybe she could score a couple hours of sleep before Jeremy—

"Could I ask you a favor?" Connie asked softly.

PJ turned back to her, caught more by the tone than the words. "Are you kidding? Last time I checked, I was living rent-free and scarfing down your food. Your wish is my command."

"You know you can stay as long as you want." Connie stared at the countertop as she said it, the pleading so quiet PJ might not have caught it. But she'd heard it once before, the night Connie cleverly negotiated PJ's return to the hometown she couldn't face. Yes, Connie might have named Davy as her reason, but in truth, and especially now as she glanced at PJ, she wore an expression that suggested it might have been for herself.

PJ sighed. "What?"

"Don't leave me with the Russians. I don't understand them. Boris . . . sometimes he scares me. He was a cop, you know. And Vera, well, I think she might be trying to take us out with cholesterol poisoning."

PJ glanced at Vera, the way her hips swayed as she hummed to herself, cracking eggs into the pan to swim and sizzle. Already grease filmed the air. Despite her high-fat cooking, Vera loved Davy, and they spent hours playing games and working on Vera's English together. In fact, maybe she and Connie should keep their voices down, in case Vera knew anything beyond the Barney song.

Boris, on the other hand, who'd already been arrested twice by Boone for sunbathing nude in the backyard, lived by his own set of rules. Usually dressed in a muscle shirt and tight nylon running pants, he started his morning with a vigorous set of push-ups and ended his days singing on the deck to a bottle of Smirnoff.

Yes, Boris scared her too.

Connie leaned close, touching her manicured hand to PJ's. "I need Boris to find a job. To do something productive." Then she hooked PJ by the arm and dragged her to the screened porch. PJ stopped at the lip of the French doors, her eyes wide on the wreckage of the backyard.

Where there once stood terraced gardens overflowing with gladiolas, roses, and a lush bleeding heart, all surrounded by an emerald lawn bathed every week by Connie's yard service, now lay mounds of glistening, rich black dirt, dug up, turned over, and ready for planting.

Presiding over it all, tied to a stake in the yard with plenty of lead, stood the goat.

PJ had no words.

"Boris is planting potatoes," Connie said in a voice not her own. "I came home last night to discover he'd spent the day furrowing my backyard." Her hand tightened on PJ's arm, even as she inhaled a deep breath. "I love Sergei. But I'm seeing blood and carnage, and I don't want the next mystery you investigate to be Boris's murder. . . ."

"Got it, Sis." PJ put her hand over Connie's tightening grip. "I'll find him a job." And then, as if she might be some sort of addict, the words rushed out. "I promise."

"I knew I could count on you," Connie said, facing her now with a tight nod. "Davy! We're off to school."

Davy bounded to his feet. Waved at PJ as he raced to the front door.

Vera swayed and hummed in the kitchen.

As PJ finished her juice, Boris came out of the bedroom. He smiled at her, showing a host of gold teeth. *"Dobra ootra."*

PJ leaned back against the door of the screened porch. *"I promise." Great, PJ, just great.* But how hard could it be to find Boris a job? It wasn't unlike solving a mystery . . . with the right clues, the right contacts . . .

This she could do.

With a quick survey of Vera's culinary skills to make sure the house wouldn't burst into flames as she slept, PJ went upstairs and barricaded herself in her bedroom, on the mission-style bed, underneath the crisp eyelet sheets. She slept, with the sun skimming the oak floor, the fresh breeze blowing across her forehead, the mattress slowly consuming her body. . . .

"PJ!"

She woke hard, sweat slicking her temples, a line of drool

pooling into the pillow. Her brain heard the voice calling, but she couldn't seem to pry her body from the sludge that trapped it.

"PJ!"

She rolled over, then tried to dig her voice out of hibernation. "Here. I'm up . . . here."

Her eyelids weighted and she drifted again, so heavy, so warm. . . .

Pounding at her door shot her straight up, the sheet falling to her waist. She'd climbed right into bed in her stakeout clothes, only managing to remove her shoes and socks. As her gaze slashed across the mirror on the opposite wall, she saw her shoulder-length auburn hair plastered to her head on one side, sticking straight up in a gnarled mess on the other. Mascara smudged under her eye added to her dazed and confused expression.

Maybe she was still asleep, trapped in some sort of a nightmare.

"PJ! It's Boone. Are you okay?"

She wrestled herself out of her covers and finally hit the floor, steadying her balance on the wooden headboard. She leaned against the door, her voice betraying her. "I'm sleeping! Whatya want?"

"Open up; I have to give you something. Hurry—I have a ride waiting outside."

She put a hand to her head, and her fingers tangled in the web of snarled hair. "I, uh, don't think so."

Silence. She heard jangling, then something hitting the floor. As her gaze traveled down to her painted toes, she saw the glint of a car key as it emerged from under her door. Boone's fingers pushed it the rest of the way through.

PJ stared at it before picking it up. "What's this?"

"It's to the Mustang. I figured you could use a—"

She flung open the door.

Apparently her decision to keep the door shut had been a prudent one because he looked at her, eyebrows raised, his lips tight and holding back a smile. "What happened to you?"

"I never said I was pretty in the morning."

"You're always pretty." He reached out for her hair—his favorite aren't-you-cute gesture—but she stepped to one side and held up the key.

"The Mustang?" She wasn't sure whether to laugh or cry. Or throw herself into his arms. "But this is your baby."

He lifted a shoulder, something sweet in his eyes. "It's probably just as much your car as mine, for as much time as we spent in it."

He didn't have to list those times, those moments when she'd sat beside him, her feet propped on the dash, sunglasses over her eyes as she tasted the freedom skimming off the open road. Or the other moments—the ones when she cuddled up next to him in the dark, watching the moon tickle the water of Lake Minnetonka on some secluded beach.

"But you love this car."

"Yes, I do."

She let her throat tighten and slipped into his arms, pressing her cheek against his chest. He pulled her against him, touched his chin to her hair. "Just promise me, nothing fancy, Peej. I don't want to see you on the ten o'clock news chasing down some adulterer in downtown Minneapolis."

She slapped his arm and stepped back. "Don't you have bad guys to find?"

"I don't know why I need to work to find trouble—all I have to do is follow you around." But he winked as he headed for the stairs. "Tonight, dinner?"

She didn't have a prayer of turning him down. Wasn't even sure she wanted to.

Not for dinner, and not, perhaps, his proposal.

A shower slicked away the cling-ons of sleep, and by the time she'd changed into a sleeveless shirt, a pair of cargo capris, and flip-flops, she felt reborn. She put Boone's key on her key ring—the one with Scooby and the gang—and found Boris in the backyard next to his unplanted potato field, sorting through wrinkled, soft red potatoes. Most had sprouted little green arms and legs like gremlins.

She refrained from mentioning that Connie could probably afford to purchase a couple hundred bushels for the amount of work Boris would put into planting, cultivating, and harvesting his crop.

In the sun next to the goat, Vera lay in a lounger. She lifted her face to the sun, unfazed by the perils of skin cancer.

PJ crouched next to Boris, swinging her keys. He looked up at her and grinned, his teeth shiny in the sun.

"Rabota?" she asked, having memorized the word for "work" back when she washed dishes for a Russian-language summer camp.

Boris nodded vigorously, motioning to the potatoes.

"No, *nyet.*" PJ shook her head. "You—" she pointed to him, then out at the great beyond—*"rabota."*

Boris sat back, studying her for a moment. His wide hands, crusted with dirt, were splayed on his knees, and his chest, still broad and tight for a man in his fifties, rose and fell for a long, silent string of heartbeats. She saw in him, at that moment, the man he'd been back in the home country, serious, even dangerous, able to bring down villains worthy of the Cold War era.

The type of crime solver she wanted to be.

She found a smile for him. What must it be like to have invested in a lifetime of crime fighting, only to discover that in another country, you were only qualified to plant potatoes? or flip burgers?

She could find him something better than that.

"C'mon," PJ said. "Let's find some *rabota*."

✳ ✳ ✳

She should have climbed back under the covers.

Four hours later, as the sun hit high stride over the earth, PJ touched her head to Boone's black steering wheel, wishing the heat might sear from her brain this propensity to make promises she couldn't keep.

It didn't help that her job applicant wore a wide-collared, seventies-style silk shirt, a pair of wool pants, no socks with his loafers, and the crowning touch—an oily green tie about as wide as her hand. He said hello like he was clearing his throat, and more than one prospective employer had cringed under his potato-planting grip.

She'd tried Sunsets Supper Club—after all, the owner, Joe, had offered her a job not so long ago, an offer that apparently he still kept on the table—then the local grocery store, meeting an old schoolmate who gave Boris long consideration before realizing he couldn't read enough English to understand how to stock the shelves. They swung by the UPS delivery place, but they needed drivers, not loaders, and Boris wouldn't even enter the fish processing plant. They finally ended up sitting in the convertible at Kellogg beach, watching children play in the sand. She was out of ideas but afraid to return home.

"Want a hot dog?" She spied a vendor with his cart pulled up in the sand. Next to her, Boris had taken off his shoes, rolled up his pant legs, and leaned back in the seat. He especially loved riding with the top down, practically letting his tongue hang out, grinning at her wildly.

She couldn't help but grin back.

Driving Boone's Mustang around town did ease the pain somewhat. And made her wonder exactly why he'd loaned her his prized possession.

Okay, so maybe she didn't have to wonder at all.

She got out, flip-flopped through the sand to the vendor, and scored them two hot dogs with Jeremy's twenty. Loading them up, she returned and handed one to Boris, who ate it with the enthusiasm of a four-year-old.

She turned and watched the sun sparkle like diamond chips on the water. Motorboats cut through the waves, skiers speeding in their wakes. One did a flip in the air. Once upon a time, she'd been a decent water-skier, doing most of her tricks for Boone, who watched her over his shoulder as he steered.

Always looking out for her, even then. Why hadn't she seen it earlier? It had probably been lost in the muddle near the end of their relationship, when she'd left town under a smoky cloud of suspicion at his guilty hand. But now, free and clear of the past, she could look at it with some objectivity.

Maybe Boone was right. Maybe they'd always belonged

together: Boone and PJ, facing the wind, side by side in his Mustang. Maybe, in fact, she'd returned home because she'd always known that too.

"I thought I'd find you here."

The voice startled her, but it wasn't Boone who sauntered up to her. Jeremy had shaved since she last saw him, and he hid any vestiges of fatigue under a pair of dark sunglasses. Now he glanced at Boris, then at the car. "I didn't realize you already had wheels."

"It's a loaner." PJ looked behind her and spotted his motorcycle parked in the lot, the helmet on the seat.

"I'll bet." Jeremy nodded a greeting to Boris, who had sat up and now gave him a long, solemn look. She would have liked to know what this former cop saw when he looked at Jeremy. Motorcycle, baseball cap on backward . . . a street hood? Perhaps only PJ recognized Jeremy as a man who had once served his country, a man who had deep, maybe even dangerous, secrets in his dark eyes. "I'd like to know what strings came attached."

"None. Boone's just helping me out."

Jeremy said nothing but after a bit gave a small nod. "Well, then maybe this will help too." He pulled a small white card out of his pocket and handed it over to her.

She took it, read *Rusty's Real Deals*, and looked at Jeremy. "The place over on Highway 12? Used to be the VW dealership?"

"Yep. Rusty'll fix you up."

PJ stared at him. "Fix me up . . . how?"

Jeremy sighed, looked beyond her. "Listen, Prin—PJ. I'm sorry about your car."

PJ flicked the card between her finger and thumb. Well, well, Mr. Jeremy Kane apologizing? Even after he'd used her for bait to catch an assassin, he hadn't apologized.

"There's three grand on deposit there. I know it won't replace your Bug, but it's all I had in savings at the moment. See if you can land some wheels." He glanced at the Mustang. "Today."

"Jeremy, I can't take your—"

"It's the least I can do, PJ. Take it."

"Listen, Boone said I could have his car for as long as—"

"I'll see you in the office tomorrow morning. Early. We have a new case." He patted her shoulder like she might be a teammate. "And it can't be investigated with . . . that." He lifted his chin toward the Mustang, then turned and walked back to his bike.

She watched him kick it off the stand. He didn't look at her as he drove away. But as she turned around, she saw him glance back and she couldn't help but smile.

Chapter *FOUR*

PJ remembered the old Volkswagen dealership on Highway 12 as the place of dreams. She'd drive by, eyes glued to the shiny new models perched on the high platform, wondering not only how the cars got up there but what it took to own wheels that packed so much joy in such a small package.

She'd scored her first Bug the summer after she'd turned sixteen, after three months of saving. It was orange and had a rip in the high black driver's seat, but she'd patched up the vinyl with glue, learned how to wrangle the clutch like a NASCAR driver, and tasted freedom for the first time. How many times she had pointed her car west before she finally made the trek to South Dakota and beyond, she couldn't count. But when she finally left, she took her love of Bugs with her, trading up as she went.

PJ drove toward the dealership, almost smelling the new-car fragrance. Or, okay, the *artificial* new-car fragrance.

Last time she'd seen the VW place, flags fluttered along the lot, the sun winking off Golfs and Jettas, a shiny round VW sign rising in blue and white like a beacon. Now the sign had been replaced by one heralding Rusty's Real Deals and looked down on a collection of both the highbrow trade-ins and what seemed every rejected, forlorn car in Hennepin County. PJ pulled the Mustang into the lot, passing high-ticket SUVs on one side and a collection of Ford Fiestas and Kias on the other, and parked next to a white-sided sales building. Beyond the rows of cars, on the other side of the lot, from a long, low building containing two open garage doors emanated the sounds and smells of a machine shop.

She dearly hoped that Rusty whoever-he-was didn't jump to the hope that she would be trading in the Mustang. If Boone knew she'd taken his baby to a greasy, throwaway car lot, he'd spend the weekend with disinfectant, singing to it in soothing tones.

She heard a "halloow!" as she climbed out of the Mustang. Boris had also exited and began wandering through the lot, looking in car windows, kicking tires. She turned and found a salesman huffing around her car, his thinning hair blowing atop a round face and tiny dark eyes. He stuck out a doughy hand toward her. "Rusty Mulligan, manager."

"Hey, Rusty, I'm PJ. My boss, Jeremy Kane, said he'd left some money on account with you."

He smiled at her, not unlike the grin of a rat, toothy and broad. "I got it. If you need any help, give Casey back in the shop a shout." He nodded toward the black hole of the garage. "I'm headed out for a bit."

PJ edged her way around the menu of cars, leaving Boris to

wander until she stood at the lip of the shop. The redolence of oil and grease seeped from the shop, and the whine of an air compressor pierced the afternoon. She waited until it snuffed out, then hollered, "Is there a guy named Casey here?"

He appeared from behind an SUV on a lift, a man in oil-soaked coveralls open to the waist, a grimy white T-shirt nearly black where it pocketed his beer belly, and a gimme cap positioned backward on his head. A smudge of grease war-painted his face not unlike the black paint of a football player. In fact, it seemed familiar as he wound up the air hose, hung it on the rack, and ambled toward her. He squinted at her and then spit a wad of chaw off to the side as he came nearer. "Can I help you?"

PJ just stared at him, at the dark stubble under the oil smudges on his face, the smile that curved up one side of his face, as if trying to make up his mind, the look of playful curiosity in his eyes . . .

"Casey . . . *Whitlow*?" She tried to keep her mouth from swinging open. Casey Whitlow, who was a year older than her and had played halfback, rushing for a state record her junior year of high school? Casey Whitlow, who'd had a full head of tousled brown hair back then, the same athlete who'd had a lineup of girls waiting to be his head cheerleader?

Casey Whitlow, who'd asked her to junior prom during her sophomore year?

She'd always found him a decent guy, even if she'd turned him down.

She held out her hand. "Uh, hi, Casey." She drew off her sunglasses and offered a smile.

He blinked at her a moment, letting his gaze travel over her, and something lit in his eyes. "PJ Sugar." Her name curled off his lips like it had taken the form of ribbon candy. "Back from the dead."

"I was never dead."

"You were gone ten years. No one heard from you."

That wasn't entirely true. She'd kept in touch with her mother. And Connie. But her absence had been long enough to merit rumors of her demise. "Well, I'm back now and looking for a car."

He cast a glance at the Mustang parked near the hut like a beacon of hope. "Is that—?"

"Yes, it's Boone's, and no, I'm not trading it in. My car got totaled this morning, and my employer, Kane Investigations, left a deposit here for me to use. Your boss told me to ask you about a car."

Comprehension came over his face, a sort of boys'-locker-room look. "I see."

Clearly Casey still had a one-track mind. Too much time spent with cheerleaders. She skipped over a rebuttal. "Three grand, I believe he said."

"Well, help yourself, PJ." His gaze lingered on her as she moved away, and he scuffled out behind her. She heard another spit and splatter.

PJ began wandering through the lot. A few pickups—newer models that had higher price tags. A collection of SUVs, a few hybrids, and an occasional sports car. Nothing, however, in her price range. And especially, no VWs.

"Hunt around in the back of the lot," Casey suggested, now examining her—er, Boone's—Mustang.

She followed his gesture and spotted Boris examining a

collection of older model cars. Boris looked up and motioned her toward him.

She let out a low groan. A Crown Victoria. Of course Boris would like it: it matched all the vehicles he saw on late-night television. Coal black and shined up like onyx, it resembled something out of an old FBI show or maybe *Law & Order*. Better yet, whoever had owned it before Rusty's Real Deals had tricked it out with a couple of dubs on the back wheels that set it up higher and would earn her props should she suddenly decide to cruise the strip.

Oh, Boone would have too much fun if she took home this car. Jeremy, too, probably.

Boris had already looked under the car for damage—or perhaps leaking oil—evidenced by the smear of dirt down one of his shoulders. He thumped the trunk with his open palm as PJ walked up. *"Prekrasnya."*

"Yeah, real pretty, Boris." She peered in the passenger window at the burgundy velour interior. It looked roomy enough to fit a small bathroom, maybe Boris's field of potatoes.

Or perhaps her bed, along with all her earthly belongings.

Hey . . . maybe . . .

No, she wasn't that desperate.

Boris turned to the door, and with some horror, PJ realized he was trying to unlock it.

"Hey!" Casey spit again as he neared them. "What do you think—?"

Boris suddenly opened the door and slid behind the wheel, oohing as he bounced on the plush seat.

Casey skidded to a stop, checked the door, then looked at Boris.

The Russian held up a piece of wire with a neat J on the end and grinned, his gold teeth blinding.

PJ admitted to a moment of admiration for Boris. She'd have to get him to teach her his tricks.

"You don't just go breaking into cars," Casey said, an unfamiliar panic in his voice, but Boris seemingly ignored him, running his hands over the shiny black dash.

"What's his problem? Is he deaf?"

"No, he's Russian. Doesn't speak much English, so don't bother insulting him. What he doesn't know won't hurt him." At least that was what she told herself every time Boris started hurling scary words at her in a rather nasty tone.

Then again, he could possibly just be calling her to dinner.

Opening the passenger door, she slid in beside Boris, who was trying out the seat, sliding it back and forth.

Casey leaned down, talking over Boris in the driver's seat. "This is a P71—probably used by the Kellogg Police Department. This baby has rear-wheel drive, a V-8 engine, and it'll take a beating. Plus, if you'll note, she's been kicked up a notch—a couple of mag wheels on the back."

Yeah, that was a real selling point.

She leaned back, stretched out her legs, and let the seat embrace her. Felt the power. Imagined driving this yacht down the streets of Kellogg.

And a Crown Vic would be a thousand times more comfortable during a stakeout, wouldn't it? She glanced over the seat. Yep, plenty of room in the backseat to camp out. She might even keep a sleeping bag in there.

PJ peered at Casey. "How much?"

Casey smiled, and she recognized it as the one he'd worn for his adoring fans when he emerged from the locker room after the game. "Well . . ." He gave her a smile. Spit again. The dark chaw landed on the wheel of a tired Camry. "A 1996 Crown Vic—it's a great deal. Blue book is $4,000 . . . but I'll give it to you for the 3K that your . . . um, friend gave you—"

"He's my boss."

He winked at her. "Right."

"I don't know. Boris, what do you think?"

He turned at his name, grinned, nodding. *"Da, da."*

"Who is this guy, anyway?" Casey shot her a frown, lowering his voice.

PJ laid a hand on Boris's thick shoulder. "My sister's father-in-law. Used to be a cop, by the way."

Casey considered him, his eyes running over him slowly. "Really. Can he break kneecaps?"

PJ gave him a look. "Funny." She shook her head. "Whatever he can do, he's not a cop here. He can't even get a job at Walmart."

"He's looking for a job?"

Technically, *she* was the one looking for a job. Boris, apparently, was just along for the ride. She shrugged her answer.

"I might have a job for him," Casey said.

"What's it going to cost me?"

Casey hung an arm over the door. Grinned. "Well . . ."

"Boone and I are dating, Case."

"Of course you are. Listen, does this guy have a driver's license?"

"It's an international license. So, yes, in a way—"

"Good. Rusty's lookin' for a guy with his skills. Tell him to be here tomorrow, 6 p.m."

Really? She studied Casey for guile on his face. "What will he be doing?"

Casey lifted a shoulder and looked off toward the garage. "Moving cars in the lot, maybe some repo work. It's sorta like . . . security."

A security agent—now why hadn't she thought of that?

Or maybe she had . . . unconsciously.

Maybe everything she did didn't have to turn into a mess with sirens and blood.

She eased herself out of the car and slammed the door, peering over the top at Casey. "I'll take it."

All she needed now were some fuzzy dice.

Boris got to employ his international license as he followed PJ home in the Crown Vic; she wasn't so brave—or stupid—as to let him drive the Mustang. She couldn't wait, however, to see Boone's face when he checked out her new ride.

And how she longed to take it out on that straight stretch on Steven's Point and see if the Vic really did have its infamous muscle.

She left the Mustang out on the street, and Boris eased in behind her, grinning widely. Employed. Empowered.

See, that's how it was done.

She entered the house, lured into the kitchen by the smells of home cooking—something frying in onions on the stove and a loaf of bread cooling on the counter. Vera had squeezed herself into tight capris and a low-cut blouse—PJ would have to wean her off soap operas—and was humming as she stirred what looked like, from this side of the room, leeches in pot.

Thankfully PJ would be eating out tonight. With Boone.

Who probably wanted an answer to his proposal. Maybe

sautéed leeches weren't so . . . No, she had to give the man an answer.

Didn't she?

At the very least she had to return his car, give him an explanation about the Vic. That would be fun.

After pouring herself a lemonade, she stepped out onto the back porch. The sun was still high enough to cast spindly shadows from the poplar and oak in the corner of the yard. The wind toyed with one of the swings, rustling the fronds of a begonia safely potted on the deck. In the wasteland of Connie's garden, the goat munched a pile of uprooted peonies.

When had she turned so . . . cautious? She'd spent years following her whims, letting them lead her like a puppy after a bone across the country and finally back home, into Boone's arms. So why wouldn't she want to marry Boone? They'd spent their high school years tearing up the streets and beaches of Kellogg, losing themselves in each other's arms, the laughter of a first love. She knew Boone better than anyone.

And Boone knew her. Knew her past and her fears, knew her scars—even the ones unseen—knew how to make her laugh.

And how to make her cry.

She loved Boone—had probably always loved him, even before they dated. At least since the seventh grade, when he'd climbed onto her bus, slouched in the seat behind her, and quietly mumbled something about going to the winter snow ball. She'd turned him down then. But not again when, three years later, he'd asked her to homecoming.

She wasn't sure she could turn him down now. Nor if she should. If she were honest with herself, hadn't she come back to Kellogg for this very reason? Boone?

She held the glass of lemonade to her forehead, letting the sweaty surface chill her.

The phone rang, and she leaped for it before Vera could pick it up. Although, last time the telemarketer on the other end actually hung up on her after hearing the barked Russian.

"PJ?" Boone, and his voice sounded wire tight.

"Hey."

"I'm sorry—I have to call off our dinner tonight. Something came up. How about tomorrow?"

Tomorrow. The word loosened something inside her and she let out a longer sigh than she intended. A reprieve. "Sure."

Silence on the other end.

Uh-oh. Had he heard her sigh and read into it more than she meant? "Really, Boone, it's fine."

"I promise I wouldn't let you down if it wasn't important."

She hated the question in his voice and couldn't ignore it. "It better be, pal, 'cause I was looking forward to taking you cruising in my new wheels."

She heard laughter, then silence.

Still, she couldn't deny the relief that splashed through her.

Until, of course, she looked at the leeches.

❋ ❋ ❋

Jeremy Kane Investigations occupied 750 square feet in downtown Dinkytown, right next to the University of Minnesota campus, over a sandwich shop that specialized in the Big Ten—salami and ham slathered with their private recipe tomato sauce—and a used-book store PJ discovered the second day of work, which stocked the complete works of Louis L'Amour. Her father would have been thrilled.

Jeremy had set up his digs on the second floor—through a gold-painted door, up stairs covered by red carpet that had been worn down to the matting, and inside the first and only door on the left. What he lacked in curb appeal, he made up for in a sharp desire for a modern and slick interior, with a stainless-steel and black leather sectional, the bleached birch table he used for a desk, and two black filing cabinets filled with nothing. Rather, he'd honed his filing system into a unique trail of manila folders that spiraled around the floor, with occasional half-drunk cups of coffee like road markers where he'd stopped to peruse an old case. His open cases were piled on his desk amid a landfill of Post-it notes, empty cheese and cracker boxes, and the occasional Dr Pepper can all littered around his laptop docking station. A spider plant on the deep windowsill blocked a view of the printing shop and gym across the street.

Jeremy had all the right intentions, however. PJ had spent the first two days (after locating her favorite L'Amour books) hanging the vista of Minneapolis and the two Ansel Adams photos stacked against the lone brick wall, filing the folders (until he freaked out and she had to replace them "just as they were"), feeding (then discarding and replacing) the spider plant, emptying the coffees, sweeping the floor, hanging a whiteboard, and generally making the place habitable.

Because, in the back of her mind, someday she too might require the use of the sofa.

But more than that, she wanted a grunt of approval, something to indicate that yes, Jeremy needed her.

Wanted her.

Believed in her.

"About time, Sugar. I've been here since seven." Jeremy didn't look up from his laptop as she crept into the office carrying a tray with two coffees—one black, the other with two pumps of vanilla and lots of artificial sweetener—from downstairs. She'd also scored a morning paper. Who knew what new business they might harvest from the crime section?

"Sorry. I couldn't find a place to park." Or rather, moor her battleship. Three minutes inside the Vic this morning told her she'd need a new mind-set to drive her hot new wheels. So much for zipping around in her precocious VW Bug. The Vic took its sweet time easing away from the curb or even a stoplight, preferring to warm up first in a low growl rather than a high-pitched *whee!* Now she felt like a sea captain, skippering her land yacht down 394 into Minneapolis, circling the neighborhood outside Jeremy's office twice before docking two blocks down in a parking space that seemed the size of a tugboat.

What had possessed her . . . ?

"Don't drop your stuff. We're going downstairs." Jeremy stood, looking military and tough in a tight Navy T-shirt and a pair of black sweatpants.

"Look who's bright and shiny—"

"Snuff it, PJ. We have work to do." He snagged a duffel bag from beside his desk.

"But I have coffee."

He took the tray, set it on his desk, and opened the door. He was down the stairs in three steps. She noticed a sticky note on the door but didn't have time to read it as she wrangled her cup from the tray—who knew when they'd be back?—and dashed after him.

Jeremy waited for her at the corner, then crossed the street. She had to jog to keep up, something not so easy if she didn't want her coffee to spill.

"Where are we going?"

Jeremy reached the opposite curb and strode down the street, past the print shop, past the bike store, then turned into the new gym with the wall of windows that displayed a class of coeds stopping traffic as they stretched.

"What? I'm not exercising!" PJ stopped at the door.

Jeremy turned, cupped her elbow, and practically manhandled her inside. "We're not exercising. We're saving your life."

"Does my life need saving?" She let him herd her past a reception desk and nodded at—or was that pleaded with?—the receptionist, who didn't even blink at the girl being accosted in the hallway.

The gym leaned toward an industrial, tough look with its painted cement floors, the stainless pipes that ran across the high ceilings, the abstract "Just Do It" black-and-white art hanging on the brick walls. Beyond a glass wall the coeds had hunkered down into a yoga position that made PJ avert her eyes.

"It does if you plan on any more stakeouts." Jeremy led her to a door marked *Ladies* and shoved the duffel into her arms. She nearly dropped the coffee on him, then wished she had when he took it, ripped off the top, and dumped the contents into a nearby planter. She dearly hoped that wasn't a plastic ficus tree. "No more coffee. I want to see protein shakes from now on."

"I don't think I like protein—"

Jeremy shoved her into the ladies' locker room. "I'll be waiting right here, so don't try to escape."

"You'd be a stellar prison guard!" She let the door swish shut behind her.

Exercising. Right. She'd sort of counted on her résumé—construction crew, stunt girl, waitress, zookeeper—to keep her fit. The last time she'd officially exercised was in eleventh-grade gym, running laps in the hope of snagging a passing grade. It had to be some sort of sadistic crime to schedule gym during first hour.

The locker room must've used the same decorator as Kellogg High—long benches; gray, wire lockers; the oh-so-attractive smell of body odor; a fog of humidity languishing in the air from the nearby showers.

PJ clutched the duffel bag and her own canvas bag to her chest and shuffled to the far corner.

Inside the duffel she found a pair of blue nylon shorts and a matching athletic shirt with the tags still attached, and a pair of socks. Good thing she'd worn her Converse. She would have hated to run in flip-flops.

Her tan was fading after two months in Jeremy's tomb. She slid into the shorts and shirt, promising herself a couple hours at the beach on her first day off.

She emerged, still toting her purse—Jeremy didn't seriously think she would leave it in a flimsy locker? It had taken her a year to accumulate the right accoutrements to survive.

She found Jeremy with his back to the door, his arms crossed, leaning one shoulder against the wall.

"I could have snuck out of here and you would have never noticed," she said as he turned.

"You think so?" His dark eyes sparked with something that looked teasing.

She didn't answer. She ran in place. "So, ten laps around the yoga girls?"

"Nope. I have something a little more useful in mind." He gestured for her to follow. They entered a room in the back of the gym, the floor covered with spongy pads on the floor, one wall filled with mirrors, another painted with Karate Kid–style action figures. A weight bag dangled in one corner, and a stack of what looked like padded armor lay on the floor.

"Should I bow?"

"If you'd like."

Uh-oh. Someone's sense of humor needed a shot of coffee.

"Take off your shoes."

PJ toed them off, kicking them toward the far wall. She watched Jeremy circle behind her. "What are you—?"

He snaked a hand around her neck, pulling her tight against his chest. She gasped, wrapping her arms around his forearm, pulling. "What's that for? Are you still mad about the stakeout?"

"I'm not mad, PJ. I'm trying to teach you a lesson. See how unprepared you were? I just snuck up on you—"

"Of course you did, you lunatic! You're my bo—well, at the very least, I don't expect you to kill me . . . or headlock me." He wasn't hurting her, though, only holding her in his sturdy arms, one under her chin, the other locked around his wrist. When she wiggled, he didn't budge. "Let me go!"

"Get away." His voice dropped a pitch, quiet, lethal. Yes, once upon a time he'd been a very scary man. "Try to break free."

PJ pulled on his forearm, yanked at his other arm. "Okay, uncle."

"Really? That's all you got, Sugar? Because you looked a lot tough—"

She slammed her heel down hard on the top of his foot.

He jerked but didn't let go. Still, he allowed a low chuckle. "Okay, two points. But if you're my hostage, a little heel stamp isn't going to help you. You're going to have to fight harder to get away."

PJ wriggled against his grip, feeling all the while the smooth planes of his chest pressed against her back. "Where are you in all this while I'm being dragged away to my death? Eating a hamburger? You're the Navy SEAL—when do you swoop in and save the day?"

"I've been disarmed by a poisoned bismark. You're the only thing that stands between Dr. Death's world domination and thousands of orphan children. Whatya going to do, PJ?"

"And I'm fresh out of pastry."

"Want a hint?"

"No, I just want to stand here all day staring at us in the big mirrors, watching you grin. You're having entirely too much fun."

Jeremy let her go. Came around to stand before her. She resisted the urge to wallop him and his hint of a smile.

"First, be aware of your weapons."

Please. Even he could see that she didn't have a prayer of hiding a gun, knife, or even a pair of brass knuckles in this getup. "I'm clean out of donuts."

"PJ, think. Elbows, knees, feet." He demonstrated some moves: jabbing, kneeing, kicking.

"Right. Weapons. But I kicked you and it didn't make a difference."

"We'll fix that. Make a fist."

"Not a problem." She tightened her hand into a fist, as menacing as possible.

He took it and rearranged it so her thumb tucked tight in the groove of her pointer finger instead of along her folded fingers. He cupped his hand over it. "This is your hammer. You want it to be tight and compact."

Then he grabbed her left arm at the wrist. "Let's say an attacker grabs your arm. Give him the hammer right on the top of his arm."

He looked at her as if expecting her to hit him. "Go ahead."

"Hit you?"

"Not hard, but yes, give it some umph."

She came down on the side of his arm.

He grunted as he let go, rubbing his arm. "I think you got it."

She danced in place a bit on the spongy floor. "I like this kind of exercise. So, how do I break out of your hold?"

He stepped behind her again. She watched him in the mirror as his gaze went over her before he took a breath and stepped up, wrapping his arm around her neck again.

"Okay, the first thing you do is tuck your chin in tight and get below my hold."

She tucked her chin down, just inside his elbow. His skin smelled clean with a hint of manly musk. "Now what?" His hold muffled her voice.

"Your attacker is expecting you to struggle. What you want to do is surprise him. I want you to step back into his hold, grab the hand that's wrapped around your neck, bend your knees a little, and deliver a hammer blow straight back with your left hand. Aim for the, uh, essentials, but if you can't, hit the nerve on the top of his leg." Jeremy shifted behind her. "Go ahead and practice, but I'd appreciate it if you'd lean more on the pretending part."

"Is that fear in your voice, tough guy?"

"Just hit me."

She pretended to hit him. "Uh, nothing happened."

"We're not done. But notice how I moved."

"I think anyone would move if I were serious."

"You're right. And while they move, you yank your assailant's hand from your neck and twist out of the hold, twisting his arm with it."

She tried the move. He let her, of course, but there was power in breaking free from his hold, like she just might be able to really accomplish it. Really defend herself. Save the orphans from the evil Dr. Death.

"Now, while you've got him here, disabled, go ahead and kick—a side kick to the knees, maybe." He flinched a little as she pretended. "That wasn't the knees."

"Just seeing if you were paying attention."

"I never take my eyes off you, PJ."

The room suddenly went very still, and she saw it again, the look he'd given her in the parking lot when he'd come up behind Boone, who'd been asking about his proposal.

Hurt? Hope?

She dropped his hand and wiped hers on her shorts.

"Want to try it again? Maybe all the moves together?" There was a crispness in his voice she hadn't noticed before.

PJ nodded without looking at him. He wrapped his arm around her neck. She could have bet her life on the fact that his heartbeat staccatoed in his chest. She cleared her throat, made a fist, and seconds later, was out of his hold.

"You had better be trying, Pizza Man."

Jeremy held up his hands, as if to say, *of course.* "Try again."

They did the move a dozen times until PJ refined her hammer punch and nearly sent Jeremy to the mat once. Good thing he was fast on his feet.

They were both breathing hard when they finished.

And she thought she'd earned a look of authentic appreciation.

"Let's try some real punches." Jeremy walked over to the netting that held the padding, picked up a thin pair of gloves, and tossed them to her, then a helmet and a body pad. He suited up with the same.

"Seriously?"

"How are you going to get used to not flinching when someone comes at you?"

She was starting to see the merit of across-the-parking-lot surveillance.

"Put your body into it, like this." He punched out, pivoting his feet. "Your power comes from your legs and your upper body."

She mimicked him.

"I don't think you need the sound effects."

"It makes me feel like a ninja. Leave me alone." She kept practicing. Watched herself punch.

"So, did you buy a car?"

"Yep."

"What kind? Another Beetle?"

"Nope." She kept punching. One, two, uppercut. Float like a butterfly, sting like a bee.

"What kind?"

"Not telling. But you'll thank me next time we go on a stakeout."

"Is it a pickup?"

"Nope." She leaned back, threw out a kick.

Jeremy stood in her peripheral vision, arms down. "Throw a few at me."

Hah! She pivoted and threw a punch at his padded chest.

Her grin vanished when he blocked her fist.

"Hey! Show me how you do that."

Jeremy showed her how to deflect punches with her arms in blocks and parries. She deflected them all, faster and faster like a kung fu master. She was the Karate Kid. *Wax on, wax off.* "I'm pretty good."

Jeremy was smiling as he threw easy punches. She blocked them, dancing on her feet. Yes, she could get into this.

She shadowboxed, jigging around the room, clapping her mitts together. "Let's see what you got. Give me something real."

He stood with his hands at his sides and shook his head, a sort of sad look on his face. "You don't want to—"

"C'mon, give me a good one. I want to see if I can block it."

"No, PJ."

"Jeremy!"

"Okay, if you—"

"PJ!" The voice came from behind her, near the door.

She turned just as Jeremy's punch flew at her.

Chapter FIVE

"You hit her!"

Through a haze of pain PJ made out Boone's voice hurtling toward her as she writhed on the mat.

Jeremy had connected with her shoulder, a jarring blow that rattled her clear through and sent her flying.

Boone dropped to his knees beside her. "PJ! Are you okay?" But he didn't wait for an answer before he lunged at Jeremy, who'd also crouched beside her. The two rolled on the floor. Boone threw a punch; Jeremy blocked it, returned one of his own.

"You hit her!"

"She asked me to!"

"Stop!" PJ pulled off a glove and hurled it at Boone, who now had Jeremy in a full body lock, arm around his neck, leg around his torso. She half debated asking Jeremy to display his escape technique but decided against it as she threw the other glove at the two. "Stop! I'm fine, and I *did* ask Jeremy to hit me."

Boone jerked his gaze up and stared at her as if she'd just told him she was moving to Taiwan. "What?"

"We were sparring. I had everything under control and would have been just fine if you hadn't distracted me."

Jeremy's hand closed atop Boone's forearm, still tight against his neck. "But in a real-life situation there will be dist—"

Boone squeezed his hold on Jeremy, who threw a backward punch at his head, then followed with an elbow to Boone's ribs. Boone huffed out a hiss of pain but didn't let go.

She wasn't sure why pride speared through her. Boone could stand up to a Navy SEAL. Still . . . "Let him go, Boone."

"Not everything is a teachable moment," Boone growled.

"I promise I'm going to be okay," PJ said, climbing to her feet. "Seriously, let him go." Besides, apology furrowed Jeremy's face as he stared at her. He'd probably *let* Boone take him down, penance for giving in to her goading to hit her.

Boone freed Jeremy, and she held out a hand to her boss. Jeremy took it, his expression unreadable as she pulled him off the floor. Boone bounced to his feet unaided.

Admittedly, Jeremy's punch had hurt. Her shoulder thudded in an endless hammer of pain as blood pumped down her arm. But she wasn't going to indict him more. She pulled off the helmet. "I *do* need to learn this stuff. Especially if I want to be a good PI."

PJ noted that Jeremy barely looked at her as he peeled off his body armor. He picked up her discarded gloves and helmet and dumped them with his into the netting.

Boone stepped close and examined her shoulder. "Can you move it? Is it dislocated?"

"I'll be fine. If anything, it'll teach me to keep my eye on my opponent."

"Oh no, you're not doing this again. Your little fight club is over." Boone pulled off her body armor and tossed it in the corner.

Now that she got a good look at Boone, he looked unhinged—reddened eyes, unshaven, and he was wearing street clothes—a pair of out-of-character ratty jeans and a T-shirt, as if he'd spent the night camped out in his pickup. Or perhaps one of those wimpy new Chevy Impalas used by the Kellogg police. He needed a Crown Vic.

"I suppose you're wondering where your car is."

"Actually, that's why I'm here. I . . . need it back."

"Oh."

"Please tell me you parked it somewhere where it's not going to get dinged by a kid on a bike or, worse, stolen. Like my truck. I came out of the gym this morning and someone had boosted it. It's gone, and I need wheels." He gave a sort of wry smile. "I'm sorry."

"Boone, that's awful! The Mustang's safe, I promise. . . ." Especially sitting in Connie's garage, where she'd parked it after Connie left for work.

"Safe and then a long pause? Uh, what aren't you telling me?" Boone looked like he might be bracing himself.

"Well, I bought a new car, so the Mustang's back in Kellogg."

Boone nodded, his smile still cautious. Jeremy had disappeared and now returned with a couple of water bottles. PJ opened hers and glugged it down. Jeremy kept a respectable distance from Boone but, as he promised, never took his eyes off PJ.

"It's a . . . a Crown Vic."

Boone's mouth opened and then closed, and she saw words forming in his eyes. Finally, his voice tight, "Don't you think that's a little cliché?"

"I like it. I feel like I'm the captain of the SS *Minnow*."

"An ill-fated tour if I remember correctly."

"Ha-ha." PJ took another drink and wiped her mouth. "How'd you find me?"

"Went to Jeremy's office. There was a note on the door."

So that's what it said. "You're really after your car? You promise you're not checking up on me?"

He stuck his hands in his pockets, his expression hardening. "I'm not checking up on you, but I'm glad I did. Apparently someone needs to keep you out of harm's way."

Jeremy's mouth tightened in a firm, say-nothing line.

"Just for the record, I tried your cell. What's the deal? It doesn't even go to voice mail."

PJ glanced at Jeremy, the keeper of her paycheck. "I didn't pay my bill. And I didn't want to have to pay reconnect charges."

Boone shook his head, his patience visibly deteriorating. "Don't you have any money?"

"I'm slightly on the lean side right now."

And as expected, Boone lasered a dark look at Jeremy, who turned away.

"So, if your wheels were stolen, how'd you get here?" PJ asked.

"I got a ride."

She tilted her head at him. "You didn't come down here for

your car keys, did you? You could have waited until tonight or swung by the house."

"Okay, I didn't," he snapped. "I came down to see . . . Well, we didn't have dinner last night, so I hoped . . ."

Hoped that she had an answer to his proposal. The truth flashed on his face, followed by a flinch. He looked away.

"We're still on for dinner tonight, right?" He asked it so softly, as if he were holding out his heart, right there in front of Jeremy.

She was opening her mouth to reply when Jeremy cut in.

"No. You're not."

PJ winced. Clearly Jeremy didn't have issues with eavesdropping.

Or cutting Boone to the heart.

Jeremy stepped beside her. "She can't have dinner with you." He seemed to relish this statement way too much, based on his tone, the way he took another swig of his drink, his dark, cool eyes on Boone.

"I can't?" PJ asked.

He wiped his mouth. "Nope. You're going undercover. Today. We have a new case, and I need you."

"I need you." Jeremy *needed* her. She so easily caved to those words, like she might be a cocker spaniel, her button tail a blur.

Good grief, she needed a support group or something.

"No, you don't," Boone snapped. "In fact, this game has gone on long enough." He walked over to the wall and picked up her bag. How strange to see it in the clutches of the man who would barely carry a backpack to school. "C'mon, PJ, I'm taking you to lunch."

"Do I get to change?"

Boone looked at Jeremy, his pale eyes icy. "How long will it take?"

"I'll just go as is." She grabbed her shoes and put them on, then took her bag from Boone. "But you need to know I'm coming back—and yes, I'm going undercover." Undercover. *Undercover.* As she glanced back at Jeremy, she couldn't help but smile.

He didn't match it, his gaze squarely on Boone, who put a hand on her shoulder and guided her outside.

They hit the street to a blast of summer air. Heat simmered off the sidewalk and scoured up smells from the sub shop alley across the street.

"How about Gopher Subs?" Boone reached for her hand as he walked to the corner and waited for the traffic light to turn. In the sunlight his hair gleamed like some legendary Norse prince, minus the battle armor, bloodied axe, and flowing cape. This Boone surprised her at every turn, from the way he'd morphed into a respectable, nearly stuffy, calm, and serious detective—despite his current out-of-character rumple—to his dedication to their future.

What surprised her the most at the moment, however, was his vitriol toward her new job. She slipped her hand out of his and walked without talking as they crossed the street and entered the sub shop.

The air-conditioning slicked over her skin, awakening the realization that she wore a pair of skimpy shorts and a sleeveless shirt. She gave a cursory search through her bag and found a rolled-up Windbreaker, which she pulled on.

"What don't you have in there?" Boone asked, barely a smile on his stoic face.

"A shower. I should have cleaned up."

"This won't take long. Grab us a booth." And before she could give him her order, Boone added himself to the line. Of course, he'd just assume she'd want a tuna sandwich. However, she'd moved on since her high school addictions. Now she liked the chicken Caesar.

Once the order came up, he slid into the booth across from her, handed over her tuna on wheat. "I'm sorry I came off so . . . raging bull. But he hit you, PJ. He *hit* you."

"I had pads on. And we were sparring. How am I supposed to develop reflexes if I don't practice?"

He unwrapped his sandwich, a dripping Philly cheesesteak. "I'm not sure I want you developing those kind of reflexes." He stared at his lunch as if it might contain the words he struggled to find. Finally, "You just don't know what you're getting into, babe."

The way he said it, soft and with a small groan at the end, made her put down her sandwich. She reached across the table and touched his hand. He covered her fingers with his thumb. Sighed.

"What is it, Boone?"

He closed his eyes a second before looking at her. "You have to trust me when I say this isn't the job for you. Enough playing around, Peej. I thought—and maybe this was stupid of me—but I thought that after the Hoffman case, you'd figure out that nosing around in crime can get you and the people you care about hurt. Even killed." He ran a finger down the side of her face. She resisted the urge to lean into his touch even as his eyes held hers. "I know I don't have the power to forbid this—"

"Forbid?"

He jerked away. Yeah, well, someone was about to lose a hand.

"Bad choice of words, maybe. How about . . . ask you not to do this? plead with you? beg you?"

"Why are you suddenly so worried about this? What's going on, Boone?"

He leaned back, raking a hand through his blond hair. She'd rarely seen him this rattled. Boone epitomized cool, right from the days when he'd stare down defensive linemen as the Kellogg High quarterback. He'd even laughed through the tattoo artist's needle the day they'd inked each other's names on their shoulders.

But now he sat across from her with a darkness in his eyes that scared her. He stared at her a long moment while she watched his chest rise and fall. "I can't go into details, but we had a murder last night in Kellogg. And it was someone we knew."

Someone they knew? Of course in a town the size of Kellogg the odds of that were great, but . . . "Who?"

He pushed his lunch to the side and leaned over the table, his voice in sleuth mode. "Remember Allison Miller?"

PJ mentally scrolled through her yearbook. "Uh . . ."

"A class ahead of us, she was a cheerleader."

PJ couldn't breathe. Yes, she remembered her—long blonde hair, an amazing toe touch. Too curvy for her age and a reputation to match. "Yes."

Boone blew out a long breath.

PJ again reached for his hands.

He surrendered them to her, holding tighter than she'd

expected. "She was working for me—sort of an informant on an investigation. They found her body last night in the Kellogg harbor." He shook his head, the memory lingering in the back of his eyes, eating his words.

PJ waited, counting her heartbeats, trying to imagine what he'd really seen and then not wanting to.

Boone stared at their clasped hands on the table, running both thumbs over her fingers. "She was beaten to death. It was brutal. And . . . the truth is, it was my fault."

"Boone . . ."

"Last time I talked to her, she said that they were onto her—but she wouldn't say who. She told me she could handle it. And I believed her."

When he met her eyes, she recognized the emotion in them. Regret. And it was aimed right at her.

"She thought she was tough enough to stand up against a group of people who played by an entirely different set of rules."

He didn't have to fill in the proper nouns for PJ to know who he was really talking about. She held on to his hands a moment longer, then sat back.

"I'm really sorry, Boone." But she wasn't Allison. And besides, she could take . . . care . . . "I really am going to be okay."

Based on his reddened eyes on hers, he didn't believe her. "Don't do this. Don't make me show up someday to fish your bloated body out of the Kellogg harbor." His voice hovered just above a moan.

"I want to do this. It makes me feel like, for the first time in my life, I could be good at something."

"You are good at a billion things."

"Name one. *One.* I have lost or quit so many jobs from one end of the country to the other that my résumé could wallpaper Jeremy's office. I like this job. I have instincts—"

"Instincts nearly got you hurt yesterday. Who knows when you'll wind up in the middle of something dangerous?"

"My instincts might have saved Geri's life for all we know."

"If you do this, I'm going to spend every waking hour worried about you. I'll think about you while I'm doing my job—"

"Don't put that on me, Boone. I'm not your wife."

His mouth tightened. Behind them, the sub clerk called out an order. The bell over the door dinged. Boone's eyes never left hers. "I am hoping there is a *yet* at the end of your sentence."

PJ's throat tightened. "Don't you see? This is my chance to do something with my life. To be someone extraordinary. To finally make my mark in Kellogg."

"You're already extraordinary."

"Not . . . to me." She looked out the window at the sun glaring on the pavement, the college students hiking home from summer classes, backpacks bumping against their shoulders. She hadn't finished college. Hadn't really finished anything.

"I want to do this. And Jeremy's got a new case for me. It's important to me."

"And you're important to me. I can't let you do this."

"Don't make me choose between you and my job." PJ wasn't sure where the ultimatum came from and wanted to snatch it back as quickly as the words tripped out of her mouth, but they hung there between them, ugly and sour. She had no choice but to cross her arms, lift her chin.

As she expected, her words, so softly spoken, hit Boone like one of her new hammer punches, evidenced by his quick flinch.

"Why?" he snapped. "Because I wouldn't win?" His eyes, unmoving, burned into her.

She saw the hurt in them, and it seared the words from her mouth.

She tore her gaze away.

With a muffled curse, Boone got up and left her there with the untouched sandwiches.

✳ ✳ ✳

Even if she added in Boone's worst nightmares and compounded them with a killer on the loose, he had nothing to worry about. PJ had to admit to the slightest simmer of frustration as she listened to Jeremy outline their next case. Her so-called *undercover* case.

"Let me get this straight—you want me to house-sit? *House-sit?* Like dust the furniture? take in the paper? water the plants?"

"And feed her pet rats, yes."

Jeremy had barely looked her in the eye after she returned from lunch, or rather nonlunch, with Boone. She'd taken the liberty of showering at the gym, finishing her sandwich, and scoring a skinny vanilla latte—after all, her coffee had gone to a very unneedy ficus—before returning to Jeremy's office. Hey, it had milk. That counted as protein.

She found him perched at his window, his shoulders squared, staring blankly into the street.

And when he started with "Maybe Boone's right . . . ," she knew she had some reparations to make on his confidence in her abilities.

"I promise to be at the top of my game. No jumping to conclusions. No distractions. Wax on, wax off." She even did the accompanying defensive arm movements.

"Sure." Jeremy turned away from the window, wearing indecision in his expression and in the way he coiled a hand behind his neck.

She held her breath for a long moment—*c'mon, Jeremy, trust me*—and finally he collapsed onto the sofa. He nodded for her to take a seat.

Yes. Finally, he was going to let her off her leash. Dance solo. Trust her instincts.

"I wouldn't let you do this if I didn't think it was perfectly safe."

Oh, shoot. But she nodded even as he leaned forward, braced his hands on his knees, and began to explain.

Thirty minutes later, she couldn't believe he'd actually debated her ability to do this job. So much for earning his respect, his admiration.

Or her own.

"So let me get this straight. You got a call from a woman who says she's under FBI protection?"

"That's right—Dally Morrison. Her FBI contact is a guy named Leroy Simmons. Goes by Lee."

"Right. And he's in charge of making sure his star witness for a drug case shows up at court in a week or so."

"Ten days from tomorrow."

"But said witness—"

"Dally Morrison, our client."

"Dally, the witness-slash-client, is in danger."

"No, not danger. Like I said, if I thought she was in danger, *real* danger, I'd never let you do this. She's just . . . let's say, upset and jumpy because another witness got killed in a drive-by shooting. But I talked with her protection agent. Even though the witness lived in Chicago, Lee thinks it was unconnected to the crime. The defendant is behind bars, cut off from his gang buddies—"

"C'mon, Jeremy, I've seen enough television to know that gangbangers have long arms."

"No, you've seen too much television. There's no evidence to connect the dots here and create a real threat."

"Maybe a little bit of a threat? Just an itsy-bitsy threat?"

Jeremy rolled his eyes.

"I just don't want my first undercover operation to be listed as house-sitting. Can't we say 'body double'? Or maybe 'witness protection shield'?"

He leaned back, his lips tightened in a firm line. But he gave the slightest sad shake of his head.

"Fine. So I'm supposed to lay low, be a shadow in her house while you . . . what?"

"I'll take Dally to a secluded location and babysit her, keep her calm so she can testify."

"Why doesn't the FBI just take her someplace safe?"

"Because Dally doesn't trust anybody, apparently. She got our name out of the phone book. But this Billy Finch is big-time in Chicago, and the FBI doesn't want her to waffle. Lee's not thrilled about it—especially the part where she doesn't want me to tell anyone where I'm taking her. But he agrees that any calls from back home or even a strange bump in the night is liable to set her off and on the run. She did this not long after Billy was arrested two years ago—took off, and Lee found her holed up in South Dakota, three sheets to the wind. He thought by moving her to Minneapolis, it would calm her down, but she's a bit high-strung. So he's agreed to let us step in, keep her calm, and help her. He needs her to stay put and show up coherent for the trial. So, you'll take her place, and I'll make sure she shows up undistracted and ready to testify."

"If you're taking her away, why does she need someone to stay at her house?"

"Because she's paranoid. She thinks that one of Finch's contacts is after her—" he emphasized his words with finger quotes—"and that whoever it is will figure out she's gone and look for her. So she wants a stand-in or she's not going. And not testifying."

"So I'm sort of bait."

"Please don't say that with so much enthusiasm. Again, if I thought you were in any danger, this wouldn't be happening. We're simply appeasing a jumpy witness's psychosis."

"You take the fun out of everything."

"Yeah, well, I think your fiancé would skin me from hairline to ankle if I got you hurt."

Fiancé. She stared at Jeremy and knew by his steely-eyed, nearly arrogant expression that he'd dropped the word with every intent of rattling her. "He's not my fiancé."

"Usually when I hear the word *proposal*, there's a *marriage* attached."

She got up and paced to the window. She could barely make out the Vic down the street. "I haven't given him an answer."

Silence boomed on the other side of the room.

"Ten days is a long time to be trapped in a house. My tan's going to fade."

Jeremy seemed to be debating his response. "There's a fence. Wear a hat and sunglasses, and you can lay out in the backyard."

"I'm not in high school."

"But you are on the job."

"On the job." On. The. Job. Like a cop. "Maybe I could wear a wig, some of Dally's clothes . . . is she my size?"

"I think you'll find that she's like you in many ways."

"I'm not sure I want to know what you mean by that. But I'll take it as a thumbs-up on my ability to do this."

Jeremy nodded, yet when she searched for the sweet assurance in his dark eyes, she came up empty.

The men in her life needed to readjust their lenses. Hadn't she confirmed Rudy Bagwell's cheating? And one shouldn't forget she'd landed Boris a job.

But ten days masquerading as another woman?

It *would* give her time to figure out the future with Boone. And perhaps erase that last glimmer of doubt from Jeremy's eyes.

"I'll do it."

"Good. And listen, there will be surveillance. Lee will keep watch over you, so you don't have to worry."

"What? Watch over me? I don't need a babysitter too."

Jeremy looked away.

"Oh, that's what you were cooking up while you were staring

out the window, wasn't it? You *agree* with Boone. Well, I don't need a bodyguard."

"Because you can take care of yourself."

"Because I have great instincts. Panther instincts."

Jeremy did a poor job of hiding a reluctant grin.

"Listen, call off the dog, and I promise if I think there's any danger, I'll call you. I promise. But *you* have to promise that the next case is something—" she discarded the word *dangerous* and went with—"sneaky."

"Sneaky it is, Panther Girl. But for this case, stay inside, make it obvious there is someone living there, water the plants—"

"Feed the rats? Seriously?"

"I think so. And most of all, stay out of trouble."

"The things you ask of me."

Chapter *SIX*

The best thing about living in Kellogg, population 3,800, was the location—nestled thirty minutes west of the congestion of Minneapolis, close enough to indulge in big-city concerts and clubs, far enough to feel like a vacation. The speed limit into town cut from sixty to thirty in a space of two blocks, during which the architecture shifted from shiny modern condos close to Park-and-Ride stations to stately estates built back from the meandering road. The road ringing the beach began a half mile out of Kellogg, then cut through the refaced downtown: an old movie theater turned haberdashery for nautical attire, a children's clothing shop, a small-town bookstore—all bedazzled for summer with planters fattened with spider plants, pansies, and geraniums.

PJ surfed through Kellogg in the Vic, taking her time, jamming to the radio, her feet itching to feel the gritty sand between her toes, maybe take a cool dip in the royal blue waters of Lake Minnetonka. The renascent smell of dinner—steaks and ribs and shrimp on the barbie—lifted off the back deck of the Sunsets Supper Club, and a family of black-hatted Canadian honkers raised their heads and watched her with their button eyes. She kept a keen eye out for Boone.

She should talk to him before she disappeared for ten days. It wouldn't be easy for him to find her.

Jeremy was swinging by in an hour to pick her up. Apparently she wouldn't need her Vic for her job. Because, *ahem*, she wasn't going anywhere.

So much for her highlighted "Witness Protection" chapter.

But maybe if she could prove to Jeremy that she could handle the mundane, he'd trust her with the exciting. He hadn't seen nothin' yet.

Chapel Hills always felt like its own enclave of culture. Manicured lawns surrounded an assortment of colonials, Craftsmans, and a few modern cube homes, their sprinkler systems rousing the fragrance of summer. She floated her skiff up to the curb in front of Connie's and threw out anchor.

Amid the opulence, Connie's neat Craftsman home seemed exactly Connie—calm, structured. An Ann Taylor kind of life, with straight lines, rich fragrances, elegance, and—

A door slammed, an explosion that cut through the chirruping birds, the whisper of wind in the pussy willow tree in the front yard. Connie emerged onto the porch, stopped at the top of the wide stairs, took one look at PJ, and said, "You!"

PJ stopped on the walk and, just to be sure, looked over her shoulder. "Uh, me?"

But Connie didn't follow up—was that an accusation or a

discovery? She turned and stalked across the expanse of porch, stopping to stand with her back to PJ.

PJ approached with caution. "Connie?"

Connie whirled, and although she'd spent years learning to control her emotions in front of a jury, it was obvious she'd need a refresher course to deal with her new home life. Her long dark hair hung in strings around her face, and mascara smudged at the corners of her eyes where she'd obviously tried to stave off a mud slide. PJ noted a rip in her hose. "You got him a job."

PJ eyed her sister carefully, spoke slowly in easy tones. "Yes. We talked about this yesterday. Did something happen?"

Connie shook her head, like the truth might be too unthinkable to speak.

"What?"

"He has to drive to work!"

PJ narrowed one eye. "Yes . . . or I suppose if he started really early, he could get there on foot—"

"Stop it, PJ; this isn't funny."

"I'm just saying, how else did you think he would get there?"

"He wants to take the Lexus." Connie shook her head again, walked over to the railing, and leaned a hip against it.

PJ dropped her bag into one of the rocking chairs. Sat in the other. Folded her hands in her lap.

"I mean, Sergei does have a car . . . but Boris says that he shouldn't show up at his new job in a car that looks like it could drop pieces on the way. He's embarrassed."

PJ's gaze went to the 1988 Montero in the driveway, the one outlined in rust. Connie affectionately—or perhaps not so affectionately—called it the greasemobile. Truthfully, Sergei rarely drove it, preferring Connie's luxury sedan.

She turned back to Connie. "You got all this in Russian?"

"Sergei translated."

As if on cue, PJ heard a slew of angry Russian—well, she was only assuming the tone was angry, based on the slammed-door clue. (After all, that's how PIs put things together.) They could be exchanging endearments for all she knew.

Connie nodded to the voices curdling the summer air. "That's Sergei and his father, showdown at the O.K. Corral."

PJ nodded. Crossed and uncrossed her thumbs.

"I don't want to be selfish—I really don't. It's just that it's my Lexus. And I worked hard for it. And I . . . I don't know why this is so hard. I thought, sure, we'll let his parents stay here, and they'll be so excited with Davy and our life that they'll fall in love with me. But I can't get past the feeling that everything I do is wrong. I cook wrong—or don't cook, and I'm constantly letting my son sit in a draft, or maybe too long in the sun, or letting him run barefoot on the lawn. Or rather, what lawn? I should have turned it into a potato patch long ago." Connie kneaded her finger and thumb into her eyes. "I don't know what I can do to get them to like me. To make them realize I'm doing the best I can. I just want them to love me like I love their son."

So maybe she and Connie weren't so different after all. They both wanted to get it right. PJ got up and wrapped her arms around her sister. Connie's bones dug into her shoulder.

"You didn't really expect it to be without a few bumps, did you? I mean, did you see the goat?"

Connie giggled, then swiped away a tear.

PJ held her at arm's length. "Sis, first, I think you're doing a great job of adjusting. They should be thrilled for you and Sergei. And I for one know that Vera is crazy over Davy. But the most important part right now is that, no, Boris doesn't need to use the Lexus. In fact—" she pulled out her Scooby-Doo key chain, working off her newest key—"he can take the Vic. He's the one who found it, anyway."

Connie followed her gaze out into the street. "That mafia car with the mag wheels is yours?"

"My new ride. You dig, homie?"

Connie laughed. "Is that why Boone's Mustang is in the garage?"

PJ dropped the key into Connie's grip. "Yeah. I didn't want anything to happen to it . . . but he'll probably be by for it . . ."

Connie's smile dimmed. "Four years of law school tells me someone is being evasive."

"Or just confused. Anyway, I'm going . . . away . . . for a few days."

"Away where? Will you be back for Labor Day? We were going to have a picnic at Kellogg Beach."

PJ retrieved her bag. "I dunno, Connie. It's a . . . let's say, a *work-related* . . . vacation." She opened the door, the air-conditioning hitting her skin as she stepped inside.

Connie was on her heels. "A vacation?"

"Who's going on vacation?" Elizabeth Sugar looked up from the book she was reading to Davy, who sat on her lap in his Fellows uniform. He ran his fingers over the pearls at her neck, counting them.

"PJ is." Connie shut the door behind them.

"On vacation? But I thought you just started your job? What will your boss think?"

"It's a *work* vacation, Mom."

Connie disappeared into the study and closed the door behind her. Voices continued to slip out from under the door.

PJ toed off her shoes onto the mat. "Jeremy knows all about it."

"What exactly is a 'work vacation'? Isn't that an oxymoron?"

Sergei emerged from the study and came right over to PJ and, without a skip in his step, leaned over and pecked her on each cheek, European style. "*Spaceeba*, Peezhay. What does that mean, *oxymoron*?" he asked, moving toward the kitchen, where Vera stood at the stove, cooking.

Elizabeth Sugar had displaced Davy and now rose from the sofa, visibly alarmed. "It means it's something that PJ hasn't thought through."

Oh, was that what it meant? A "for your information" was just forming on PJ's lips when another Russian emerged, this one from the back porch.

"*Prevyet*, Peezhay."

She'd met Sergei's cousin Igor only once, but she'd never forget his low, movie-thug voice, the mafia garb—head-to-toe black, complete with squared-off shoes to match his squared-off shaved hair—nor the way he looked at her. Not unlike the eyes of a snake. Even now, his gaze trailed up her as he worked on an apple he'd plucked from the bowl on Connie's table.

She turned away. "*Prevyet*. And believe me, I've thought it through, Mom."

"You've barely been there two months and already you're taking a vacation?" Elizabeth rounded the sofa, Davy following her with the opened book. "How are you going to get Jeremy to trust you?"

"It'll get her away from Boone." This from Connie, who followed her father-in-law from the study.

Boris held PJ's key to the Vic, his smile bright. "*Spaceeba, maya* Peezhay."

His PJ? Maybe yesterday's excursion around Kellogg and into the province of his new employer had bonded them. When he smacked a kiss onto her cheek, she didn't mind so much.

He did look slicked up—wearing yesterday's suit and shoes—for his new job. He waved as he opened the door to leave and nearly walked into Boone, hand lifted, ready to knock.

"Get her away from Boone? Then why is he here?" Elizabeth shook her head and stalked past PJ toward the kitchen.

"Get away from whom?" Boone asked as he walked into the foyer. A shiny pink gift bag dangled from his grip.

"Nobody." PJ whirled toward the direction of her retreating mother. "And I did think it through!"

"Think what through?"

PJ turned back to Boone. "My *work* vacation."

"You're going on vacation? I thought—"

"Stop."

His mouth pursed in a tight line. "Then you're still intent on following through with this?"

"PJ's leaving?" Davy had stopped on the word *vacation* and now dropped his book. "No, I don't want Auntie PJ to leave!"

Ah, see, this was why she loved Davy. He leaped toward her, and because she'd honed her instincts, she caught him midflight. He wrapped his legs around her, framed her cheeks in his hands. "Don't leave, Auntie PJ!"

"I promise I'll be back, little man. Two weeks, tops. And then we'll go to the beach, okay?"

"Promise?"

"Scout's honor." She held up two, then three fingers.

He popped her a kiss right on the lips.

"With that kind of action, no wonder you turned me down," Boone said, a soft smile on his face as PJ put Davy down.

"I didn't turn you down."

He considered her a moment. "No, I guess you didn't, did you?"

"No."

"Please don't. And please forgive me for . . . walking out on lunch."

How was she supposed to stay mad at a man who came to her house to apologize, especially bearing gifts? She pointed to the bag. "That for me?"

"It's for both of us." He handed it over.

She looked inside. "A cell phone?"

"I can't stand not being able to get ahold of you. And if you can't pay your bill, I will."

"Boone, I can't accept this."

"Think of it as my concession to this double life you lead."

"Shh . . ." Thankfully, Connie had scooped up Davy, leaving her to parley with Boone in private—or at least in semiprivate. Igor still leaned against the doorway, eating the apple.

"Let's go outside," Boone said.

PJ followed him onto the porch, digging the phone out of the bag. "I don't know what to say."

"I have a list of suggestions, if you're consulting me." But he said it with a smile. "Just promise to call me if you—and I can't believe I used the word *if,* but I'm holding out hope—*if* you get into trouble. I'll be there."

"Like Superman?"

He lifted a shoulder. "Like the guy who loves you, even if I don't understand this new PJ."

For some crazy reason, the words made her eyes film. His words, his appearance today at the sub shop, rushed at her and she remembered in his tone his fear that, indeed, she'd end up like Allison Miller.

Her ultimatum suddenly hung ugly and weighted at the end of the memory. "I . . . I'm sorry for my stupid words today. It's not that I wouldn't choose you."

"I don't want to talk about it."

"Oh."

"How long are you . . . uh, going on *vacation?*"

"Ten days or so."

He looked as if she'd hit him. "Ten days?"

"Boone! I was gone for ten years and you hardly blinked. Ten days is nothing."

Behind him, she heard a lawn mower fire up, one yard over.

"I did blink. And now that you're back, ten days is an eternity, especially when I don't know where you are or what you're doing. Or who you're doing it with."

She raised an eyebrow.

"Okay, that might have come out wrong. But I don't trust Jeremy. He doesn't . . ."

"Look after me enough? protect me? He's my boss, Boone, not my bodyguard."

"I still can't pry the image of him hitting you out of my brain."

"Let it go. I'll be fine. I promise."

"There you go, making promises again." He ran a finger under her chin. "Make me this one: promise to call?"

She caught his hand. "Yes. And I also promise that when I come back, I'll have an answer for you."

"Would that include a promise to switch careers, maybe become a librarian?"

She rolled her eyes but let him pull her closer as he wrapped his hand around her neck and bent low to kiss her.

"PJ, you about ready?"

Boone froze, his eyes just inches from hers, and shook his head, his face grim as Jeremy bounced up the stairs. Oh, the growl hadn't been a local lawn mower but his motorcycle. She peered past Boone and spotted Jeremy's bike parked on the street, two helmets on the seat.

Boone stepped back from her, caught her hand, then her gaze. "Ten days."

She nodded and noticed he barely acknowledged Jeremy as he passed by him.

"Ten days for what?" Jeremy asked, watching Boone retreat.

Ten days to figure out the rest of her life.

✳ ✳ ✳

"She scares me a little bit." PJ leaned in close to Jeremy as they stood on the sidewalk, where PJ had retreated after ten minutes inside Dally's 1920s yellow one-and-a-half-story home.

"Please tell me, what do Dally Morrison and I have that is remotely in common? Because that girl in there . . . well, what exactly do you see as similar? The long mane of inky black hair or perhaps the lip piercing, or maybe it's the tattoo on her stomach that says, 'Born to party.'"

"It was more of a thematic statement than a physical comparison. And keep your voice down." Jeremy leaned against his motorcycle, arms folded against his chest, clearly unmoved. "I don't want her taking off into the night."

"Thematic, huh? Then of course you mean her preference for leather in August? Maybe she and Rudy need to form a club. Or perhaps you're talking about the exotic animal furniture in her living room. I felt like I was walking into Wild Kingdom. And let me warn you now that if you open your mouth and have the audacity to say we're both exotic or something equally stupid, these feet are walking."

"Your approval on her decorating choices is not a part of the deal, PJ."

"Did you see her pets, Jeremy? I counted five chinchillas— and by the way, they aren't rats. They're disgusting little creatures that spit and scream. The only possible thing you can say right now to keep me from laying out in traffic is that Dally and I are the same size." She propped her hand on her hip and dared him to disagree.

Jeremy held up his hand in a conciliatory gesture. "Pipe down, Panther Girl. First of all, if anyone can take care of the spitters, it's you, the girl who used to clean rhino cages. And no, I wasn't referring to your taste in clothing or decorating. But if you want me to get particular, she does have your big green eyes, and your sort of . . . flamboyant style."

"I am wearing a pair of yoga pants and flip-flops. The height of flamboyancy." She shook her head. "Do you see anything in my attire either skintight or with the words *Hot Babe* written anywhere, especially lower than my belly button?"

Jeremy leaned back, running his gaze over her as if complying with her request.

"That was rhetorical." PJ took a step closer.

Not even the dusk hid the small smirk playing on Jeremy's lips.

"Isn't there another way we can protect her? You can't leave me here. It smells like the San Diego Zoo in there, and I swear I saw one of the leopard lampshades move. You don't expect me to sleep in her bed, do you?" Oh, where was her Vic when she needed it? "C'mon, Jeremy, have a heart."

He was so obviously clamping his lips against a laugh that she held up her hands in a sort of surrender as an alternative to smacking him.

His smile faded as she stalked down the sidewalk. Three blocks to the east, the homes had begun a nice bend toward luxury as they hugged the Minneapolis lake chains, and the influence had seeped into Dally's neighborhood. Her small neighborhood of bungalows and cottages poised at the edge of restoration, with a few homes displaying remodeling signs in their manicured front lawns. Bookending one side of Dally's beguilingly conservative home sat an equally cheerful, light blue Cape Cod with lush variegated hostas leading up either side of a flagstone walk. On the other side, a derelict low-roofed Craftsman with a half porch and a chain-link fence jailed an unwelcoming rottweiler who had been losing his mind since PJ and Jeremy's arrival. He'd now worked up foam around his jowls that sprayed spit like a Gatling gun from his dark lips as he darted the length of the fence and back.

A few Kias, Geos, and now and again a Caravan clogged the street, as well as the alley behind the house, save for a lone restored black Charger with racing stripes parked next to Jeremy's bike. How Dally Morrison ended up in this neighborhood . . . well, someone at the FBI hadn't been doing his homework if he was hoping to help her blend.

Dally's front door squealed open, and she came out under the porch light, straight black hair (and now PJ noticed a streak of red—maybe that's what Jeremy was referring to) trickling down over curves strapped in by a black vest. The slightest tummy bulged out between the bottom of her vest and the top of her low-rise jeans, highlighting a belly button ring like the Hope Diamond.

She stood with her hands on her hips, her expression not at all hinting at patience. "Are you two done talking about me?"

PJ glanced at Jeremy, who merely raised his eyebrows at her.

Fine. "I better get double merit points for this."

Jeremy followed her back inside.

Dally met them in the kitchen, where she ripped open a package of sugar-free gum. "Just quit smokin'," she said as she took two pieces and crammed them into her mouth. She offered one to PJ, who gave a quick shake of her head.

The kitchen displayed a contemporary charm PJ hadn't expected in the black counter-height square table with matching plum-covered chairs, the black marble counters, the white cabinets. Unfortunately she'd been focused on the zebra-patterned chairs in the living room, the shiny black sofa, and the leopard-print rug.

But, moving again into the living room, she noted that Dally hadn't limited art to just her body—she had plenty left over for the walls. PJ stared for a long time at an eight-foot dragon mural on the side wall, complete with fire, spikes down its tail, and eyes that drilled into her.

"So, you're going to be me, huh?" Dally examined PJ up and down while PJ matched her gaze, memorizing the way Dally chewed with her mouth open; her cherry red lipstick; the pink, green, and red flower tattoo that started at her right shoulder and trailed down her arm, ending in what looked like two bright splotches of blood on the back of her hand. Her eyes had been traced in about a pound of black liner, yet in them PJ saw the slightest hint of approval as Dally stepped back and nodded. "I s'pose. Of course the girls at the Scissor Shack won't be fooled, but if you try and do something with that hair—maybe you can find one of my hats—"

"What's wrong with my hair?"

"For one, it needs highlights, but the biggest issue is that it's red, hello." She gestured to her own appearance. "I'm assuming you're not color-blind."

PJ felt Jeremy's hand settle on the small of her back.

"No. You're right. Maybe I can . . . temporarily . . . dye . . . it." PJ's voice cracked slightly on the word *dye*. She would have preferred a wig.

"Whatever. Listen, the deal is, you be me. Whatever it takes. Which means I s'pose I have to give you permission to wear my threads. I've spent a lot of time cultivating my fashion; do not make me look like a geek. Most of all, puh-*leeze* do not get any dye or peroxide on them. I can't replace some of the vintage pieces."

PJ let those words settle a moment. "I'm sorry . . . did you say 'dye or peroxide'?"

"I know it's tempting not to wear an apron, but I always do. I care about my clothes and my stuff. So I'd appreciate if you'd do the same."

PJ looked at Jeremy. His eyes flicked to Dally, then back to PJ as he leaned close. "You have to go to work."

"What?"

"What he's saying is that I work at the Scissor Shack." Dally eyed Jeremy like, *good grief, didn't you brief her?* and PJ matched it. For a second, she could agree that she and Dally were exactly alike—tricked into one of Jeremy's schemes.

He held up his hands. "She just told me when I got here."

"I tried to get someone to fill in for me, but ten days is too long. I canceled most of my appointments. And the others are simple set and drys. I'd suggest not taking any walk-ins, but you'll be fine."

"Set and drys?"

"You'll be fine," Jeremy repeated, patting her shoulder.

She worked her hand into the hammer fist.

"But what I'm more worried about is the Rockets. We have four big games coming up over the next week and a half—including a triple-header this Saturday—and my team is going to be ticked if I'm not there."

"The Rockets?" PJ turned to confirm Dally's words with Jeremy as Dally left to retrieve something from the other bedroom.

"The Rockets?" PJ mouthed again. Jeremy wore an unfamiliar apprehensive expression. "It better not be something like Roller Derby or—"

"I play catcher." Dally returned and dropped chest padding, leg guards, a mitt, and a mask into PJ's arms, then shoved a sheet of paper into her hands. "I figure if you keep the mask on and only take it off in the dugout, no one will see you. Jeremy told me that you used to play . . . ?"

PJ looked at the equipment, relief swooping through her. "High school. We went to state."

For the first time since PJ had entered her world, Dally smiled. "Perfect. I made a list of the signals." She pointed to the paper.

Signals? "Uh, I played shortstop."

Dally's smile dimmed. "You *can* catch, right?"

"Of course I can catch. But I'm more useful out in the field."

"Excuse me, but the catcher is the most important position next to the pitcher." Dally snatched back her equipment—or at least most of it. The mask tumbled onto the floor. "You told me she could play."

Oops, Dally had gone right over her head to the boss. But seriously, all the catcher had to do was hold out the glove, give a target to the pitcher, right?

"She can play."

"Not if she doesn't know how to call the pitches." *Now* the words were for PJ.

"I can call the pitches." PJ said it almost on reflex, but how hard could it really be? It was softball, for pete's sake, not the major leagues. A pitch was a pitch, and just because she hadn't called pitches in high school didn't mean she couldn't figure it out now.

"This isn't going to work." Dally turned to Jeremy, something dangerous in her eyes. "If she blows it, I could get kicked off the team. Do you know how hard it is to get on the Rockets? And we have a tournament this weekend. You told me she could play, that she'd have no trouble calling the pitches. What were you thinking?"

Jeremy didn't flinch, didn't even look at PJ. "She can. Don't worry; your persona is in good hands, Dally."

Where he'd conjured up his confidence, PJ wanted to know because she could use some too.

Especially as Dally turned, saying nothing, her black-lined eyes searching PJ's. "Listen, if you blow this for me—" her eyes communicated the threat before her lips said it—"you'll wish you and your flip-flops had just stayed home in Preppyville."

Preppyville? PJ tightened her jaw, glancing at Jeremy. He wore a shocked, panicked, please-don't-blow-this expression on his face. Which, of course, was the last thing she needed because she couldn't let him down. Not with the way he'd stood there and defended her. She heard the words forming in her head, felt her mouth opening, and then, "No problem, Dally. I won't let you down. I promise."

"I promise."

Dally didn't acknowledge PJ's words, just stared first at her, then at Jeremy. He met her gaze with even eyes. Her voice was small when she finally sighed and said, "My life is in your hands."

Chapter *SEVEN*

PJ couldn't decide who won the overprotective prize.

Dally held up her chinchillas one by one, kissing them on their pointed snouts, saying, "Be good for Mama."

(Which implied what? That they weren't normally good? What was a bad chinchilla like?)

Meanwhile Jeremy took PJ aside and not only made her confirm his cell phone number but also threw a couple karate moves at her for her to wax on and wax off.

"Methinks someone is a little worried here. What happened to 'I wouldn't let you do this if I thought there was any danger'?"

"Just for me, couldn't you write the number down?"

"No. A great supersleuth never writes down the numbers. It's up here in the vault—" she tapped her head—"218-555-8919. Got it."

He shook his head, then pulled a worn wallet from his back

pocket. "I meant to give this to you earlier." He opened it and worked out a slick black card. And on it, in shiny silver letters right under *Kane Investigations*, was her name. *PJ Sugar, Associate.*

Her own credit card. "Seriously?"

"I'll pay you when we get back in the office. I just wasn't thinking. I'm sorry I forgot, PJ."

She was still staring at the card as his hand closed over it. "Just for emergencies, okay? No new cars or shopping sprees at Macy's."

"Does emergency pizza count?"

"Your life better be at stake." But his smile was warm as he handed it to her.

They sat on the steps outside Dally's house, hidden in the shadows of the black wrought-iron fence and the overhang of the porch. He'd refused to turn on the front light in case neighbors were watching.

PJ had most definitely seen a curtain drop from a window of the unassuming blue house next door, so who knew what congregation ogled them from the haunted house with the rottweiler, who still manned his post, eyeing them from somewhere in the tall grass like a lion in the Serengeti.

Still, even with Jeremy's face lost in the shadows, she could trace it without looking—dark eyes, square jaw with a scrape of whiskers. The aroma of leather and mischief lifted off him to fragrance the night.

She might miss him, just a little, over the next ten days.

"Just don't do anything out of the ordinary. Like . . ."

"What? Cut hair? Play softball for one of Minnesota's top teams?" Dally had taken no small measure of time filling her in on every teammate and their positions, as well as their idiosyncrasies, not to mention putting her through another thorough grilling about the finer points of catching and the various call signs. Apparently the Rockets were top contenders for an amateur title this summer, having clinched the title last summer.

No pressure there.

PJ had nodded but refrained somehow from making more promises.

"What makes a girl get that many tattoos?" Jeremy asked into the night. So, he too had noted the gallery of images on at least the exposed parts of Dally's body: a cat—or was it a chinchilla?—on her ankle, a butterfly with a broken wing showing over the back of her jeans, the flower curling down her arm. Great, the height of August, and PJ'd spend the next two weeks wearing long sleeves.

PJ's hand went to her tattoo of Boone's name, and Jeremy saw the gesture. "I suppose you don't want to tell me how you got yours?"

She couldn't see his eyes, but his tone was so soft, she couldn't stop herself. In fact, hidden here in this strange neighborhood with the oily alleyway smells, the barks of unfamiliar dogs, the taste of adventure in the air, it didn't feel so much like giving away a piece of herself as trying out some new identity. A person who wasn't afraid to let someone see her scars, her dreams.

Her tattoos.

"It was a birthday present for Boone. He turned eighteen a month after me, and at the time I thought we'd be together forever. It was his idea and everyone seemed to be getting tats.

It was the beginning of the craze. I agreed to something little. His is bigger, but of course, you usually can't see it."

"It says Princess?"

She could feel Jeremy's smile in the dark.

"No. Just a big *P* and *J*."

He swatted at a mosquito on his exposed forearm. "So does he know what they stand for, the *P* and *J*?"

Jeremy's seemingly innocent tone brought her back to one of their first meetings, when he'd tried to cajole out of her the real names behind the *P* and the *J* of her initials. But she'd spent the better part of twenty-eight years hiding that identity. Perhaps, in a way, it was just one of many things she was afraid to reveal.

Or maybe it was the only one that she *refused* to reveal. Because lately she'd done a breathtaking job of living her dreams, her hopes, even her past out loud and in living color. Not unlike a tattoo.

"No, he doesn't know."

"Not even Boone, huh?"

"Nope."

"Okay, let me give it another shot. We went through the Patty variations, and of course it's not Peanut Butter and Jelly or Princess."

"Although really, it should be, if the world was fair."

She felt him chuckle next to her, a tenor staccato.

"Let's just focus on the *P*. How about . . . Priscilla?"

"Nope."

"Pamela?"

"Nope."

"Poppy? Patsy? Phoebe? You will tell me if I get it, right?"

"I haven't decided yet."

"I think I'll have to go back to Fast-Pitch, based on your upcoming softball career."

"Thanks for that, by the way. If I lose Dally's catching position, you might have to put *me* in hiding after this is all over."

"If that's what the job demands." His foot tapped hers, and she flashed back to riding behind him on his motorcycle, her hands locked around his flat stomach, her chin propped on his shoulder, her life in his hands. There was something about Jeremy that made her trust herself. When he looked at her, his eyes seemed to see so much more of her than she saw of herself.

He reached up and touched her hair, running two fingers through it. "Don't dye it. Wear a wig."

She wasn't sure what to say to that, nor what to do with the feeling of loss when his hand dropped away. "Hey . . . do me a favor and be careful. . . . I mean, I don't trust her."

"What do you think's going to happen, PJ?"

PJ stared ahead, distracted by the sound of hip-hop from a car wheeling by. "I don't know. Maybe I'm just jealous."

His sharp silence beside her made her still. Oh, wait; she hadn't meant to say that, had she? "I'm just kidding." She added a laugh—too high—on the end of her words; it made her wince. "Really, I didn't mean that."

His voice was so quiet, she could barely hear it above her heartbeat. "I hope you did."

Dally appeared at the screen door. "You ready to go, boss?"

"That's my line," PJ said, leaping to her feet. She caught Jeremy's eyes on her as she swung the door open and followed Dally through the house to the back.

Dally left through the alleyway in the darkness, Jeremy leaving after her and then scooting around to the alley on his bike to load her on the back and whisk her into the night.

PJ tried not to dwell on how that had been her a few hours ago, holding on to Jeremy as they flew through the streets of Minneapolis, a tight bullet of crime-stopping power. She listened to the duo from the back step until the motor blended into the blur of night sounds; then she went inside and stood in the quiet living room, next to the zebra chair, with the dragon watching her from above.

From next door, a body emerged into the night, slinking past the overhead light. PJ made out a bulky form through Dally's side window and watched as it climbed into the Charger. The machine bullied out into the darkness.

Then the neighborhood went quiet, and all she heard was the *scritch, scritch* of the chinchillas and the lonely ping of her own heartbeat.

Ten days to talk to no one but herself.

She retrieved her duffel bag from Dally's kitchen and carried it through the house, checking out the bathroom—aquamarine with a dragon on the transparent shower curtain—and then to the bedroom in back.

Surprise, surprise! Tough-talking Dally had a pink bedspread on a white French provincial bed. The zebra-striped pillows PJ could have guessed at, along with the one black wall painted with a huge purple dragon with red eyes. But the question of how she might sleep with Puff staring at her was answered by the rich red velour curtains that framed the four-poster bed. She couldn't help but wonder at the girl behind the tattoos when she took in the three pink walls. A matching dresser contained framed photos—many of Dally, her arm slung over shoulders of compatriots, mugging for the camera.

PJ opened the closet door to check out Dally's shoe supply and discovered (of course) a closet full of leather, animal prints, and—jackpot!—a bin of multicolored Chuck Taylor sneakers.

Maybe she could like Dally a little.

And she couldn't forget that Dally was doing all this so she could put away a drug dealer. PJ had to give the woman credit for doing the right thing.

It took PJ all of five minutes to unpack—a few pairs of jeans, a couple pairs of shorts, T-shirts, tanks, and a sweatshirt, the last of which she pulled on as she padded out into the main room.

The quiet enveloped her, pressed inside her. She found the remote and turned on the television, flipping through the channels. Over three hundred channels and she couldn't find a thing? Even the oldies channel offered nothing but a James Coburn movie. She slumped down on the black leather sofa, turned off the television, and scanned through the day, starting with Boone's disheveled appearance at the gym.

She couldn't believe Allison Miller was dead. She closed her eyes, listening again to Boone's words: *"She was working for me—sort of an informant on an investigation. They found her body last night in the Kellogg harbor."*

She hadn't thought about Boone using informants, but being a detective, of course he did. Worse, she couldn't believe they had actual killers, the kind who dumped pretty girls into the lake for the fish to feed on, in Kellogg. Her one run-in with a murderer had been of the international variety, and she'd labeled it a fluke.

Clearly Boone would see and know things that she didn't about the state of crime in Kellogg. And clearly he would have seen things that might keep a man up at night worrying about his girlfriend.

So maybe she should cut him some slack. She didn't exactly want to end up like Allison Miller.

Allison Miller. Bouncy, blonde Allison. PJ remembered her the way the entire high school probably did: easy. In fact her on-again-off-again boyfriend, Casey Whitlow, had cemented that reputation.

Casey Whitlow. Huh, she hadn't thought about him in a decade, and here he'd crossed her mind twice in two days. He wouldn't have had anything to do with her death, right?

That wasn't fair. Just because he hadn't turned out like his shiny high school career predicted didn't mean he'd become a murderer. Look at PJ—she wasn't nearly the trouble that she'd imprinted in her classmates' minds. . . .

Okay, maybe she wasn't a great example. And she should probably stop jumping to conclusions.

Getting up, PJ wandered to the kitchen, opening Dally's pantry. Cheese Nips, pretzels . . . She decided she had been too hard on Dally when she found a half-eaten box of Cap'n Crunch. Returning to the living room, she stood in the darkness, crunching on cereal, and watched as the furry chinchillas dug themselves into the sand, bathing in it. Not unlike PJ's relationship to the beach.

She watched her reflection in the glass windows, measuring her image against Dally's. Perhaps, from a distance, she was just a conservative version of Dally—wild red hair instead of the long, dyed black variety, one tattoo instead of eight or ten, standard ear piercings, and clothes aimed at comfort rather than an outcry of personal fashion.

How exactly was she supposed to get inside Dally's skin and impersonate her without knowing her?

PJ opened a few doors. The one to the hall closet—empty. The one to the basement—not a chance. The one next to the bathroom—stairs.

She stared up at the black hole a long time, her foot poised on the bottom step. The space above smelled of age and old lace, and when her hand traced the wall, she found no light switch.

Maybe . . . in daylight. She closed the door.

Still crunching on cereal, she returned to Dally's room, hunting for clues. She studied the pictures on her dresser. One taken in a hair salon. One of the girls—now *that* was red hair—stuck her tongue out to reveal a silver stud, while posing with a hang-loose gesture. The other, a peroxide blonde with hair caught in the eighties, filled out a light blue apron with the words *Scissor Shack* on the front. Her smile was sweet, and PJ guessed she might be the proprietor.

Another picture showed Dally with her softball team. PJ recognized the redhead from the first photo, her long hair in braids, this time "peacing" the camera. Dally crouched in the front in her catcher's garb.

A smaller picture in a silver frame showed Dally standing in front of Mount Rushmore and leaning against a sharp-dressed man, although the picture was too small to make out any features.

If the roles were reversed, what would Dally find to clue her into PJ's life? She'd unpacked her duffel onto the bed. With the exception of her Bible—stuffed with bulletins from the Kellogg Praise and Worship Center—nothing revealed PJ's true identity.

She stared at the bedroom mirror—gold-plated, with ornate sculpting around the oval edge. Compared to Dally, she felt nondescript. Even her simple *Boone* tattoo lacked pizzazz next to all Dally's color.

She'd never considered herself . . . well, boring before. In fact, most of the time she thought of herself as messy, a patchwork of so many different dreams she didn't know which ones belonged to her.

Or maybe she just saw herself through the lens of her failures.

Closing up the Cap'n Crunch box, PJ went to Dally's closet and sorted through the clothes. She picked out a jean miniskirt, a black fringed vest, and from the dresser, a pair of long tube socks with pink stripes, which she paired with black high-top Converse.

The mirror didn't quite reach her legs, so she pulled up a chair and posed. With a hat, and yes, a wig, maybe she could pass for Dally.

She might need some gum.

And another tattoo or two.

Oh, who was she kidding? PJ stepped over onto the bed, flopped down, and stared at the ceiling. She hadn't a prayer of impersonating Dally.

Sometimes she had enough trouble being herself.

She closed her eyes, listening to the hammer of dread in

her chest. *Lord, I don't know how I got myself into this. What was I thinking?*

Again, she'd let her mouth run away with her good intentions—thanks, probably, to the hint of desperation in Dally's voice, despite her steely exterior.

But oh, how she wanted this PI thing to work. God had sorta dropped it in her lap and she'd grabbed it with both hands, clutching it to her chest with the desperation of a last chance.

She was tired of defining herself by her mistakes. By the things she almost got right.

She wanted to be extraordinary.

She wanted to be amazing.

She wanted to do this right.

She wanted to keep all the promises she'd made. Especially to herself.

She couldn't disappoint herself . . . couldn't disappoint God . . . again.

Please help me keep my promises.

She wriggled out her Bible from where she'd lain on it, noting that she'd crumpled the bulletins. She smoothed one of them, focusing on the verse from one of last month's sermons. 1 Peter 1:3—"Praise be to the God and Father of our Lord Jesus Christ! In his great mercy he has given us new birth into a living hope through the resurrection of Jesus Christ."

She'd once heard mercy defined as not getting what she deserved.

Yeah, well, tonight, sleeping in a fuzzy pink bed with a beady-eyed dragon leering at her, she needed all the mercy she and her big mouth could get.

✳ ✳ ✳

PJ must have been missing her Vic. Strange, because although she'd dreamed of her Volkswagen in the past, she had always been at the wheel, navigating some uncharted beach trail.

But somehow she knew it was a dream because, otherwise, how could her new car be plowing through the waters of Lake Minnetonka, churning up spray in its wake, PJ at the wheel even as she watched from shore? She lay on the sand, baking in the sun, the heat pooling on her skin in droplets of sweat as she cupped her hand over her eyes. She waved to herself. Herself waved back. She could almost taste the spray of water on her face.

Then the car turned toward the shore. She sat up. Its headlights were on, and now they seared her vision like the sun as the vehicle yachted straight for her. The PJ at the helm continued to wave, but the PJ on shore had climbed to her feet. She tried to yell, but the words glued to her throat.

The car kept coming, cutting through the blue and white bobbered boundary to the Kellogg swimming area, taking out a floating yellow buoy, the wake like claws upon the water.

The car hit the shallow area, and she heard grinding as the tires chewed up beach. Water hit her face. *Stop!*

As the Vic gathered speed and arrowed out of the water, PJ turned to run. Her breath sawed in her lungs and a scream lodged in her throat. *Stop!*

She reached the edge of the grass, the engine roaring in her ears as she turned and saw the Vic grinding up her footprints in the sand.

She dove for the grass, and something bit her leg. She landed, knees scraping on the sand, and scrabbled to her feet. But the teeth held. *No!* She looked down to find a rope burning into her leg. The end trailed back into the sand, where she'd come from, where the Vic now gunned toward her.

She grabbed the rope, pulled, fighting to yank it from its anchor, seeing the Vic now leap from the sand, the motor growling as it hung above her, the greasy engine like a snarl of snakes ready to drop. She curled into a ball and—

A scream woke her. High-pitched, over and over. PJ sat up, shaking, listening to more screams and frenetic chirrups.

The chinchillas. PJ flipped back into the pillows, hearing them run around their cage, leaping from one ledge to the next, the *scritch, scritch* of their tiny feet against the wood chips.

A thump.

Most definitely *not* a chinchilla. She sat up again.

Another thump.

PJ gave up trying to control her heart as it slipped out of her grasp and ran away with her imagination.

Something—something *much larger* than one of Dally's rat-looking rodents—was creeping through Dally's house.

Maybe Dally wasn't paranoid about someone being after her. PJ slipped out of bed onto her knees, gave a look at the window, and then groped for something, *anything*, to use as a weapon.

Where, oh where, was her phone when she needed it? And as for Jeremy's phone number . . . 911 was the only thing that entered her brain, followed by the urge to simply hide under the bed.

She saw movement—a shadow across the open space outside her cracked door. Big movement attached to a big person.

Help . . .

Her frantic search for a weapon under the bed unearthed a plastic cup, a paperback book, and tweezers. Yeah, she'd pluck him to death.

Keeping low, she crawled across the room, her chin nearly on the floor, her breath coiled tight. Her gaze fell on a lump in the corner—Dally's catcher's equipment. At least she'd have armor.

PJ pulled it with her behind the bed and wriggled on the chest padding. Added the helmet.

In a full-out frenzy, the chinchillas were obviously losing it, screaming and spitting. From the hall, PJ heard fumbling, the squeal of a door opening—that would be the stairs. Footsteps scraped up the steps.

Oh, what she would give for a weapon. She peered at the corner, praying. And saw, tucked into the round mitt like a lump of gold, a softball.

Sort of like a rock, right?

She snaked her way toward it, her hand closing over the ball as the attic door closed. Footsteps thumped again in the hallway.

She hadn't played shortstop for nothing. Her eyes glued on the shadowy slice of the bedroom door.

The door eased open.

She hauled back and let the softball fly.

It connected square on—or at least she thought it had because she heard a cry and then cursing. She launched herself onto her feet and ran at the door, intending to slam it shut. A hand snaked out and grabbed her arm.

Hammer fist. Almost like a reflex, she pounded once, hard,

on the side of the intruder's arm. He cursed but, instead of letting go, yanked her toward himself and out into the hallway.

It didn't work; it didn't work!

The words screamed inside her head even as she ducked and drove her shoulder into the man's chest.

He huffed out a breath. She smelled garlic, along with a cloying, almost sickly sweet menthol body odor.

On reflex, she drove her knee up as hard as she could.

He howled and released her. She kicked out, catching him in his belly, pushing him back.

Then she dove for Dally's room, slammed the door shut, and locked it.

As the chinchillas screamed, she slumped down into a ball and joined them.

Chapter EIGHT

"Be there. *Be there!*" PJ stared at the phone, unearthed from the abyss of her bag. Why did she carry such a black hole? The digital numbers glowing in the darkness of the bedroom confirmed that yes, she had dialed correctly.

The phone rolled over again to a very dispassionate voice that cared little for the fact that she'd nearly been manhandled and said, "Please leave a message at the tone."

Just in case it wasn't Jeremy's number—so much for her keen memory skills—she left a relatively calm, low, inadvertently breathy message that went something like "You'd better have a good reason for not answering, because . . . because . . ." Then before she could burst into tears, she hung up.

She pressed the cell phone to her forehead, as if by magical powers it might summon help.

Apparently God wasn't heeding her prayers. Was it only a couple hours ago that she'd been on her knees, figuratively at least, begging for a way to keep her tangle of promises? Maybe she should be more specific. *Less* trouble, not more.

At the very least, she could use a divine reminder that she wasn't alone. In a strange house. With someone trying to kill her . . . *er*, Dally.

The only bright spot—besides the digital phone numbers—was that Dally hadn't been paranoid. Although, perhaps that wasn't such a bright ray of hope at all.

What if this was one of Billy Finch's thugs? Her hammer fists and softball throw wouldn't quite do the trick.

The chinchillas had stopped screaming ten minutes ago, and if she could just hear over her heartbeat, she might be able to discern if the intruder had left the house.

She stared at the phone again, one name still thrumming in her head. Oh, she didn't want to call him. Didn't want to fuel Boone's so easily kindled hysteria about her profession.

But right now she could use someone with big shoulders and possibly packing a real weapon to walk through her door. Perhaps she'd even let him camp out on her doorstep for the entire ten days.

She had no doubts that Boone, if invited, would do exactly that. A surge of warmth curled over her.

"Hello? Dallas, are you okay?"

The voice sounded far away or perhaps just feeble. PJ wiped her eyes with the heels of her hands, pulled on the catcher's mask, and scrambled to her feet. "Who's there?" She pressed her ear into the crack of the doorframe, keeping her voice tight. No need to betray the fact that she held on to the knob to keep from collapsing.

"It's me, Dallas, dear. Gabby, from next door. Are you okay? I thought I heard screaming."

The next-door neighbor. PJ unlocked her door, flung it open, and rushed out, nearly leaping into the arms of her rescuer.

Or fellow victim. The woman screamed and clocked PJ hard upside the head with whatever solid object she gripped in her hand.

PJ just knew the mask would come in handy. It skewed sideways as she jumped back. "Hey!"

A light flicked on and the woman on the other end of the blunt object held out her flashlight like a lightsaber or perhaps a stun gun. "You're not Dally! Stay where you are!"

PJ obeyed. The woman—her second assailant of the increasingly short night—resembled someone's grandmother, the kind who made cookies and candles, who tucked small children in bed and sang them sweet melodies. Wisps of shoulder-length white hair sprang wildly around her head; the smallest touch of pink lipstick buttressed the corners of her mouth. Standing a chin above PJ, she wore a white terry-cloth robe over a cotton nightgown with a pink ruffle at the bottom. Her bare feet—with a hint of pink polish on the toes and covered in grass stains—peeked out the bottom.

Talk about unlikely rescuers.

"I'm not moving." PJ raised her hands, pit-stopping on the way up to peel off the catcher's mask and hold that above her head too.

Why, she suddenly wasn't sure. The elderly woman was as unarmed as she. In fact, a quick scan of the bedroom uncovered the softball three feet away in the splattered soil of a damaged geranium. PJ could probably dive for it and come up with a clean shot.

"Who are you?" her rescuer/newest threat barked. She pointed the beam of her flashlight square into PJ's face. "And where's Dallas?"

PJ lowered her hand to ward off the light, blinking away the dark splotches. "I'm her . . . friend. Sort of. Dally's not here."

"What do you mean, 'sort of,' and what's all the screaming over here? I thought someone was being murdered!"

Yeah, well, that wasn't so far from the truth.

In the living room, the chinchillas had awakened and started to scold them.

The woman poked her head into the hall—"Hush!" Then, back to PJ, "Hate those things. But I'd rather see them alive than made into some sort of muff for Paris Hilton." She lowered her light a bit and twirled it impatiently, as if waiting for an answer to her question.

"I think there was . . . a . . ."

"For crying in the sink, you're shaking all over."

The woman advanced toward PJ and a sturdier hand than PJ expected wrapped around her arm. "Now just take a deep breath. You look like I felt hiding out in the subways of London during the blitz, like the world might come crashing in any moment."

The blitz? As in World War II, the bombing-of-London blitz? Either PJ had traveled through time or this woman with the grip of a trucker was up into her eighties.

She flicked off her light. "What were you thinking, leaving your front door wide open? Don't you know there could be prowlers around here?"

PJ couldn't agree more. She nodded, not sure where to start. "Now, what's your name?"

PJ briefly debated an alias. But she certainly couldn't pass herself off as Dally, and she wasn't sure who else she might pretend to be, so . . . "PJ. PJ Sugar."

"What kind of name is PJ? Those are initials. What's your real name?"

She heard Jeremy's teasing in her head. *"Poppy? Patsy? Phoebe?"* She hated how she longed at this moment to hear his low, calm voice calling her anything he wanted to. "It's just . . . PJ?"

"Hmm. Not going to tell me, huh? Well, my name's Gabby Fontaine. I live next door." She walked out of the bedroom with PJ trailing behind. In the kitchen, PJ sank into a chair as Gabby chased the night away with the overhead light. "I don't think Dallas has anything stronger than apple juice—she's done a good job of licking her addiction— but maybe a cool glass of water?" She turned back to PJ, one hand on her hip, a thin brown line where her eyebrow might be raised high. She looked like someone PJ should know, an old teacher perhaps. She certainly made PJ want to sit up straight in her chair.

PJ nodded, feeling her body begin to settle back to earth now that the lights were on, the nightmares shooed into the shadows. "You didn't happen to see anyone run out the back door, did you?"

Gabby turned from the sink, her mouth half-open. In the fluorescent light, her hair—PJ could see that most of it was pulled back into a hair clip—had a slightly orange hue. "You *did* have a prowler." She plunked down the glass and reached for the phone hanging on the wall.

"Are you calling 911?"

"No, the cops will take forever to get here. I'm calling my grandson."

"No, you don't have to go to all that trouble." PJ got up and depressed the ringer to cut off the call. The last thing she needed was a crowd to identify her as Not Dally and blow her cover on the first night. "I'm fine. Maybe it was just a dog or something."

Yeah, right. A five-year-old child could tell she was lying.

Gabby stared at her, not blinking. "Isn't that strange—a dog opening a closed door. But I don't suppose there's any sense in waking up Sammy if you're okay."

PJ reached for the water. Her hand still shook.

Gabby watched her drink, watched the water dribbling down PJ's chin. Her judgmental silence bore down against PJ in her hazel eyes, the way she pursed her lips.

She took the glass from PJ's hand. "You know, Sammy's a big kid—"

"I'm fine, really." Truly, she could now probably stand on her own without falling over. She even tried out a few steps, back toward the living room. For a moment, she stood there, reenacting the actions of the assailant, putting movement with the sounds she'd heard—the opening of doors, the creak of the stairs as he went up. Those didn't seem like the movements of someone intent on killing Dally in her sleep. Whoever had been here was looking for something.

PJ turned to Gabby, who had followed her and now posed with her arms folded over her bathrobe in the doorway to the kitchen. "Tell me, does Dally have a boyfriend?" Maybe it had been an old flame, sneaking back in to retrieve . . . what, his baseball cards?

Gabby narrowed one eye. "Who'd you say you were?"

"I . . . uh . . . I'm a cousin? A distant cousin."

"From?"

"Chicago." PJ scrolled through Dally's résumé. "I'm here to sort of house-sit while Dally is . . . on vacation."

Gabby stared at her—no, probably through her, dissecting all her pitiful lies, while PJ resisted adding a further incriminating nod to her words.

"That's not like Dally, to run off and not tell me. We have a standing breakfast date."

That must've been on Dally's list—which PJ had yet to read. "Right. She mentioned that."

One brown line up again. But Gabby finally nodded. "No, no boyfriends recently. Well, none that I'd call a boyfriend. . . ."

"Anyone you *wouldn't* call a boyfriend?"

"I'm not sure what to call him. He just seemed way too familiar with Dallas, showing up at all hours of the day, staying over. In my time, ladies were more . . . discreet. Of course, I knew girls who had boyfriends like that. Even my own Sebastian would sometimes come over late, but never for . . . well, you know."

She said the words like she might for a jury, with a fierce glint in her eye.

"You know this guy's name?"

"Uh." Gabby put her hand to her forehead and for the first time hinted at her age as she frowned and for a long moment stared around the room as if suddenly not knowing where she might be. "Uh . . ."

"It's okay. Just let me know if you think of it." At eighty plus, the woman was allowed a few blank spots.

"I'm sorry. It'll come to me. But she did try to hide him, like I wouldn't know something was going on."

PJ put a face to the dropped curtain next door. "Do you live in the blue house?"

"Well, of course—you don't think I'd leave my yard in such a terrible mess . . ." She shook her head as if realizing her words. "Yes, I live in the blue house. I've lived there nearly fifty years, since we moved back from England."

PJ strained to hear a trace of English accent. She deduced the other half of "we" as Sebastian.

"Do you think this mystery man of Dally's might have a reason to sneak into Dally's house? maybe a reason to hurt her?"

That question was obviously too much for Gabby. She pressed her hand against her chest, fingers wide, mouth opening. PJ noticed polish on her nails. "I don't . . ." Then, "You're not a cousin, are you? You sound like a cop." She said it short, like "pop," with a tone of derision in her voice. "Why would a cop be here? Where's Dally?"

She pushed past PJ and into the living room, where she stood staring for a moment, as if waiting for Dally to materialize. Then she whirled and poked a thick, slightly arthritic finger at PJ. "If you've hurt her . . ."

PJ would have to let the woman in on at least a partial story if she didn't want the cops on her doorstep in the imminent future. "Listen. Dally's fine. She's with . . . my friend Jeremy. I really am house-sitting. Watching after . . ." She gestured to the pile of agitated fur in the cage.

"Flopsy, Mopsy, Cottontail, etc.," Gabby said, not smiling. "I want to talk to her."

Yeah, well, me too.

"What was that?"

Oops, she hadn't meant to say that aloud. "I called them, but Jeremy's not answering. I'm sure they're fine."

Gabby seemed to be measuring her words.

PJ unclipped the catcher's padding, slid it off, and set it on the sofa.

Gabby's eyes softened. "That *was* screaming I heard. You were pretty scared, weren't you?" She nodded toward the padding.

PJ lifted her shoulders in a quick shrug. But her stomach could still take flight any moment. "Strange house, strange neighborhood. I might have overreacted."

"Not at all." Gabby drew a deep breath and ran her gaze up and down PJ, taking in her yoga pants, the T-shirt. "Alrighty then. You get your shoes on. You're spending the night with me."

"Uh . . ."

"No arguments. My daughter fixed me up with a nice pull-out, and it's time I used it. Hurry up now. What kind of neighbor would I be if I let you stay here alone . . . especially with stray *dogs* roaming the streets. You probably wouldn't sleep a wink. Besides, that's hardly a warm welcome to the neighborhood, is it?"

PJ had to admit that God answered in mysterious ways.

✳ ✳ ✳

PJ had traveled back in time. She could trace the years back to the midfifties just by standing in Gabby's family room.

The carpet had been pulled up, or maybe never laid, and a gleaming oak floor hosted a brown oval braided rug. An old

RCA television console took up one wall, with fuzzy, green cloth speakers the size of today's flat screens on either side. The top was propped open for the phonograph, and a bookshelf beside it held what might be a hundred LPs, the first one a mint condition Everly Brothers *Greatest Hits*.

The two-cushion, lime green sofa could be called vintage on eBay, but PJ suspected it had been new when Gabby and Sebastian placed it against the far wall facing the television. A caramel-colored La-Z-Boy in the corner, worn on the footrest and the arms, suggested a retirement purchase.

Pictures, free of dust, hung on the walls—black-and-whites of stoic ancestors, and a grainy sepia, obviously blown up, of someone who could only have been the family matriarch with her Edwardian dress and grim, take-no-sass posture. Two senior pictures, the wide-collared shirt and orange print dress dating them as seventies-era graduates, perched atop the bookshelf, and behind them on the wall hung a shot of Gabby and a distinguished gentleman sitting up primly for the camera. She looked about fifty in her rust-colored pantsuit, her hair blonde and layered.

But the picture that caught PJ's attention and beckoned her forward was what looked like a professional shot, with a pose reminiscent of a vintage Hollywood actress, maybe Lauren Bacall or Audrey Hepburn. In this black-and-white photo that hung on the wall next to the kitchen entrance, a twenty-year-old Gabby Fontaine leaned into the camera with barely a smile and all the beauty of a movie star.

In fact, as Gabby emerged from a back room, blankets in her arms, PJ could still see it—the straight posture, the slight play of a smile on her face.

"Oh yes, that was me. It's hard to remember back that far."
She disappeared into another room.

PJ followed her. "Were you an actress or something?"

Gabby was taking the cushions off a couch in a room that
contained only a small metal desk in the corner. An orange
macramé cat with big black eyes leaned against the wire
straight-backed chair angled out from the desk.

Atop the desk sat an eight-by-ten glossy shot of the man in
the other picture, his dark hair slicked back, one foot up on
the fender of a Hudson, leaning on his knee as he smiled for
the camera. It resembled a James Dean photo.

"Your husband was very handsome."

"Yes, he was. He did some acting—that shot was from one
of his commercials. But he gave it up for the family. We didn't
have children until later, and he sold insurance for most of his
life. I lost him to diabetes way too early."

"I'm sorry to hear that."

Gabby pressed two fingers to her lips, then touched the
photo. "We were married for forty-three years."

Forty-three years.

Four-plus decades. Could she be married to Boone that
long? That's what he was asking, wasn't it? The rest of her life.
Could she love Boone Buckam for forty-three years?

Better yet—could he love *her* that long?

Above the sofa hung another string of pictures, these more
recent—maybe late nineties. Two boys and a girl, faint replicas
of Sebastian and Gabby.

"My grandchildren. My son, Tripp, never got married, but
my daughter, Evelyn, did. That's Evelyn's son Sammy." She
pointed to a boy with skater-length blond hair.

"You have a nice-looking family."

PJ helped her pull out the bed and grabbed the other end of the sheet. She was weighing her stupidity at following an old woman she barely knew into her home. But at Dally's house, she would have spent the night in a strategic position in the living room with all the lights on, clad in the catcher's armor, white-knuckling the softball to clobber any hint of an assailant. In her heightened condition, who knew if the chinchillas would live through the night?

No, better to accept Gabby's divine hospitality and confront the demons from the night in the light of day.

Gabby spread out the comforter, a blanket with faded roses, and slid a yellowing white pillowcase with a crocheted edge over a pillow. "My family thinks that I've lost my mind. That maybe they should be making decisions for me."

She tossed the pillow onto the bed. "Just because I forget things sometimes. Like where I put my reading glasses or a brooch." Her hands went to the emerald at her neck. "You know, I can still remember the day they were born, even remember the day Seb gave me this necklace on our first anniversary. I remember every birthday and even their anniversaries. Just because occasionally I forget to turn something off or maybe end up at the grocery store with no memory of how I got there . . . but perfectly safe, mind you." She shook her head. "I am eighty-four. I'm allowed to forget my teeth once in a while."

PJ suppressed a grin.

Gabby turned and pulled the curtains over the window. "I'm sorry I don't have a shade in here. Have to get that. You close that door and lock it if it makes you feel any better." She gave PJ a small smile. "I'm right down the hall if you should decide to do any more screaming."

Without thinking, PJ reached out and hugged her.

Gabby held her awkwardly at first, then patted her back. "There, there. It'll all look different in the morning."

Yeah, sure it would. Tomorrow she had to become Dally Morrison.

PJ closed the door behind Gabby and climbed onto the lumpy sofa bed, staring at the ceiling. One glaring truth wouldn't let her close her eyes.

Someone *was* after Dally. And they just might succeed in getting PJ first.

Chapter NINE

Bacon. She smelled frying bacon. PJ's stomach leaped to attention even before she could pry her eyes open.

Where was she? She stared at the window, the sunlight trumpeting through the light blue curtain. A sparrow's chirping suggested a cheery morning.

Gabby. She was in her neighbor's guest room.

Because she was Dally Morrison. Oh, this was already getting way too confusing.

She'd slept with her cell phone gripped in her hand and now flipped it open just to confirm that no, Jeremy hadn't called. She could be lying dead under a bridge in the Kellogg harbor, and Jeremy would be having breakfast at IHOP trying to distract Dally.

Clearly it was up to her to find out who wanted Dally dead. Or at least scared and perhaps hurt. Mostly because they'd aim for Dally and take out PJ.

She hadn't packed a bag last night, so she finger-combed her hair and promised herself she wouldn't breathe on her hostess as she folded up the blankets and the sofa and then tiptoed into the hall.

Gabby was at work in her sunny yellow kitchen wearing a purple leisure suit and a frilly green apron, cracking an egg into a cast-iron pan when PJ entered. She'd smoothed on another layer of lipstick and the finest powder on her wrinkled cheeks, and she wore a pair of clip-on gold earrings and the necklace with the small emerald pendant. She emanated an old-world elegance and smelled like PJ's mother's old powder puff.

PJ pulled up a chair at the Formica table. "Good morning."

"It's 9 a.m. Did you know that?" Gabby turned, holding a spatula. "Dally is usually up at seven."

"Sorry," PJ said.

A gray Siamese jumped on the table and glided over to PJ, purring.

"Simon, get off the table," Gabby said, shoving the cat away.

PJ picked him up and set him on her lap, running her hand over the soft fur.

"He loves to get up on things, get a regal view of life. But he knocks pictures over and pushes things onto the floor. Troublemaker."

As if he'd had enough of the slander, Simon leaped from PJ's lap.

Gabby turned back to the stove. "You might as well come clean, because I've been tossing this around for the better part of the night, and I feel it only fair to tell you that I know you're here because of that Chicago thing."

PJ stared at her, scrolling through the transcript of last night's conversation. Had she . . . no, she hadn't mentioned Billy. . . .

Gabby rounded, a don't-bother-to-lie look on her face. "I told you, Dally and I have a standing breakfast date. And she wouldn't miss it unless something was really wrong. And then I remembered—her trial's coming up. She has to testify against that creep she used to date, and she's probably scared, isn't she?"

"Uh . . ."

"And I'll bet you're a cop, aren't you? Supposed to watch over things . . ." She waved her spatula. "House-sit."

"I'm not a cop."

Gabby could probably make a CIA agent talk, the way she used her hazel eyes as lasers.

"Fine, I'm a private investigator." Sort of.

Only, at this rate of confession, she wouldn't be a PI long. Good grief, maybe she should just take out an ad in the *Star Tribune*.

"I'm standing in for Dally."

"What, so you can get killed?"

"I hope not. But why do you think someone wants to kill Dally?"

"If you could put someone behind bars for life, don't you think you'd be a prime target? Of *course* someone's trying to kill Dally."

PJ knew it; *she knew it!* She wasn't sure, however, exactly how she felt about this knowledge. . . . There was a sort of catch-22 to her always being correct about international assassins and dark-alley thugs.

"Who—?"

"Well, Billy Finch of course."

"He's behind bars," PJ said, trying out Jeremy's argument.

"Oh, sure. Don't tell me that he can't figure out a way to get to her. I watch television."

PJ hid a smile as her gaze went to the console in the family room.

"I have a black-and-white in my bedroom. Sebastian used to like to watch it after he was bedridden." She shook the spatula at PJ. "I don't like this scenario. Not one bit. You here by yourself, pretending to be Dally . . . that's what you're doing, isn't it? I think the word is—" she lowered her voice—"*bait.*"

"Bait?" To hear Gabby say it, plain out like that, made a finger of dread crawl up PJ's spine. And it was a little unnerving how easily Gabby put those pieces together.

"You know, Finch's boys will think it's you—"

"I think if Billy Finch wanted me—or Dally—dead, we'd already be that way." PJ took a napkin, began to fold it into tiny squares. "I'm perfectly safe." If she kept saying it, in that exact tone of voice, over and over, she might just believe it.

"I think I need to call Sammy."

"No!" PJ leaped to her feet, crossed over to Gabby. "Listen. I know some . . . self-defense. And I'm pretty fast on my feet. But more than that, if too many people find out that Dally is gone, then she *will* be in danger. I'm just going to lay low, keep my doors locked. I'll be fine; I promise."

Gabby flipped first one egg, then the other. After a moment, she slid them onto plates. She added bacon, then slipped off her apron and turned back to PJ, the plates in hand.

PJ took a plate as Gabby sat down at the table and poured PJ a glass of orange juice, then one for herself.

PJ picked up her fork, but a hand on her arm stopped her. Gabby turned her hand over. "Let's bless the food."

PJ took her hand. The skin was soft, and Gabby ran her thumb slightly over PJ's grip. And when she threw in a few words for PJ's—and Dally's—safety . . . well, PJ was probably just overtired from last night's activities. She blinked back the moisture in her eyes as she raised her head.

Gabby patted her hand, then picked up her fork. "Now, tell me everything. Where are you from, Miss PJ, and don't even breathe the word *Chicago*."

PJ filled her in on how she'd returned to her hometown after ten years of wanderings, omitted the run-in with an assassin in her hometown, but somehow found herself revealing Boone's recent proposal.

"But you haven't told him yes?"

"I don't know what . . . I mean, that's a big decision, and I'm not sure." PJ finished off her egg, washing it down with juice.

"Do you love him?"

"I've loved him for a long time. And I always pictured us together. But the truth is, there's something about saying yes that sort of cuts off my breathing."

"Oh, my."

"I just feel, sometimes, that Boone only sees me the way he wants me to be, not the way I am."

Gabby considered her for a long moment, her hand going to her gold necklace, playing with the emerald pendant. "I was engaged to someone else before I met Sebastian. Clark was working as a walk-on for MGM back in the glory days of the silver screen. I was young and impressionable, and I had bright-light dreams. He was a smooth-talking extra who thought his smile and the cherry red carnation he always wore in his lapel might make me swoon at his feet. I fell in love with him the first day I saw him. He drove up in a convertible Karmann Ghia—he was parking it for a studio exec—and I thought, *Now there is the man for me*. Dashing and rich, with a bright future ahead of him.

"Oh, I wanted him to love me. So I didn't tell him how terribly poor I was, living hand to mouth, working in costuming, waiting for my big break. I 'borrowed' costumes when he took me out on dates. We'd dated about six months, and I'd already accepted his marriage proposal when one night I saw him stepping out with one of my coworkers, a girl who had a role in an upcoming Ginger Rogers movie.

"I was devastated, and I hid in the costume room, furious at myself for being so stupid. Sebastian found me there. He was working set construction at night and walking on as an extra during the day. I'll never forget that night, the smell of sawdust in his hair, the way he sat on a crate, those blue eyes seeing me in my darkest place. Then he asked what a beautiful girl like me was doing hiding under a rack of dresses, looking like I'd lost the world. Sebastian touched my hand and said the words that saved my life: 'You know, just because he seems like the right guy doesn't mean he is.' I wept even more because I realized that I'd been holding my breath all along, waiting for disaster. And when Seb took my hand, I knew I could breathe again.

"Of course, Seb just wanted to marry me instead. He'd been watching me on set and hoped that I'd come to my senses. It was no accident he found me in that costume room. He didn't tell me that for years. By then, he didn't have to."

Gabby took PJ's plate and piled it on her own. "Now then, we're going to have to do some work if you're going to be impersonating Dally Morrison. Let me tell you, you're in for a ride."

PJ opened her mouth, still trying to absorb Gabby's story. "I, uh . . ."

"You didn't think I was going to let you do this by yourself, did you? Now listen, if being Dally will keep her alive, then you're going to be Dally. My concern is how we're going to keep you out of trouble."

Yeah, well, someone should start a club.

* * *

With the exception of the wide green eyes, the remnant freckles from her youth, and the heart-shaped face, PJ barely recognized herself.

In fact, she did a better job of recognizing the cronies in Dally's pictures. Now at least she had names for those faces.

Stacey Dale ran the tattoo and body art shop attached to the Scissor Shack. With her long red hair and her infectious laughter, PJ could understand why the place was called Happy Tats. Stacey and Dally were cut from the same cloth. Stacey wore a tight black shirt covered in skulls, dangerously low wide-leg jeans, and a pair of red open-toed Vans. Still, from the moment PJ walked into the Scissor Shack with Gabby, Stacey had been all enthusiasm and not in the least horrified that PJ wanted to impersonate her best friend.

"Are you sure we can't just dye it? This wig will get *soo* hot under your baseball cap and mask." Stacey smoothed the long black wig with her fingers, the nails painted black.

"I like my hair. Besides, I'd also have to put in hair extensions."

"And those aren't cheap." This from the Scissor Shack's owner, Linda Button, a blonde who embodied every nuance of the word *buxom* in black spandex leggings under a voluminous white tuxedo shirt rolled up at the arms. "The wig's all I can afford to donate for the cause, sisters." Linda stood behind PJ with her hands on her hips, surveying the final product. "You reproduced the magnolia tattoo real well, Stace."

PJ's persona had transformed before her eyes as Stacey airbrushed Dally's magnolia tattoo onto her shoulder, trailing the stem down her right arm and punctuating it with two red dots of blood on the hand.

"What does the flower mean?" PJ asked.

"Well, the magnolia is a symbol of nobility and strength, but that strength has come at the cost of her own blood. Dally got it after Chicago. It's sort of a reminder of all she's gone through, and everything she is today. She has a motto: *Every day the choices you make tell you who and what you are.* But it isn't without struggle, hence the blood, despite the beauty. I helped her design the tat—it's one of my favorites. Are you sure you don't want me to give you a real one? Or maybe we could doodle this one up a bit?" She surveyed PJ's left shoulder. "Who's Boone?"

"The man she's trying to figure out if she should marry," Gabby piped up from her spot under a dryer as she flipped through a women's magazine. She'd accompanied PJ to the Scissor Shack, a block and a half from her house, walking in her spongy shoes at a pace that shocked PJ and made her hope to be as spry when she reached her eighties. It had taken the clout of only one of Dally's longtime Scissor Shack clients to convince Stacey and Linda to transform PJ from conservative Kelloggian to inner-city rocker.

"You don't know if you should marry him?" Stacey asked, plopping herself down in one of the four black chairs. The place had an elegant chic about it, from the black sinks and chairs to the blue walls and the white oval French country mirrors at each station. The place was small, to be sure, but embodied a neighborhood charm that evoked the sense of juicy gossip shared over a perm and color or a set and dry.

Stacey slid one skinny leg over the other and leaned in like PJ might have some sort of delicious backstory.

"I just haven't made up my mind yet," PJ said. "He was my high school sweetheart, so of course, I love him. . . ."

"But do you want him to be the father of your children?" Linda asked.

"Children?" PJ looked at her in the mirror. Linda was eating a granola bar and nodding. "I haven't thought about children."

"Well, first comes marriage . . ." Linda lifted black penciled eyebrows.

Gabby closed her magazine and pushed up the dryer. "Let's keep her alive first, shall we, girls? She can figure out if she wants to marry Boone once we catch whoever broke into Dally's house last night."

Linda shot her a look, midbite. "We?"

Stacey drew both legs up onto the chair, her face bright, accented by the half-moon tattooed over her right eyebrow. "*We*, of course. Who knows Dally's life better than Linda and me?" She nodded at Linda. "I'll bet it's Missy Gainer. Remember, Linda, how hot she was after Dally botched her hair?" She added a minute inflection to the word *botched*.

Stacey turned to PJ. "It was gorgeous. The most delicious deep purple I'd ever seen, and with Missy's dragonfly tattoo on her neck, it made for beautiful wedding shots. But Missy wanted lavender, and anyone knows that when you're starting out with hair as dark as Missy's, you have to strip out the black, which makes it more porous and more susceptible to color. Dally even told her that, but oh, Missy was furious. And of course, poor Dally couldn't go back and lighten it because the hair would have been damaged—anyone could figure that out. At least anyone who isn't . . . you know—" Stacey ran her two pointer fingers in small circles around her head—"loony."

"Missy isn't loony," Linda said. "She's just . . . zealous."

"She accused Dally of trying to steal her fiancé." Stacey hopped off the chair. "C'mon—Rick's no prize. I don't care if he is built like Mr. Universe. Me, I like thin guys who don't spend every moment at the gym, flexing. More importantly, Dally's not the kind of person to steal another girl's man. Besides, Dally has—" she lowered her voice, turning it soap-opera breathy—"a mystery man."

PJ laughed, and even Linda cracked a smile.

"Who is her mystery man?" PJ asked.

"Oh, she's not telling," Linda said, finishing off her Dr Pepper. "But I do know they broke up. Dally came in a couple weeks ago all red-eyed and teary saying she hated men."

"Yeah, I get that way about once a month," Stacey said. "Doesn't mean she broke up with him."

"Well, I haven't seen him around," Gabby said as she moved over to Linda's chair.

Linda began to unroll Gabby's hair.

Stacey leaned close to PJ's ear. "And she should know."

"I still have my hearing, little miss."

Stacey gave Gabby a grin, all teeth, then turned back to PJ. "Missy swore to Dally, right here in this very chair, that she'd get her back for destroying her hair two days before her wedding. And I believe it too, because once Missy followed a second baseman from another team to Jack's Bar over on Fifty-second, and used her car for home-run practice." She widened her eyes. "Scary girl."

Next door in the tattoo studio, the bell over the door jangled. "Uh-oh, the artist is on duty." Stacey patted PJ's knee. "The tournament starts at one o'clock. Warm-ups at high noon. Don't be late."

The tournament?

Stacey seemed to sense her pause because her smile dimmed. "Wait—you can play, right? I mean, we're one game short of the top ranking. We can't lose. Dally wouldn't let someone take her place who couldn't play. . . ."

PJ swallowed back a shard of panic. "Sure. Sure. No problem. Played in high school. And I learned all the calls."

Stacey narrowed her eyes at PJ. "Don't make me regret turning you into my best friend."

PJ shook her head, and Stacey winked at her as she headed out the door.

"You'd better climb off that chair and get over here and let me teach you how to fix Gabby's hair," Linda chimed in. "She's in here nearly every other day, and if there really is some thug from Chicago sitting outside with his binoculars, it won't do to have me unrolling her. Gabby doesn't let anyone else touch her hair."

"Then maybe I—," PJ started.

"Grab a brush, kiddo," Gabby said, not looking up from her magazine. "Oh, look at this; Paris has a new video out."

Chapter **TEN**

"You do this every day?" PJ held a plastic bag filled with a box of soy milk, a carton of eggs, a can of peaches, and a bag of peanuts as she walked home beside Gabby, past tiny bungalows and boxy Cape Cods, most with new siding and rich landscaping. The sun still blasted heat into the day, desperate as it fell into the horizon.

PJ couldn't figure out why her neighbor had stayed all day watching PJ learn to set and comb out hair. Maybe a sort of inherent protectiveness for Dally and now PJ.

The two walk-ins didn't know Dally, so she hadn't had a smidge of opposition to her fake identity. However, she'd discovered it felt different imitating a person, rather than just a persona. It was one thing to pretend to be a golf pro or a massage therapist—things she'd done to solve her last crime. This felt more . . . deceitful.

She kept having to remind herself that she was trying to

save Dally's skin. Still, she'd been relieved that she hadn't been forced to attempt the lie for Linda or Stacey.

Not that she could have. But could she lie to the entire softball team?

This gig felt more ludicrous with every passing moment.

"I walk every day, but not always to the Scissor Shack. I go to the library or the park. Dally meets me there sometimes, and we have a picnic."

"You two do a lot together."

Gabby reached out to drag her hand along a chain-link fence they were passing. She slowed slightly, letting her breath catch up. PJ hadn't realized they were walking so fast. She just wanted to get home and out of the wig that had indeed begun to itch, sweat beading along the back of her scalp.

"Dally needed a friend. She was so alone when she moved here. Didn't know a soul." Gabby took PJ's arm as the fence ended. "Don't you have anyone who is missing you right now?"

"My sister, Connie, maybe. Her son, Davy. He's four. I suppose my mother might wonder where I am. But I was gone for so long before, I don't think I've been home long enough to miss."

"I don't think that's the criteria. Who do *you* miss most right now?"

Jeremy. The name poured into her mind. Jeremy, with his dark smile, the way he looked at her with eyes that suggested mystery and sometimes pride.

And as quickly as the thought crashed over her, guilt followed. Oh . . . she should have been missing Boone.

"You were thinking of your man, weren't you?" Gabby lifted her hand to wave at a neighbor.

PJ said nothing.

The sun had fallen low over the rooftops, casting long, boxy shadows over the sidewalks. They passed a yard where three children danced through the sprinkler. Across the street, a neighbor stood at the foot of his driveway in slippers and a pair of Bermuda shorts, holding a newspaper, watching them.

"That's Bernard Lewis. He works nights. Probably just getting ready for his shift. Wife died about three years ago. Has a daughter who comes around about as often as Evelyn, although she's of course much younger."

They'd reached Gabby's front walk and PJ turned in to it. "Don't you ever drive anywhere?"

"Not anymore. Evelyn picks me up for church. And Sammy takes me to the shopping center if I want to go. An old lady like me doesn't need all that stress."

"Did you sell your car?"

"Oh my, no!" Gabby reached into her purse, an ancient white handbag with a gold clasp. She pulled out her keys. "It's in the garage out back. Was Sebastian's pride and joy. I couldn't part with it. Sammy keeps it tuned up and running for me. Just in case I want to cruise Lake Calhoun." She winked at PJ before she put the key in the lock, turned it. "Will you stay for supper?"

PJ followed her inside and put the bag on the table. "I need a shower. And I should probably track down Jeremy."

"Jeremy? Who's that?"

"He's my boss."

Gabby stood there silent, her gaze on PJ's face. "Oh, I see." She said it with a tight smile, her eyes sparkling. "He's not the one who'll find you hiding in the costume room, is he?"

"See you tomorrow, Gabby."

Inside Dally's house, PJ closed the front curtain that looked out on the street. Then she stripped off the wig and Dally's crazy clothes. An hour later she sat in the kitchen polishing off a cup of pudding she found in Dally's pantry. The house felt more her own after twenty-four hours. From the side window, she occasionally saw the curtain at Gabby's window rustle. No doubt the woman would be on high alert tonight—PJ's own private security detail.

She tossed the pudding container and stood for a long time in the bath of refrigerator light, wishing for a pizza. Closing the fridge, she settled for the dregs of Cap'n Crunch in the box on the counter. Turning off the kitchen light, she opened the front door, hiding in the growing darkness and letting the summer evening caress her skin. The sun had vanished, and at its departure, the crickets had begun to sing, the fireflies pulsing in the velvet twilight.

She wondered what Connie was doing—most likely wrestling dinner down Davy, who, after two weeks alone with PJ, had turned into an amateur junk foodie. Vera was probably in the kitchen frying something inedible. Boris would be at work, hopefully loving his new job.

Boone . . . was it a bad sign that he walked into her thoughts last? Maybe she should call him, at least tell him she missed him.

She did miss him. Missed sitting on the porch with him after a hot day, sipping lemonade, hearing his laughter as she told him stories of Davy or Boris and Vera. Missed his hand in hers as they walked on the beach, their feet in the warm sand. Missed the tangy smell of his aftershave, his sturdy hands on the wheel of his Mustang as she lifted her face to the sun, the wind tangling her hair.

Yes, she could probably love him a very, very long time.

But be the father of her . . . *children?* Did she want her own mini Boone to leap into her arms? Someday, perhaps. And yes, Boone would be a great father, remembering the way he tousled Davy's hair. In fact, with very little effort, she could see the house, Boone's car in the driveway, even a curly-haired boy with Boone's smile . . . although where she fit into the picture she hadn't quite figured out.

She closed the door and wandered into the living room, staring at the dragon peering at her in the faint lamplight. "You don't scare me."

The chinchillas were waking, snuffling about in their cage, jumping from one ledge to another. She suddenly remembered that Dally's instructions about their care had included a mandate to let them out for an hour a day so they could run around—"supervised, of course."

Supervised chinchilla care.

Well, she supposed . . . She set the cereal box on top of the cage and opened it to reach in, maybe let the white one out—

It bit her. Hard, spearing down in the webbing between her thumb and finger.

"Ow!" She yanked her hand back and closed the cage. "Fine. No hour of exercise for you."

She retrieved the cereal box, turned on the television, cruised over to the old movie channel, and watched five minutes of the Duke, then channel surfed to a reality cop show and turned it off.

She had enough drama in her life.

Lying back on the sofa, staring at her toes, she thought of a pedicure, then the Scissor Shack, Linda, then Stacey and her words about Missy. Would Missy really come after Dally for a bad dye job? And what about Missy's husband? Could he be Dally's mystery man?

What if said husband—Rick?—and Dally did have a thing and he'd snuck into Dally's house to erase all evidence . . . including Dally?

What had the intruder been hunting for?

She got up and opened the television cabinet. Looked under the sofa. Pulled up the cushions.

Then she opened the door to the attic and looked up into the darkness. A long string dangled from a lone bulb above the stairs.

She eased her way up, the third and seventh steps groaning under her weight, and found a light switch as she neared the top. She flicked it on and gasped.

This was an attic and more. An extended wardrobe room.

Truthfully, when PJ had stared at Dally's supply of clothing yesterday, she'd run Dally's warnings through her head and wondered what all the fuss was about. Now she stood at the top step, the Cap'n Crunch box in her hand forgotten.

Dally had a wardrobe that rivaled a fashionista's from Fifth Avenue. An oval stand mirror stood in the center of the room, and along the walls hanging racks held enough leather to outfit the entire Harley-Davidson rally in Sturgis. Next to that hung faux fur: lime green leopard, pink and black zebra, orange and yellow tiger stripes, and a vest of white rabbit and silky . . . chinchilla?

Beyond the fur hung a dozen or more vintage-looking gowns: beaded chiffons with matching boas and headwear. Fringed flapper dresses from the twenties. Long, opulent satin and velvet gowns from the thirties. Wedding dresses from the forties. Strapless cocktail dresses from the fifties.

Apparently Dally's flamboyant style didn't stop at her body art.

On the other side of the attic, a dressmaker's stand wore a creation that looked even older, with a high-sashed waist and a straight skirt, a simple boat neckline and long puffy sleeves. Beside it, a sewing table held a fancy machine, and next to that sat a book titled *Vintage Replications*.

Dally Morrison was a seamstress. More than that, she had real talent.

And what was even better, she had a great sense of shoe fashion. Vintage high heels spilled from a box near the stairs.

PJ liked Dally Morrison more and more every day.

Leaving the cereal box at the top of the stairs, she looked through the dresses, finding a pink lace and tulle gown complete with a sewn-in crinoline and a faux—she hoped it was faux—white rabbit stole. It even had a pair of long white gloves pinned to the hanger.

What was a girl to do?

PJ wriggled out of her T-shirt, shucked off her yoga pants, and pulled the dress over her head, losing herself for a moment in all the fluff. When she emerged out of the top, she'd transformed into a . . . princess? She zipped up the side closure and twirled, watching the skirt levitate. Rooting through the box of shoes, she found a pair of gold high heels—probably the wrong era, but she didn't care. Then she pulled on the gloves.

"Oh, do you want to take me to dinner? Really? Ask me to the ball?" She pursed her lips and posed before the mirror, a few shots that Marilyn Monroe would have been proud of, then of course accepted this dance from Boone, or maybe someone else, and let herself be led around the room. "Sure, I'll dance with you too." She switched partners and finished the dance, accidently knocking over a stack of books piled below the sewing table.

She bent down to restack them and discovered they were all tawdry romances. Not only that but the top one was half-read, an unmarked envelope stuck between the pages.

An envelope.

With a letter.

She opened it, the dance forgotten.

> *Dear Dally,*
> *You made your choice. Now I have to make mine.*
> *I wish things could be different.*
>
> *~ R*

R. As in Rick? As in Missy's husband? Was this Dally's "mystery man"? Was this who had broken into her house? Rick, looking to find and destroy incriminating evidence?

A thump downstairs made her freeze. She listened and heard it again. Her heart had already fled through her mouth, and she grabbed the railing before her knees followed and left her in a heap on the floor.

Another thump.

Someone was in the house.

Again.

She flicked off the lights and wished desperately for her phone. Okay, okay, this time she'd speed-dial Boone, she promised.

She reached out in the darkness for a weapon—any weapon—and her hand closed around the Cap'n Crunch box. No, that wouldn't work.

The shoes.

She pulled off the beautiful gold stilettos, holding one in each hand, and tiptoed down the stairs. The third step creaked and she froze.

Another thump, this time followed by a rattle.

The chinchillas began to scream. *No, no, no.*

With a howl PJ leaped, shoes at the ready.

The prowler jumped off the cage and right at PJ, landing on her face, hissing. PJ screamed and pushed the cat away. It landed on her feet and shot off into the back of the house.

"Simon!" PJ gasped, shaking, the shoes still gripped in her hands. The softball lay in the middle of the carpet—one mysterious thump. Next to it lay a book Dally had left on the television. The other thump.

"PJ?"

The voice behind her startled her and she whirled before she had a chance to think, to stop, to consider. She just reacted, fast and hard, and whacked the man with the heel of her shoe, right above his ear. "Stay back!"

"Ow!"

See, this was what came from skulking around in the semidarkness. Predators and boyfriends could sneak up with impunity.

"Oh, Boone!" She dropped the shoe and launched herself into his arms.

"I really hope this means you're glad to see me."

She buried her face in his neck and inhaled the sweet safety of Boone. *Boone.* Yes, *yes*, she'd missed him! First.

She pushed away from him. "What are you doing here?" Then, "Oh no, you're bleeding!"

Boone clutched the side of his head. "I think you took off a foot of skin. It hurts."

"Don't bleed on the carpet!"

"Is that all you can say?"

"Don't get it on this dress either." PJ headed for the kitchen and turned on the light so she could examine the pink dress.

"I'm hurt here." Boone followed her into the kitchen, grabbed a towel, and held it to his head.

PJ opened the freezer, looking for a bag of peas or corn. Of course, Dally, a girl with PJ's exact eating habits, had only a half carton of peppermint chocolate-chip ice cream. She grabbed the ice tray and closed the door.

Boone stared at her, eyes wide. "Good grief, PJ, are you undercover as a debutante?" He took her arm. "Is that a tattoo? What in the world . . . ?"

"It's paint," PJ said, pulling out another towel.

"Paint? What kind of person are you impersonating?"

"I don't want to talk about it."

"You don't want to talk about it? You came after me with a pair of heels! Is the neighborhood that rough?"

She was a little more vigorous than she intended cracking the ice tray on the open towel. Cubes flew across the counter, hit the toaster and a rack of mugs. "You have no idea."

"Apparently not."

She folded the towel, then opened a drawer and sifted through the utensils, unearthing a meat mallet. "How'd you find me? Did you track me here? Do I have a homing beacon pinned to me?" She gave the ice a whack, breaking it into little shavings.

"I'm a little afraid of you right now."

She rounded on him and held up the mallet.

"Your cell phone. It has GPS, and I used the police computer to find you."

"That's unbelievable. Simply . . . completely . . . You don't trust me at all, do you? What did you think, I'd take off, disappear into the wind?" She gave the ice another pummeling and chips flew off the counter, onto the floor.

Boone took a step back. "Well . . ."

She glared at him. "Seriously? You want to go there?"

"No, of course not. The GPS is part of your phone system. And frankly I'm just a little relieved to know that if you got attacked in the middle of the night, you'd inflict some damage."

"I'm not going to feel bad about your bleeding." Only she did, a little. She folded the towel and handed it to him, taking the other from his grip and tossing it in the sink. Just imagine if she'd connected with his eye? The thought turned her weak, especially when she caught a glimpse of the blood dripping down from where she'd gouged him. "What were you doing sneaking in here anyway? I could have killed you."

"Your door was open and I heard you scream—or at least yell. Scared the wits out of me. I thought someone was in here beating you to death."

"It was the neighbor's cat. And that wasn't me screaming; that's the chinchillas."

"The what?"

"Don't ask." She wiped up some of the ice debris and pushed it into the sink. "How'd you get in here?"

"I told you—the back door was open."

"I know I closed it."

"Do you think I broke in?"

PJ grabbed the door handle, examined it. Closed it. Sure enough, it didn't latch. She put a hip into it. Now that tidbit of information might have been more useful than chinchilla tips from Dally. Frustration flushed into PJ's voice as she turned back to Boone. "Please, why exactly are you here?"

"I . . . wanted to see you."

She stared at him in the kitchen light, seeing how as usual he looked pressed and put together, not at all frayed at the edges, the blue in his shirt deepening his eyes. And it was probably a crime to smell freshly laundered this late at night. "It's only been a day, Boone."

He looked sheepish and lifted a shoulder. "I missed you."

She wasn't sure what to say to that. "You look like you're going to church or something."

"Yeah, well, you look like you're going to a cotillion."

"We touched on that." She peeled off her gloves and lifted the ice pack, then winced at the wicked scrape above his ear. "Sorry about . . . No, wait. I take that back. I'm not sorry. Serves you right."

"I'll have to admit, you are pretty tough, even in a dress." He touched the lacy gown. "Don't get me wrong. I like it."

"It's Dally's—the woman I'm standing in for. Apparently, as

well as being a biker chick, hotshot catcher for the Rockets, an avant-garde hairdresser, and best friend to her eighty-year-old neighbor, she's also a seamstress. Has an entire room full of pretty dresses to accentuate her all-leather-and-fur attire."

"Really?" He stepped back and ran his gaze over her. "I'd like to see some on you."

"You're not even supposed to be here. What will the neighbors think?" She feigned gossip, putting a hand over her mouth. "Dally's got a new guy."

His expression darkened. "Does she have an old guy? someone I need to worry about?"

She went into the living room. "Uh . . ." The last thing she needed was Boone worried about someone who may or may not be an old boyfriend. "Supposedly there's a mystery man, and Gabby seemed to know him, but he hasn't been around—"

"Who's Gabby?"

"She's the eighty-year-old neighbor lady."

"I thought you were supposed to just lay low, pretend to be sick or something."

"She came over last night when she heard the screaming."

She stopped on *screaming*, realizing she'd gone too far, especially when Boone's hand fell away from his wound, his smile fading. "Please tell me it was the chimichangas?"

"Uh . . ."

"What was the screaming for, PJ?"

She made a face. "It wasn't that big a deal."

"Explain the screaming."

"There might have been a prowler—"

"I knew it! I knew Jeremy would leave you here, and then

you'd get hurt. I don't like it. I'm taking you home." He'd already tossed the towel in the sink.

"Stop, Boone. I'm fine. I'm not hurt, and as you can see, I can inflict damage when I need to. Besides, I promise that Gabby is on high alert. And I can't leave. Now that I know Dally's right, that she's in danger, I have to complete my mission."

"You aren't in the Marines, for pete's sake." Boone took a deep breath. "Do you know who it was?" He looked like, if she said yes, he just might do some prowling of his own.

"No. It might have . . . been an old boyfriend. Maybe. Or not. Whoever it was, he smelled really bad, like ointment, or medicine, and garlic."

Boone wore something akin to horror in his expression. "I don't even want to know how you got close enough to smell him. But that settles it; I'm staying."

"Boone . . ."

"Don't think I'm moving off the sofa until I know you're safely tucked into bed, the doors locked like Fort Knox. I might even sleep in the car." As if to put a point to his words, he plopped down on the sofa and patted the pillow as if checking its suitability.

Boone's vehemence touched her. Only last night she'd longed for him to be here, for his aura of strength to permeate the house. "You really shouldn't be here. My mother would be over here with my father's golf clubs if she knew."

He relaxed his posture a fraction. "I know. But your reputation is safe with me."

Now. It certainly hadn't been ten years ago.

As if Boone read her thoughts, he smiled. "Especially if you try on another dress for me."

PJ narrowed her eyes at him. "Not a chance, pal."

She went to the attic and changed, rehanging the dress. Boone lay, eyes closed, breathing deeply when she returned downstairs. She sat on the coffee table and nudged him awake.

Boone opened one eye and took in her T-shirt and yoga pants. "That's much better."

"You're so unromantic."

"Oh, I'm romantic, honey. I just like the plain old PJ, the one I know and love. The one who can't stay out of trouble."

She wasn't sure why those words made her throat tighten. She managed a smile though. "I did miss you."

"Even though it's only been twenty-four hours?"

"Yes. Now give—what are you doing here anyway?"

Boone suddenly looked tired, his hair as mussed as she'd ever seen it. "I got my truck back."

"Already? That's fast work for the Kellogg cops."

"Hey, now."

"Present company excepted, of course."

He sat up. "They found it this morning just down the street from the health club. Only thing was—it was stripped, right down to the wheels. My insurance company is totaling it."

"Oh, I'm sorry, Boone."

"I'm not." He ran a hand down her arm, met her eyes. "You know I was thinking maybe I wouldn't replace it. I'll buy a junker to drive around town."

"But you love your truck."

"Not as much as I love you. What if I used the insurance money for us? You know, put a nice little down payment on a house—like this one. You'd like that, right?"

PJ closed her eyes, hating the burn in her chest, the painful pleading in his voice. "I don't know what I want, Boone."

He pulled his hand away, stared at her a long time without moving. "Did I say something wrong, PJ?"

No. Yes. She didn't know.

"Why do you want to marry me?" Her question came out so softly, she wasn't sure he heard her.

But the frown on his face said that he had. "Because I've loved you for as long as I can remember. And because you love me too."

When she didn't answer, he added a small "Don't you?"

His question made her want to crawl into his lap and take him in her arms. She nodded, her vision blurring.

He said nothing for a long time, but finally, gently, he took her chin and turned her face to meet his. He brushed the tear from her cheek with his thumb, but his voice wavered slightly. "Okay. I get it. I won't rush you."

She rubbed her arms, suddenly chilled and very, very tired. "You'd better go. But I don't want to wake up and find you camped out in the Mustang outside."

"No promises," he said as he kissed her on the cheek. "Make sure that door latches when I leave."

Chapter *ELEVEN*

Boone had evidently opted out of sleeping on the streets or in his car. PJ stood in her Superman pajamas drinking milk from the carton, having slept hard, the crease of the cell phone now embedded like a road map to frustration in her cheek. If Jeremy didn't start answering her voice mails . . . well, she might start thinking that she'd have to rescue *him*.

Her stomach growled and she glanced through the living room to see if she could detect a light or perhaps movement over at Gabby's house. What time was it, anyway? Her stomach growled as if she hadn't eaten for a week. She could sure use some breakfast. Eggs, bacon . . . especially since she'd finished off the Cap'n Crunch.

At least her door had remained latched and locked the entire night. Not a prowler to be seen or smelled.

She wrapped her painted arm in saran wrap and took a shower, then stood before the bedroom closet and tried to think like Dally. Big. Expressive. Outrageous. She chose a pair of orange and black leopard pants, a red shirt, and a pair of black-and-white Vans that she felt sure Stacey and Dally would approve of. Then she braided her long wig into two pigtails, added a green Army hat, and pronounced herself sufficiently Dally-ized.

She might even fool Gabby.

She'd definitely fool Boone.

And she couldn't deny a sort of intoxicating freedom in being this other person, as if she could say or do whatever she pleased—without consequence.

PJ sprinkled some food into the chinchillas' cage. They didn't move from their pile of slumbering fur. She'd heard a few yips and growls last night before dropping off in hard-stone slumber.

Exiting out the back door, she went around the alley and through Gabby's backyard. A T clothesline—four lines deep—suggested the bygone era of crisp, sun-dried sheets, and under a gnarled maple the scars of a rope swing had never grown over. A slanted cellar door evidenced the first incarnation of walk-out basements, and the white metal furniture on Gabby's tiny patio had weathered a thousand storms, the green print on the cushions faded into a faint hue of lime over grimy white. She would have liked seeing the overgrown flower boxes under the picture window in their glory days. She could picture Gabby's family here—like the Brady Bunch—grilling in the backyard, Sebastian in plaid shorts and a green shirt holding a fork in barbecue mitts, Gabby in her print day dress bringing out cookies and lemonade as a pigtailed Evelyn swung in the tree swing.

PJ knocked at the door. "Gabby?"

No answer, but she heard music, something big band and lively, with saxophones and trumpets, and it conjured hazy images of the *Lawrence Welk Show*. She knocked again and this time tried the knob. It turned, so she stuck her head inside and then entered the kitchen. "Gabby?"

"In here!" The voice sounded muffled, and for a second PJ thought maybe Gabby had fallen. What if she'd broken her hip? As she passed the family room, she spotted an LP spinning on the old console, the sounds crackling even as—oh, Frank Sinatra—crooned something sultry.

"Gabby?"

"I'm in the bedroom."

PJ passed the guest room and found Gabby in the back bedroom.

Her room had been transported straight from Nixon's era. Green shag carpeting, blond furniture with prim lines, a bureau with a large mirror, and matching side tables with green opaque lamps. The bed had already been tidied with a white chenille coverlet, and two appliqué pillows featuring brown owls with orange beaks lay propped against the headboard.

It could have been taken from a vintage seventies magazine page, Twiggy stretched out on the bed.

Only instead, Gabby was stretched out halfway *underneath* it.

"Gabby!"

The scenario before PJ seemed a slap of reality after her previous image of pit bull Gabby, the neighborhood enforcer. This version was elderly and frail, dressed in a green housecoat, her blue-veined legs sticking out the bottom, ghostly append-ages of their former elegance. Pink velour slippers cast from her feet sprawled near the side of the bed and one end of the white spread had been tossed up over the pillow.

"Are you okay? Did you fall?"

"No." Gabby winced as she wriggled farther under the bed, her face upturned against the frame, her arm extended as far as it could go.

"What are you doing?"

"Oh, I'm such a silly," she said, her voice slightly muffled under the tomb of her double bed. "I was reading last night, and I'd forgotten to take off my earrings, so I set them on my night table. And wouldn't you know it, this morning Simon jumped up on the table and the earrings went flying. One is way back there."

Gabby wriggled herself out and slapped off dust accumu-lated on her hands. "I wouldn't worry so much, but Seb gave them to me, and if I don't wear them, I'm afraid they'll go missing. I seem to put my valuables down places and then forget . . ."

PJ bent down and pressed her cheek to the floor—it smelled like some perfumed powder one sprinkled to freshen old carpet—and peered into the shadows. Sure enough, Gabby's emerald earring lay in the center of the darkness, right beyond fingertip reach. "Let me see if I can reach it."

"I'll get a broom." Gabby climbed up off the floor and then, to PJ's surprise, did a brief soft-shoe right there. "Oh, I just love Frank, don't you? When he looked at me with those baby blues, I would have promised just about anything." In that moment, she wasn't a woman who wore years in the lines on her face, dressed in clothes more appropriate for a senior center, but a young and fresh girl, her eyes shiny and full of something bright only she could see in her rearview mirror. "I loved the way he laughed. He just made a girl feel beautiful."

"You knew him?"

But Gabby was lost, caught in a memory, waltzing out of the room.

PJ turned over onto her stomach, stretched out, closing one eye. Her fingers nicked the earring, and she used her middle and pointer finger like tweezers to pull it toward her. Finally her hand closed around it. She sat up, holding it in her hand.

She got up and went to the jewelry box, open on Gabby's dresser. It sat atop a long rectangle doily next to a picture of Sebastian in thick seventies glasses.

PJ dropped the earring into the box, then sifted through the collection of clip-on earrings and other jewelry. A sapphire brooch in a gold setting and a pair of three-drop pearl earrings, a cocktail ring with tiny rubies, and the emerald pendant on the chain Gabby had worn yesterday. She held it up to the mirror.

"I knew it."

The tone, more than the words, made PJ shift her gaze toward the doorway.

While Gabby had a natural elegance even at her age, this woman clearly worked for it with her coiffed golden brown hair, ivory pants, and brown sweater with a touch of gold at her ears, neck, and wrists. PJ had the sense of speaking to a very expensive bar of Godiva chocolate.

"Excuse me?"

"Don't give me that lip, young lady. I know exactly what

you were doing." She strode forward and grabbed PJ's wrist with a manicured hand, shaking it until the necklace dropped into her open palm. "I knew that one of these days I'd catch you red-handed."

"What are you talking about? I was just looking."

"Oh, I'm sure that's exactly what you were doing pawing through my mother's jewelry. Good thing for her I take an inventory. I know exactly what pieces have gone missing, and now I have reason to go to the authorities." The woman said the word with a crisp airiness that conjured images of English bobbies.

This certainly couldn't be . . . "Evelyn?"

"Oh, brother." She dropped the jewelry into the box behind PJ and closed it with a click. "You can drop the 'who are you?' act. You knew I was having work done. I am sure my mother could talk of nothing else." She changed her tone of voice, imitating Gabby. "'In my day, a woman aged gracefully.' Well, in her day, there weren't younger women throwing themselves at her husband."

"That's what you think, Evelyn. There were plenty of young ladies who would have liked to take Seb home, but he wasn't the kind of man to wander. Besides, back in my day, men and women pledged themselves for life." Gabby stood at the bedroom door, holding the broom. Whatever song had been in her expression earlier had died. "Maybe you should consider spending more time at home and less time trying to get me to sell the house and move into an old folks' home." Gabby entered the room holding the broom out to PJ. "Oh, did you find it?"

PJ smiled at Evelyn. "Yes, I found your earring, Gabby." She took the opportunity to accentuate every word. And smiled again, showing lots of teeth.

"Thank you, Dally."

Dally. PJ glanced at Gabby, who gave her a quick wink before Evelyn turned on her.

"Mama, you know you can't take care of this place. Who knows what could happen to you here all alone?"

Clearly the "what could happen" had everything to do with Gabby's tattooed neighbor.

"Oh, fiddle-dee-dee. Sammy's here almost every night. And Dally keeps an eye on me, don't you, sweetie?"

"I'm sure she does." Evelyn pursed her lips.

Gabby ignored her and leaned the broom against the wall. "We were just talking about the old days of Frankie and Gregory."

"Gregory?"

"Peck," Evelyn said under her breath. She caught PJ's eye and lowered her voice to a whisper. "Don't encourage her. She thinks they were close personal friends. They took her dancing."

"I should make you a Cobb salad. I got the recipe straight from Sally at the Brown Derby. We would go there sometimes, all of us, after shooting—"

"C'mon, Mama. I'll make you some brunch." Evelyn put her arm around her mother, guiding her to the hallway.

PJ began to follow, but Evelyn rounded on her. "My mother is not in her right mind, and you should know better. The last thing she needs is you encouraging this Hollywood nonsense."

"She wasn't in Hollywood?"

"My mother was a housewife from inner-city Minneapolis. Do you seriously think she lived the life of a Hollywood starlet? Look around you."

PJ saw a home filled with love. The height marks of Gabby's children and grandchildren were etched in the woodwork near the kitchen. Evidence of a life invested in cookies and cleaning and caring.

"I don't know. There is that one picture—"

"It's an agent shot. Her only one. She's had it there for as long as I can remember, a constant reminder of her empty dreams. She never knew Frank or Gregory or Rita—"

"Hayworth?"

"Of course. Apparently, she was one of Rita's favorite makeup girls."

"Maybe it's good she has such a vivid . . . uh . . . past. If only in her mind, then." Only PJ didn't think Gabby seemed the type to invent a past. "How do you know she made it up?"

"I'm her daughter. Don't you think I would know if my mother had been a Hollywood starlet? Even a small screen one? Besides, she didn't start conjuring up actual stories until after my father had passed. It's like she wants to re-create the romantic life she wished they had."

"Your mom seems pretty content with her life."

"Dallas, I know she likes you, but don't pander to her. It's because of you that she won't go to the home. She thinks you're . . . a sort of granddaughter." Evelyn poked her finger toward PJ. "But I'm not fooled, missy. I'm watching you." She turned and strode down the hall.

PJ followed, listening to Frank sing "Pennies from Heaven," seeing Gabby now swaying to the music as she pulled out her cast-iron pot. Evelyn reached out to help her, and Gabby wrestled it from her hands.

Was Gabby losing her mind?

Which meant, what? If she wasn't, then where was her jewelry disappearing to? Or if she was, had she imagined seeing Dally's boyfriend? Maybe she did belong in some senior living apartment.

Suddenly Gabby looked up, mouth open, and said, as if seeing her for the first time, "Dally, what are you doing here?"

"I'm, uh . . ."

"You have a softball tournament. Right now!"

⁕ ⁕ ⁕

The last time PJ had played softball, it had been against the Minnetonka Blue Devils in the last round of division championships, and she'd played shortstop. Sometimes she could still smell the cut grass in the outfield, feel the scrape of diamond gravel beneath her cleats, hear the buzz of early evening gnats around her head. In her memory, she saw Boone astride his bike in the parking lot, distracting her from the game.

That night, two outs, bottom of the sixth, two on base, they were up by one run. She saw him go around the fence and perch in the stands. Tonka's star was up, a home-run hitter who had been PJ's nemesis for three years. But prom was only a week away, and she had breathy prom night promises on her mind.

She glued her eyes on the batter as the first pitch went wide.

Boone waved.

She ignored him as the batter swung at the second. The ball popped up for a foul.

The third dropped inside, another ball.

And then Kacy Olson sat down next to Boone.

Cute Kacy Olson.

She'd had her jealous eyes on Boone since sixth grade.

The fourth pitch connected just as PJ's gaze went to the little tramp trying to steal her man. The ball flipped up high, too deep to be an infield fly, but PJ wasn't going to let it out of her reach.

She backed up, glove high, feet scrubbing through the dirt, into the outfield. "Mine!"

Behind her, the left fielder was running hard to dig it out. "Got it!"

She had her eye on the ball, her glove up, backpedaling—

She slammed into the left fielder just as the ball ricocheted off the top of her glove, bounced on the grass, and rolled toward center field.

Tonka won by three.

She rewrote that moment over and over, sometimes late at night, seeing herself jump and nab the ball or, better yet, letting it pass over her head, trusting her left fielder.

In neither scenario did she end up the pariah of the Kellogg Mavericks.

Now PJ could taste the old pregame adrenaline, a roil of half fear, half hope as she flew into Dally's house, unearthed her softball uniform from the laundry basket—the clean laundry, thankfully—pulled on the polyester over her wig, added the cap, grabbed the cleats and equipment, and took off for the softball diamond three blocks away.

She was getting a do-over.

So it was at catcher. She could play catcher. It had to be a thousand times easier than shortstop, right? Just squat and catch the ball.

Oh, and call the pitches. She tried to remember the signals as she jogged toward the field. She paused in the parking lot at the lip of the park to put on her equipment and pull herself together.

Her debut as Dally. She would simply wear the catcher's mask, and no one would know the difference. Positioning the cap backward on her head, she pulled the mask down over her face.

The ballpark had three fields, two already in use. A bat cracked against a ball and a cheer sweetened the humid afternoon. The smell of hot dogs reminded her that she'd missed breakfast.

The Rockets were warming up in the infield, throwing the ball around. Whoever had picked the black uniforms should be strung up from the oak tree in the park behind them because PJ already wanted to wade into Lake Nokomis, sparkling blue, pretty, and tantalizing just beyond the fields.

But no. She was here to win. To be Dally Morrison, superstar catcher.

For a second she wished Jeremy were here to see her be a PI, the undercover girl who got the job done.

She found Stacey stretching out on the grass, a fashion statement with her bright red hair and the way she'd cut her shirt short to reveal her stomach and ruby belly button charm. Apparently PJ had dressed Dally down in her basic uniform and hat.

Whoops.

Stacey looked at her. "You're late."

"I forgot."

She shook her head, making a face. "Listen, if you want, I can get a pinch catcher in. I talked to Morgan—don't look at me like that; I didn't tell her anything, only that you weren't feeling like yourself—and she said she'd love to fill in for you."

PJ crouched before Stacey, looking around, then lowered her voice. "Dally said that if she—I—didn't play, then they'd cut her from the team."

"They wouldn't cut her for one game. Just maybe bench her for the season. But what's worse: you messing up her position or the entire game?"

PJ debated this in silence, weighing the personal ramifications and just how seriously she should take Dally's threats. "I'll play."

"You swear you can do this."

"It's amateur softball! But yes, I learned the calls, and I have played softball before. No problem."

Stacey narrowed her eyes. "Apparently Dally didn't fill you completely in on Karla."

"Karla?"

"Maybe it's best you don't know. C'mon—she's warming up with Morgan. You'd better stake your territory."

PJ followed Stacey over to the catcher's box, where a girl with short blonde pigtails crouched behind the plate.

"Morgan has her own fan club," Stacey said. She gestured to a group of young men in the stands.

PJ noticed more fans assembling, some wearing Rockets T-shirts, a few older folks, maybe from the neighborhood, maybe relatives. She wondered if Gabby had ever attended one of Dally's games, then if Boone might show up.

Even though she hadn't mentioned the game.

The pitcher looked like she could have played for the majors, with arms that filled out the sleeves of her black Rockets uniform. She chewed a wad of gum, her dark eyes under her cap sizing up the imaginary batter, leaning low over the ball that she held out in her mitt.

"Who's—?"

The pitcher suddenly straightened and in a split second delivered the ball to the catcher in a roundhouse fast pitch that made a satisfying and frightening thwack in Morgan's glove.

PJ jerked. "That was fast."

"Aw, she's just getting warmed up. Karla's pitches have been clocked nearly as fast as the pros."

"Professional softball?"

"Baseball." Stacey gave her a disgusted look, then shook her head. "Heaven help us." She waved as Morgan threw the ball back. "Morgan, Dally's here."

Morgan took off her mask as she stood. "Hey, Dally. I was just filling in." She offered a smile to go along with her sunny voice, and as she passed by PJ, a cheer went up from her devoted fans.

PJ crouched down behind the plate, her thighs protesting. The minute she settled into a crouch, her balance shifted and she clunked into the dirt on her backside.

"Oops."

Stacey was watching her, eyes wide with horror. "Please."

PJ held up a hand to the pitcher—Karla. "Sorry! I haven't stretched out yet."

"Don't talk," Stacey growled.

PJ patted her glove. "Give it to me, Karla!"

"Seriously. Not a word."

PJ closed her mouth. Stacey was nearly as scary as Dally.

Karla stared at her, as if waiting for something. PJ held out her mitt. Waggled it. Whacked it with her hand.

"Call the pitch," Stacey said under her breath.

Call the . . . Right. PJ sent the sign for a fastball, the only pitch she really recognized. Karla sized her up, stepped back, and let it fly.

PJ tried to hold steady, but she couldn't move under all this gear in this crunched-up position, and as the pitch came at her, she couldn't help but pull back. The ball hit the dirt where her glove had been and bounced up hard, thwacking her mask. She tumbled back again into the dirt.

Stacey turned away, wincing.

Karla delivered something that looked like a glare.

"Hey, Dally, you back off the wagon or something?" the first baseman shouted.

"That's not funny!" the second baseman said, as PJ scrambled for the ball and threw it.

PJ nearly cried with relief when it sailed in an arch straight for Karla. She lifted her hand in an apologetic wave.

C'mon, PJ. She crouched again, held out her glove, sent the same sign, and this time focused on Karla's pitch. The ball sailed toward her, dropping at the last moment right into her glove. Pain veined up her arm and she held in a howl.

But as she threw the ball back, she saw Stacey nodding, a tight smile on her face.

She had to learn to move in this getup. And see. The

black lines of the catcher's mask crisscrossing her face and the padding right above her eyes cut off her vision. She tried another fastball—maybe she'd do the entire game with fastballs—and it went wide. She lunged for it and nearly took out the coach, who was advancing to the plate to call the team in.

PJ fringed the huddle, listening to the pep talk, trying not to flee. Especially since their opposing team, the Hornets, were equally ranked. Apparently the winner of today's three-game tournament went to the division play-offs.

As she walked away, the coach, a woman who reminded her of a den mother, with her softly rounded body and the curly brown hair sticking out of her hat, gave PJ a kind look and pulled up beside her.

"Listen," she said quietly. "I know you and Karla have tried to patch things up, but this game is bound to dredge up memories and, well, if you sense Karla getting out of control, you let me know."

Huh?

"Maybe I'm overreacting, but I just don't want a repeat of last year. That's all we need—for the Rockets to make the papers again. It was hard enough to get the grocery store to sponsor us this year, but more importantly, we need Karla for the play-offs. She can't break her probation or we'll be in trouble, so . . . just keep an eye out." She patted PJ on the back. "Good luck out there, kiddo."

PJ froze as the woman walked away. She stared first at the coach, then back at Karla, who was warming up in the bull pen, swinging her arms.

Pro . . . *bation*?

Stacey met her in the dugout. "I got Morgan to hit for you—I used the bum knee excuse."

"Bum knee?"

Stacey leaned close. "Karla. It's not a pretty story."

PJ clasped her hands over her knees as she sat in the back of the dugout, too afraid to cheer.

She was a dead girl.

They ended their first at bat with no runs. PJ manned the plate, watching Karla march to the mound, a wad of gum in her cheek—or maybe that wasn't gum.

"Batter up!"

PJ crouched as the first batter stepped up. She gritted her teeth and flashed the fastball signal at Karla, who then stared down the batter and pitched.

Thwack. PJ realized she'd closed her eyes, but yes, the ball landed in her mitt. She stood up to throw it back, then saw Stacey furiously shaking her head. Oops. Apparently catchers didn't stand up to throw.

PJ tried a drop ball. It came in short. PJ nabbed it and this time stayed down to return it to the mound. Next to her, the batter was digging her cleats into the dirt, mumbling under her breath.

So maybe she'd stick with the fastball. PJ gave Karla a target and—

The batter swung. The air whooshed right above PJ's head, and her entire body jerked as the batter connected with the ball. She searched for the hit in the field, but it seemed to have vanished. Then Karla was running toward her, gazing above her.

Uh-oh.

PJ looked up just as the ball landed three feet from her with a poof of dust and spiraled into the backstop.

"Foul."

Karla had stopped ten feet away from PJ. "You playing here? And what's with the string of fastballs? Get your head in the game."

PJ sprang to her feet, nodded, and picked up the ball. She threw it back without comment.

Karla caught it, but instead of turning back to the mound, she stopped and pointed at PJ, her eyes like bullets as she communicated what PJ interpreted as death, maiming, and pain.

Probation.

Karla struck the next two out—mostly with fastballs—before PJ got another chance at a foul. She saw the ball pop up, leaped for it, and barely missed it as it banged off her glove and dribbled out. Thankfully, it was a tough catch.

Still, a voice rang out behind her from the bleachers as she settled back into her position. "You trying to kill me, Catch?"

PJ shot a glance into the stands and nearly missed another bullet from Karla. All nine rows had filled now, with friends, parents, babies, husbands . . . She saw no one she recognized.

They closed the first inning with no runs.

The Rockets managed to score two runs on the Hornets, and by the end of the second inning, PJ decided she could probably do this. Choose a pitch—she hadn't the faintest idea how to call them—make a target for the ball, catch the flies . . . sure, no problem. Except she felt she might choke on her own tightened breath.

She managed another inning, this time reaching out and swiping a quick foul that earned her an out and a cheer.

By the fourth, sweat tidal-waved down her back, her face, and bathed her catcher's mitt in slimy odor. She trembled every time she crouched down, her legs having turned to lava. And it didn't help that every time she signaled a pitch to Karla, the pitcher either rolled her eyes, frowned, or gave a her a steely-eyed look that sent a cold drip of fear into PJ's stomach.

Karla had stopped growling at her or questioning her intelligence in the dugout. Which could only mean that she was saving up her fury for some after-game retribution.

PJ levered her mitt out, hating Jeremy and Dally, hating Kellogg, Minnesota, her life of crime, and especially Boone, who had practically goaded her into PI work.

"Strike three!"

PJ watched another batter go down. Two outs. One more.

A line drive to short. Stacey scooped it up and arrowed it to first. How hard was that? Try playing catcher.

She collapsed in the dugout, rubbing her thighs.

"Why don't you take off your mask?" This from the first baseman, a petite girl with a blonde crew cut.

PJ shook her head.

"You're really acting weird tonight, Dally. Not one taunt out of your mouth—usually you and Karla are going at it, razzing the batters."

Tag-team batter harassment. No wonder Stacey told her to keep her mouth shut.

She nodded, and the first baseman moved away to torment someone else.

One-two-three, the Rockets went down fast, too fast for PJ to catch her breath.

"Okay, let's hold 'em," Coach said as PJ trotted out past her. "Hang in there, Dally."

Yes, hang in there, Dally. Hang in there.

As if someone in the stands had heard her mental cheering, a voice rang out, "Go, Dally!"

Again she turned and scanned the crowd.

There. *There*—beside a kid finishing a hot dog and a blonde with bug-eye glasses and a straw hat—the guy trying to look nondescript in a red baseball cap and a pair of wire-rim dark glasses.

Jeremy.

She nearly whipped off her equipment and leaped into the stands, hands outstretched to strangle him.

"Dally! Batter up!" Karla's voice had the edge of a bowie knife.

She would just have to kill Jeremy after the game.

Batter one came up to bat. PJ crouched behind the plate, not looking at Karla as she sent her a curveball signal. Karla walked her on a full count.

"C'mon, Karla," PJ shouted and received a frown.

Maybe she could change Dally's image. Offer the glove of friendship, so to speak. She patted the palm of her mitt, then flashed her a drop ball. She'd been going in alphabetical order for a while now. Curveball, drop ball, fastball, knuckleball, screwball.

The pitch came in hard, and PJ refused to let out a yelp.

However, her encouragement seemed to rouse Karla. She struck out the next two batters.

Two outs, one on base.

The next batter stepped up and whiffed the first two pitches.

"Batter, batter, batter. *Sw-ing*, batter!"

Stop, Jeremy.

The batter swung at the third pitch, a hard crack. PJ was on her feet in a second, but it fouled out of the third-base line.

One more. PJ held her mouth shut, not wanting to rile Karla. She sent out the signal and patted her glove all the same.

Karla sized up the batter, narrowed her eyes, and round-housed the ball. It came in fast and high, a perfect arch.

The batter stepped back, waited for it, and swung.

It connected with a tinny crack, as if the wood caught only the edge. As PJ jumped to her feet, the batter tossed her bat and took off for first.

The ball sailed high into the infield, just a few feet from PJ. "I got it!"

She raced after the ball, hearing in her periphery, "Mine, mine!"

The sun glinted into her eyes, dotting her vision with black, stealing the ball, but she judged it and a second later it appeared just beyond her hand. She dove, arm outstretched, yes, *yes*—

It would have been a stunning catch, with PJ landing prone in the grass, her prize in the leather. Except a body hit her just as the ball touched her glove.

She landed in the dirt with a bone-jarring grunt. The ball thudded into the grass and rolled away.

Karla groaned at her feet.

"Pick it up!" Stacey came diving in from short.

PJ hit her knees and crawled toward the ball just as Stacey scooped it up and threw it to first.

But the runner had already rounded first and was halfway

to second. She slid into second as the first baseman picked the ball out of the air.

Just as the leading run touched home.

"Safe!"

A cheer went up from the Hornets' side of the bleachers.

"You!"

PJ rolled to her back as Karla landed on her, knees on either side of her ribs. "What, you gotta be the star?"

"Karla, I—"

Karla grabbed her mask and with a snarl ripped it off.

Unfortunately, and to Karla's horrified shock—an expression that PJ relished despite the obvious disaster—her wig skewed aside, even as PJ reached up to hold it in place.

And then it was just Karla holding the mask, her mouth open in a wide-eyed snarl as she said in a low, horrified whisper that felt like a knife to the heart, *"You're not Dally!"*

Chapter TWELVE

PJ didn't know what was worse—her cover being blown, at least to Karla and the team, losing the game after the Hornets took the lead, or looking up into the stands after Stacey shoved Karla away (probably saving her life) to discover that Jeremy had vanished.

With the blonde, who no doubt had been Dally and was probably right now plotting how to ambush PJ in the dead of night and leave her bleeding in some alley.

She already felt mangled after the chewing-out she'd received from the coach, Karla, and even sweet Morgan. *"What were you doing playing catcher in the most important tournament of the season?"*

Worse, she'd been banished to the sidelines, her face burning, her jaw aching from Karla's follow-through, sweltering under her stupid wig that she'd managed to keep attached to her head. Stacey had rounded them up for a quick huddle while PJ pulled herself back together, and maybe, hopefully, no one in the stands or on the opposing team had heard Karla's under-the-breath accusation.

As the game ended, the team's disappointment rang in her ears, and the sun poured out wrath upon her shoulders. She just wanted a soak in the tub, a bowl of Moose Tracks ice cream, and a compensatory phone call from Jeremy, not necessarily in that order.

And to make matters worse, Morgan, her—er, *Dally's* stand-in, had not only missed two fouls but been flattened by a slide into home during the bottom of the fifth inning in the third game and sprained, if not fractured, her ankle.

PJ had gone in and finished the game for Morgan, holding her breath as Karla slammed pitches into her glove for the last strikeout.

She shook her hand, realizing she had no business pretending to be Dally Morrison.

She was way out of her league.

Again.

At least she knew how to buy pizza. She dearly hoped eight large double pepperoni and mushrooms and six supremes counted as an "emergency business expense."

The pizza parlor was a dive that resembled one of the untouchable bars in Kellogg, the kind with rusty pickups in gravel drives and neon beer signs the only hint of color. Inside, however, it reminded her of Hal's Pizzeria, with the window overlooking the kitchen, as well as the cherry red booths and the twang of eighties tunes from a glowing jukebox.

"So let me get this straight." This from Morgan, who sat sandwiched between two loyal fans. They had consumed a large deep-dish, enjoying the boon wrought by their attachment to Morgan. She had her bandaged ankle propped on one of the lucky men's legs. "You're Dally's cousin from Chicago, and you're filling in for Dally while she's visiting relatives in Mankato?"

PJ glanced at Stacey where she sat crammed into a red booth, levering out her own deep-dish pepperoni. Stacey gave PJ a quick smirk. Thanks to the fast-thinking redhead, PJ hadn't had to cop to the truth and in fact only had to nod her head to Stacey's tall tale, woven before PJ even had a chance to open her mouth. Thankfully, it also meant that because they packed out the pizza joint, for a brief respite, she could take off her wig. It lay like a skunk beside her on the booth seat.

PJ gave a short nod, painfully aware that her circle of lies was not only widening but spiraling a knot of guilt deeper into her chest. It hadn't seemed so hard to change identities when she'd done it anonymously. Now she was actually producing embellished fabrications that she had to keep straight. For a good cause, however. Namely, Dally's life.

She certainly hoped Dally remembered that, wherever she was, conjuring up ways to inflict pain on PJ.

What was the key to a good lie—base it on truth? She turned to Morgan's question. "Actually, I'm more like housesitting. But I did play some ball in high school, so . . ."

Morgan's footrest groupie slid out from the seat, gently putting down Morgan's foot and grabbing her empty cup. He picked up PJ's also. "Diet Coke?"

PJ nodded.

"I guess it makes sense, Dally not wanting to lose her position, but you'd think she could have told us. We're her team, after all." Morgan took a bite of her pizza. "Good thing you know how to play softball, PJ, or we would have been in big trouble." Not a hint of sarcasm in her tone, and PJ wondered if she'd actually had her eyes open while watching the game.

Karla apparently had. And confirmed it by shouting, "She'd better learn to be a real catcher before the next game or you're playing, Morgan, busted ankle or no."

Morgan turned a shade paler. She leaned forward. "You do know how to call pitches, right?" Her voice trembled, and she shot a glance at Karla. "She sorta scares me."

"Get in line," PJ said, gesturing to the welt on her jaw, where Karla had connected before Stacey had pulled her off. Apparently, once a punch left the pocket, it had to complete its trajectory. At least according to Karla. Two games and six hours later, it had stopped throbbing, and now only ached when PJ opened her mouth. Like, to consume comfort pizza.

Dally forgot to mention the hitting when she covered the game rules.

Morgan's fan returned to the table, setting the drink down before PJ.

Morgan's voice lowered. "I'll make you a deal. I'll teach you how to call pitches if you'll play."

"I thought you wanted to play."

Morgan sat back. "I do. Just . . . enough to warm up. But I'm a mess during the actual game. If you couldn't already tell." She gave a resigned shrug. "This is my third injury this season."

"She's a great cheerleader, though," one of her fans said.

PJ pressed her lips together, fighting a smile. "I'm sure she is." She reached for a piece of pizza. "By the way, that's a deal, Morgan." A pepperoni escaped off the piece and PJ grabbed it and tucked it into her mouth. "So, do you know Missy Gaines?"

Morgan didn't even blink. "Sure. We've played together for years."

"But she's not on the team this year."

Morgan lifted a shoulder. "She and Dally have an old rivalry for the same position. Dally beat her out this year. But she still comes to our games. In fact I saw Missy just last Saturday, talking with Dally after one of our games. It looked like they were getting into it. Then Missy took off like she wanted to run Dally down with that old Impala of hers." She leaned close again. "She scares me too."

"Did you hear anything they said?"

"I know I heard the word *die*."

Two witnesses to Missy's threats—Stacey and Morgan— and a note. Had Dally and Rick gotten back together recently enough to stir up trouble?

Maybe she needed to have a little face-to-face with Rick, even slap down the note she found at Dally's. Or better yet, talk to Dally herself. Preferably from a safe distance, like over the phone.

She pulled the cell phone from her bag, stared again at the blank listing of calls received. She'd dialed Jeremy twice after the game and again only netted the cryptic monotone message.

She'd give him a monotone message. . . .

As the door opened, the hues of dusk swept into the room. A bulk filled the door, and the form seemed familiar. PJ watched the man, or rather oversize college student, stride across the room straight for them.

He wore a look that matched Karla's as he lumbered up to their table. "Morgan?"

Although she'd been smiling already, her entire face lit up. "Sammy!"

With a look, Sammy made Morgan's two bookends practically vaporize. He held her ankle as he slid in, barely fitting under the table. Then he leaned in and kissed Morgan on the lips. "Hey, babe."

PJ couldn't place the guy, but she knew she'd seen him before—or at least the impressive girth of his shoulders. Add to that the angular jaw, those hazel eyes, the high and tight haircut deserving of the Marines. No wonder Morgan's fan club ran for the hills. Only he had a smile for Morgan that didn't match the menace of his frame.

"This is my boyfriend, Sammy," Morgan said, her eyes shining.

He held out his hand to PJ. "Sammy Richland."

Morgan had a boyfriend? Then what was all the flirting with her fan club?

Or maybe Morgan didn't consider it flirting. Maybe she wasn't cognizant of her own powers. She wrapped one arm around Sammy's and gave a pout. "You missed my game."

"Sorry, sweetie. I had some stuff to take care of."

As he said it, PJ noticed the slightest sheen of sweat on his forehead despite the air-conditioning of the restaurant. Steroids?

Oh, that wasn't fair. Just because the guy had the build of a tank didn't mean he didn't come by it honestly. "What do you do, Sammy?"

"He fixes cars—he's amazing. Mostly it's antiques. He tears them apart and then puts them back together again."

Sammy lifted a shoulder, the slightest blush appearing on his face. "It's a hobby. I'm hoping to open my own shop when I get enough cash together. For now, I pick up cars where I can, fix them up, sell them again." He tossed a clump of keys on the table, a shiny black Dodge logo glinting in the mix.

And bingo, just like that, PJ placed him. "You're Gabby's grandson."

His face lost his grin and he nodded. "You know my grandmother?"

"I, uh, sorta live next door."

"She's Dally's cousin," Morgan said.

He leaned forward. "Really." His eyes ran over her, suddenly not friendly at all.

PJ nodded, aware that her gesture felt stiff.

"So, what did my grandma tell you about me?"

It was the way he asked it, softly with the edge of a filet knife, so sharp to almost not be noticed, that chilled her. And when he added a smile, she didn't believe it for a second, because his eyes bored into her, giving her roughly the same look he'd given Morgan's fan club before they beamed away.

Nothing. Oh, she hadn't spoken aloud. "Nothing," she managed. Followed by a smile. *C'mon, smile. Smile!* There it was.

He sat back, snaked an arm around Morgan.

PJ realized she'd been holding her breath. "I think it's time for me to get home and get a bath," she said to Morgan.

She wasn't sure whose eyes—Karla's or Sammy's—burned into her neck as she replaced her wig, waved to her team, and exited into the cooling, dark night.

With the shadows trailing her and the breeze shimmering in the trees, the wig didn't feel nearly as horrifying. Still, the

heat from the day radiated through the cement walk, reeking
of oil and weeds that lined the path home. She cut into the
alleyway, her feet scuffing up dirt and pebbles. The rottweiler
next door met her with a black wet nose shoved through the
chain-link fence. He growled.

"Yeah, get in line."

She wasn't sure what Sammy was afraid she knew, but suddenly she had a horrible feeling that Granny Gabby didn't
have the first clue who her precious Sammy really was.

Or where her jewelry might have disappeared to. It fit
together with a resounding smack inside her head, just like
one of Karla's fast pitches into PJ's glove. Sammy might be
stealing from his grandmother for drug money. Or . . . what
if he had something to do with Boone's car-theft ring? *I pick
up cars where I can, fix them up, sell them again.* Was that a
euphemism for stealing?

Okay, even she could see the stretch there, but at the least,
she'd have to keep an eye on him.

Gravel crunched behind her as a car rolled down the alley.
She scooted over to let it pass.

It stopped behind her.

She heard feet scuffing toward her and was just turning
when a hand came over her mouth.

"Hey!"

And then an arm snaked around her waist. Her equipment
bag thumped to the ground in the middle of the alleyway. The
ground fell away and she kicked back. "Hey!"

It came out *Mma, mma!* Followed by her ineffective punch
that landed in midair. She threw another and this time hit
something, but her attacker didn't slow. Her ankle caught on

the edge of the back fender right before her assailant shoved her . . . into the trunk.

And closed it.

＊ ＊ ＊

She was not going to cry. Not. Going. To . . . PJ wiped the moisture from her cheeks, aware that she still trembled. She was exhausted from kicking first the trunk and then the seat, hoping this was the kind of car trunk that folded down for skis and the like, but no, not a hint of a budge.

They'd been driving for nearly an hour, and on the highway, no less, at speeds that most likely could get her killed even if she did manage to jimmy open the trunk and leap to freedom.

And what was that smell? Putrid, as if she'd been thrown in next to someone's year-old gym bag filled with sweaty socks and soiled shoes. And on top of it all, the cloying stench of ointment that smelled vaguely familiar, but she couldn't place it. Maybe she'd died and gone to olfactory hell.

Why hadn't she hung on to her bag? Then she'd have a cell phone—and yes, she'd most certainly call Boone. Beg him to forgive her, maybe even take him up on that librarian suggestion.

She might even say yes. A brilliant, write-it-in-the-sky *Yes! I'll marry you.* Because clearly he was the only one who cared that she might die protecting—or in place of?—a woman who didn't in the least deserve it.

Okay, that might be a little strong. Maybe Dally had saved an orphan from getting run over or donated a kidney or something. Still, it seemed unfair that PJ might be taking the fall for someone who would never appreciate it, never realize the cost to people like . . . Davy. And Connie.

And even Jeremy. Who would never realize what he'd lost either.

She tasted salt and wiped again.

She hoped Jeremy felt bad when he found her mangled, murdered . . .

So maybe that wasn't the best line of thinking.

The driver turned off the highway, judging by the way the car slowed. She pulled off the wig and curled into a ball, suddenly dreading the end of this ride.

"Help!"

Sometimes she hated how her instincts always, regardless of how she tried, landed her in the middle of trouble. Or in this case, in the dark, smelly, humid tomb of a trunk.

PJ didn't expect rescue—probably didn't deserve rescue for her stupidity. It just felt good to remind herself not to give up.

Please, God, please . . . I'm sorry I jump into things without thinking and get in over my head. I promise to think—please help me think!

The car had turned onto gravel, from the grinding under the tires. PJ felt around the trunk, her hand connecting on a bag at her feet. A gym bag? She rummaged inside and found nothing but dry, wadded clothing, not even a tennis ball.

She'd just have to use her hammer fists.

The car came to a stop.

PJ braced herself, ready to lash out the second the trunk opened.

Only, it didn't. The driver got out, slammed the door. Foot-steps crunched on gravel . . . and faded away.

No, no, *no*—he was *not* leaving her here. "Come *back*!"

Nothing.

She kicked the trunk lid. "Coward!"

Then she put her hands over her eyes, gritted her teeth, and let the tears flow.

"PJ can take care of herself."

No, she couldn't! She couldn't! Apparently, however, God wasn't taking care of her either.

A cramp seized her calf and she flexed, massaging it away, slowing her breathing. Everything hurt. Was the air starting to thicken? She gulped in deep, pained breaths. Could someone suffocate in a trunk?

That was it. Next time Jeremy offered her an assignment, she wouldn't wish for guts or glory. Only a quiet surveillance assignment from a safe distance.

Maybe, *surely* she could kick out the seat.

She spent a half hour attempting just that, wounding her hands, her knees, and drenching herself in furious tears.

"God, I'm sorry for thinking You abandoned me. Help! Please, send someone—Boone, Jeremy—*anyone*."

She lay back, hands wrapped around her waist, just trying to breathe.

"Wait a second, PJ! I'll get you out!"

She froze. Held her breath. Great, now she'd gone completely over the edge, her own paranoia starting to speak back at her.

Then she heard scraping, the grind of metal on metal. As if someone was trying to wrench open the trunk?

"Jeremy!"

"Calm down, Sugar. I'll have you out of there—" The trunk popped open.

PJ launched herself from the recesses of her smelly catacomb straight at Jeremy's dark outline.

He didn't even flinch. In fact, he dropped whatever implement he'd used to free her and held her tight, his arms locked around her even as he staggered away from the car. His breath rushed out fast and uneven. "I got you. I got you. *I got you!*"

She was shaking, she knew that, but she couldn't speak.

He held her, his face in her neck. "Oh, thank You, God. Thank You."

PJ had no words, just clung to him—that sturdy, muscled, powerful, safe, rescuing Jeremy who had read her mind and—

"How did you find me?"

He still hadn't released her and now met her eyes, his dark and furious. "Lee. He had the house staked out. Good thing he put out a BOLO for you and the car, or you would have . . ." He closed his eyes and touched his forehead to hers.

He was shaking a little too.

"You scared me," he said softly. "*Really* scared me this time." Then he swallowed and slowly drew away. Her feet found the ground. But she didn't let go, and neither did he, his hands tight on her arms, holding her up.

"Lee?" she asked, her voice coming out parched.

"The FBI agent—Dally's contact. He was parked just beyond the alley when he saw you get nabbed. He didn't see the assailant, only you being shoved into the trunk. By the time he got out of the neighborhood to follow, he'd lost you. But he got the plates. And a camera at the entrance caught you pulling into the park. Lee called me the minute they got the address. Like a miracle, I was only a few miles away."

Like a miracle. And no, she didn't care that he'd had her tailed, despite her protests. For once, she was thrilled at Jeremy's lack of confidence in her.

She pulled in another shaky breath. "He didn't see who did it?"

"Sorry."

A breeze lifted her hair from her neck. For the first time she realized she was standing in the middle of a gravel lot, the wind hissing in the dark trees, the sound of a river spitting in the darkness. "Where am I?"

"Taylors Falls." Behind his voice she heard the whine of sirens. Jeremy pulled her close again, his arms locked around her shoulders. "This was a bad idea. A really bad idea. I'm not sure I've ever prayed so hard. I maybe have even bargained a little."

PJ let him hold her, let herself sink into his embrace. And for a second she thought she felt his lips brush her hair.

Jeremy had come for her.

Like he . . . cared.

Only—"Where have you been?" She tried to sound more angry, *was* more angry, but it came out exhausted. She'd have to try again. "I've been calling and calling." She pushed away from him.

Even in the padding of darkness, she recognized his frown. "I haven't gotten one call. I've had my phone with me the entire time. In fact, I was getting worried that I hadn't heard from you."

Worried that he . . . ? She blinked at him. Held out her hand. "Lemme see it."

He dug his cell phone out of his front pocket and slapped it into her hand. She opened it and scrolled to the recent calls. Two from L Simmons, and then, nothing.

Not one of her frantic calls.

She closed the phone. "218-555-1989?"

He took the phone from her. "218-555-8919."

She took a breath, then cleared her throat. "Maybe I'll write that down."

Jeremy gave a short nod and pocketed the phone.

"Someone is after Dally," she said after a moment.

A police cruiser came screaming into the lot. Headlights flashed across the car, illuminating the green paint, the battered exterior of a Chevy Impala.

"And," PJ said, looking at the car, "I think I know who."

Chapter THIRTEEN

PJ stood in Dally's kitchen, her shoes crunching through a pile of sugar now attracting a brigade of ants, and stared at the destruction of Dally's house. Sofa cushions upturned, pictures knocked over, books opened on the floor, pages crumpled . . . and, as she stepped over the piles and picked her way to Dally's room, even her closet torn apart. The debris from her dresser was scattered across the floor—picture frames, jewelry, with undergarments spilling from the open drawers.

Jeremy stood behind her, one hand on her shoulder—it seemed impossible for him to not have a hand on her arm or her elbow, as if he might lose her or she might dematerialize into the night. She would admit to liking it, although she'd attribute that to her quickly fraying composure. His touch seemed to somehow hold her together.

Dropping her bag—retrieved from the alley—onto the

bedroom floor, she picked up a black leather skirt. "Dally's going to kill me."

"She won't know."

PJ snorted. "Look at this mess. Someone wanted me—or Dally—out of the way so they could toss the house. And what were they looking for? Did they find it? Don't you think this deserves a serious, under-the-hot-lights interrogation? C'mon, Jeremy—she's not telling us everything. I know you and Lee didn't believe her, but you have to now. Someone *is* after her, and I'm not sure it's Billy Finch, no matter what Dally claims." She narrowed her eyes at him. "The thing is, if we don't find them, they won't get Dally— they'll get me."

He pursed his lips, something simmering in his eyes. "I won't let anyone get you."

She stared at him. "Uh, I don't see how you're supposed to protect me, hiding Dally wherever. Besides, this isn't the first time someone's broken in, Jeremy. The other night—"

But the horror on his face cut her off. "Someone broke in the other night? Why didn't you call me?"

She gave him a look of profound incredulity. "Seriously?"

"I'm calling Lee. We're calling this entire thing off."

PJ grabbed his wrist even as he dug into his pocket. Behind him, the morning sunlight had just begun to gild the wood floor of the living room, and in the shadow against it, Jeremy looked tired, lines forming around his mouth, his brown eyes weary, whiskers darkening his face.

"No. Don't do that. I'll stay at Connie's until we change the locks and clean this place up. You can ask your buddy Lee to hang around outside. I'll be extra careful."

"But maybe your cover is already blown. This might be unnecessary—"

"Or not. But if we give up now, we'll never know who is after Dally, and maybe she *will* be frightened enough not to testify."

Jeremy stared at his phone. Weighed it in his hand. "Billy Finch tied up the family of a drug dealer who crossed him and then lit their house on fire and let them burn alive. One of the victims was a five-year-old boy."

PJ said nothing.

When he looked up at her, his eyes were reddened. Tired. "Dally told me that. And some other things. Finch needs to stay in jail."

"And Dally needs to testify."

He pocketed the cell phone, wrapped a hand around the back of his neck, and turned away from her. "But not at the expense of you getting hurt."

She watched his shoulders, tense under his black shirt, rise and fall with his breathing, his worry.

"Talk to her, then. Get a list of who might want to hurt her. Besides Billy, that is."

She expected a quick nod, an easy agreement. Instead, he sighed, long and hard. Which made her wonder exactly what made her request so difficult. Did he believe Dally over PJ? Or . . .

"How are you two getting along?"

She said it so quietly, it might have been just a thought, but he turned, a strange expression on his face. "Fine."

"Any . . . excitement?" She wasn't exactly sure what she meant by that, but she had to add, "Are you *distracting* her?"

A smile edged up his face. "It's been . . . uneventful."

Uneventful? "As in boring uneventful or peaceful uneventful?"

"Let's just say that you add a little more life to any situation. And there are no donuts at the safe house. She's a lot more distracted by what she thinks you might be doing to her clothing, her catcher's position, and her chinchillas."

"Who spit, by the way."

He raised a dark eyebrow to match his smirk. "So, who is this Missy person? the one who owns the Impala?"

She'd named for Jeremy a sketchy list of suspects on the motorcycle ride back to Minneapolis, a ride that seemed to bathe her in comfort as she locked her arms around his solid waist. Occasionally he reached down and wrapped his hand around hers, squeezing. And once he'd touched his prickly cheek to hers, propped on his shoulder, whether by mistake or on purpose she didn't know. At the time, she didn't care.

Now, standing in the kitchen, seeing him radiate some sort of poorly disguised panic, yes, she wanted to know exactly what was behind his rather-tender gestures.

Or maybe that was too much information on an already-cluttered night. "Missy is a patron of Dally's salon. Dally wrecked Missy's hair a couple days before her wedding and Missy vowed revenge. And apparently she has an old Impala. Her husband, Rick, is some kind of bodybuilder."

"Hence the smelly gym clothes."

"You had to bring that up." She rubbed her hands on her arms. "You know, now that I think about it, the guy who attacked me the other night smelled the same way—a sort of menthol-ly ointment odor—the same smell as the clothes in the bag."

"You think it could be Rick?"

"Dally had a boyfriend she recently broke up with. Maybe it was Rick. You should ask her."

"We also need to check Missy's whereabouts. And if she still has her Impala."

"While you're at it, check out Karla, the Rockets' pitcher. She has a record of some sort. There's also Sammy Richland, Gabby's grandson. He's into something, but I don't know what."

"Any other neighbors—perhaps the mailman?—who strike you as suspicious?" His eyes had turned warm.

"Don't mock my instincts. Remember what happened to the last mailman who underestimated me."

"And your stellar roundhouse kick." Now he'd broken into a full-out smile.

She held up her dukes as if to punch him.

He lifted his hands in surrender. "As you wish, Fast-Pitch. I'd forgotten how persuasive you are. Sort of like a pit bull."

"Are you trying to say you might miss me a little?" She wasn't sure why she'd said it. It just spilled from her tongue before she could catch it.

Before she wanted to.

Jeremy's smile dimmed, leaving behind only a stillness in the air as he swallowed hard and stared at her with something in his eyes that looked almost hungry. "I should probably get back to Dally."

Right. Dally.

If he wanted to spear her clear through to her backbone, he couldn't have found sharper words. She'd obviously been inside a smelly Impala too long and had been reading into the emotion of the moment. He was her boss, all this concern only professional.

PJ felt suddenly hungry and tired. "I should go talk to Gabby."

"It's too early. Call her after you've had some sleep."

"You're probably right. Can you take me home?" She picked up her bag, shoved the wig inside, and hoisted it over her shoulder.

Jeremy followed her out to his motorcycle. She climbed on the back, resisting a long moment before giving in to the need to put her hands around his waist. He started the engine and rode stiffly through the early morning, without talking, even at the stoplights.

A golden sun half-mooned over the dark waters of Lake Minnetonka, spilling out orange in a frothy layer over the horizon. The clear sky screamed of sand castles on the beach, a dive into the cool blue of the lake, perhaps even ice cream dripping down her chin as she shared a cone with Davy.

Jeremy motored through Kellogg, into the Chapel Hills neighborhood, and pulled up in front of Connie's still house. PJ had the urge to wake up Davy, maybe head to church, and spend the morning thanking God for another miraculous rescue. She didn't bother to ask Jeremy if he'd be there.

She climbed off the bike and started to walk up the flagstone steps.

"PJ."

She turned, sighing, running a hand through her hair. "I need a nap."

His eyes were on hers. He opened his mouth as if to say something. She looked away, at the sprinkler hiccuping on the lawn across the street, the mist turning to a rainbow in the languid morning air.

When he said nothing, she glanced back at him. That hungry look again roamed his eyes, and she filled in for him. "Thanks for rescuing me."

Then she turned and walked up the steps, listening, but not hearing his bike pull away. Not, at least, until she was safe inside her house, leaning against the door, wishing she knew how to stay out of trouble.

"Auntie PJ!"

The voice made her look up, and sure enough, Davy scampered down the stairs, dressed in his Spider-Man pajamas, his hair in a wild nest. He stopped at the edge of the stairs, poised to launch himself at her. "Do you play baseball?"

Then he jumped.

She caught him and nearly went down with him in a heap.

Baseball? Oh yeah, she still wore Dally's outfit. Minus the wig, of course. Good thing, too. She didn't want to scare the child.

"Yep, I've been playing baseball," PJ said as she nestled his little body close. He smelled of sleep and fresh-laundry innocence.

She breathed it in, eyes closed.

"Peezhay?" Sergei came down the stairs in a T-shirt and a pair of lounge pants. He rubbed his eyes, his hair as wild as Davy's.

Davy slid out of her embrace and ran to the kitchen, climbing on a stool. From the guest quarters on the other side of the kitchen, Vera emerged wearing her short orange bathrobe, her hair in a net. She raised a hand in greeting as she tousled Davy's hair.

How PJ had missed this. Missed the friendly simplicity of Connie's home. No chinchillas screaming at her, no bumps or smells in the night.

No one throwing her into the back end of a car.

No one confusing her with strange, hungry looks.

Footsteps thumped behind her on the porch; then the door opened . . . and in walked Boris. He wore his predictable dark suit and turned his back to her as he shut the door.

"*Prevyet*, Boris," she said, switching to Russian, one hand on the banister. "How's the new job?"

He said nothing, just turned back to her. All activity in the room stilled. Vera dropped the frying pan onto Connie's high-end stove.

Boris sported a rather angry-looking black eye, swollen as large as a plum, along with a wicked scrape along his chin.

"Cool," Davy said.

"*Shto sloocheellas!*" Vera gasped, nearly running from the kitchen.

PJ's Russian had improved greatly over the past month of living with the Russians, but even she didn't need to speak the language to understand Vera's panicked *What happened?*

"*Nichevo*," Boris muttered, catching his wife's hands and pushing her away.

Nothing? Nothing happened? PJ wasn't buying that. She'd seen nothing and this wasn't it.

Sergei had retrieved a bag of frozen peas from the freezer and handed it to his father. Boris slapped it over his eye and let Vera lead him to a chair. Davy beheld him as if his grandfather had morphed into a Marvel character. Super Boris.

PJ slumped down on the stairs, head in her hands, listening

to their conversation, comprehending little. Something about work and a misunderstanding.

Great. As Boris's handler, she should probably be expecting a call from Rusty any moment.

As if on cue, or by some cosmic power, her cell phone rang. She pulled her bag toward her and dug out the phone on the second ring.

But no, not Rusty. Boone.

And he sounded just as frazzled as she felt.

"Am I reading this wrong, or was there a BOLO put out on someone matching your description, stating you'd been . . . *kidnapped*?"

✳ ✳ ✳

PJ slept like a slug. Hard. Sprawled out in the center of the bed on top of the white chenille bedspread, with the eyelet curtains free from their sash and blowing summer into her room. She'd changed out of the softball uniform and collapsed on the bed, promising herself she'd get up and ready for church as soon as she . . . got . . . some . . . shut . . .

"Peezhay!" The pounding at the door drilled through her head—*bang, bang.*

Go away and come again another . . .

"Peezhay, you have a ghest!"

Her eyelids weighed an elephant each, and her body refused to respond to the alarm in her brain. Someone had glued her to the bed or tied her hands and feet and . . .

"PJ? It's Connie. Are you okay? Sergei said you didn't answer. Someone is downstairs for you."

Yes, she knew. Boone had come to wrest her out of a sound and needed sleep, to harangue her about her unfortunate and terrifying late-night trip to the border of Wisconsin. Okay, it couldn't have helped that she'd said a short "Yep," followed by a sleepy "but I'm okay," right before she ended his call with "I'll tell you later."

Later apparently wasn't soon enough.

"I'm . . . here . . . Con . . ." She still hadn't managed to open her eyes.

"Okay, that's it; I'm coming in."

She heard a key in the lock and pried her eyes open—way, way open—before Connie barged in. "You're still sleeping? It's noon, PJ! You missed church!" She moved into the room, picking up the soiled and smelly softball uniform, holding it with two fingers, and dropping it into a hamper near the wide chest of drawers. "What in the world . . . ?"

"I was . . . up late." PJ managed to push herself up. Scrubbing a hand down her face, she caught a glimpse of the destruction in the mirror across from the bed and grimaced.

Connie, who looked tidy as usual, her dark hair in a high ponytail, drew back the loose curtain and fitted it into its holder. "Does it have something to do with the smelly softball clothes?"

PJ flung an arm over her eyes where the sun roared in. "Not really."

"Is that another tattoo?" Connie stood above her, eyes on PJ's arm. "You didn't—"

"It's paint, Connie."

"Oh, good. The last thing you need is another tattoo. You know you're going to have to live with Boone's name on your arm the rest of your life."

Thank you for that reminder, Connie. That was the very issue she couldn't seem to get out of her brain.

"And how long are you here? Are you still on a *work vacation?*"

"Just long enough to sleep. Which, at this rate, might be a week or so." PJ yawned. "Tell Boone that I don't want to see him until 2020."

"It's not Boone." Connie sat on the bed, grabbed PJ's arm, and pulled.

"You do a great Elizabeth Sugar impersonation."

"Where do you think I learned my tricks? Now get up and do something with your hair. Igor is a really nice guy." She patted PJ's leg, rose, and closed the door behind her.

PJ didn't move, staring at herself in the wide mirror. Igor? Sergei's cousin? Uh . . . "Connie?" But her sister was gone— along with her mind. Because in what world did Connie ever think that she wanted to see Igor?

She was about to flop back onto the bed, dream this nightmare away, when Connie's voice passed by the door. "I know where you live. Comb your hair and get downstairs."

PJ tumbled out of bed, thankful for the cool wood of the floor on her bare feet. Splashing some water on her face in the bathroom, she let it trickle down her chin, staring at the woman who looked suddenly eighty. Or maybe just felt like it.

Eighty. Gabby.

Gabby! Who would be waiting for breakfast or at least her breakfast date. What if PJ didn't show up? Would Gabby call the cops? or worse, Sammy? She didn't know why that thought ran an icy finger down her spine.

She dragged her bag off the bedroom floor and plopped it

on the bed, digging out her cell phone. Dialing information, she tracked down Gabby's number, then connected through. The phone rang and rang while PJ padded into the hallway and past Davy's room. She stopped, noticing through Davy's window what looked like Boone's black pickup. Oh, swell. Now she had two men to contend with downstairs.

Worse, her Vic seemed to be missing from its parking place in front of the house. Boris, working overtime?

She closed the phone, trying not to panic. What if Gabby had fallen? or maybe gone over to Dally's to find her, right into the waiting arms of PJ's assailant back to finish the job?

And what about the chinchillas? Had she fed them before leaving? What exactly would Dally do if her chinchillas expired?

And what if Gabby saw the house in its current condition? She'd be worried, horrified . . . What if she had a heart attack?

"PJ!"

"I'm coming!" She gripped her cell phone as she padded down the stairs. Maybe she should go over there . . .

Except she didn't have a car.

She did, however, have one tidy-looking mafia boy standing in the foyer, holding . . . were those roses? *red* roses? A half dozen, by her quick count.

Igor grinned, his ebony eyes sparkling with delight. "Khello, Peezhay."

She lifted a hand and glanced at Sergei, who perched against the back of the sofa, his arms across his overly muscled chest, grinning like a proud father. Where was Boone? Maybe she'd imagined his truck.

Oh, wait, Boone's truck had been stolen. Or totaled. Or something.

Still shaking off sleep, she took the roses. *"Spaceeba."*

Igor smiled wider, approving her use of Russian.

She buried her nose in the flowers, not sure what else to do.

"I khave something to show you," Igor said, reaching out as if to grab her arm.

She stepped away but nodded. "Sure, Igor." She glanced toward the kitchen for help, but Vera sat with Connie at the table. They both grinned like a couple of teenagers.

Igor opened the front door, stood back, and gestured outside.

PJ led the way out to Connie's front porch.

"I bought a truck." Igor was all smiles, nodding as he spoke. "Just like American man," he said while rolling his *r*'s.

Oh, so the black machine outside belonged to Igor.

Lifting the keys, he dangled them. "Vant a ride?"

Good grief. This proved it—men were the same world-wide.

"Uh, Igor, I dunno . . ."

"Just short ride."

What on earth had given this man the idea that she might be interested . . . ?

She turned back to the house and saw Connie and Vera with their noses pushed up to the window. And then she got it.

Bonding. Connie, desperate to get Vera to like her, had fixed up her single sister—aka prey—with a fellow Russian. PJ sighed and gave a tiny wave.

Connie waved back. Vera clapped.

"Please?" Igor asked in the pleading tone she'd heard Boris use on Vera, not unlike a kid begging for a Popsicle.

"Okay, just a zip around the block." Or . . . "Actually, I could use a ride into the city. Okay?"

Igor just about did a jig right there on the sidewalk.

PJ had a moment of remorse. She didn't want to lead the man on. But if Connie needed her . . .

"Let's go." PJ hustled down the walk before she could change her mind, threw the roses into the front seat, and climbed in.

Igor woke up three steps behind her and had the truck revved in seconds.

"Nice wheels," she said as Igor turned the corner. She ran her hand over the sleek black dash, the leather bucket seats. "Really nice wheels."

Igor grinned like a ten-year-old.

It had that artificial new-car smell, and PJ used the recliner to put her seat back. "It reminds me of Boone's truck, the one that got stolen."

"Is my truck."

"I know that, Igor."

But he looked at her, a sort of wounded expression on his face. "I pick up this morning. Uncle Boris find for me."

She clasped her hands between her knees. "Why did you get this truck? I thought you had a car."

"I sell it for truck."

"Why?"

He stared at her then, an inscrutable expression on his face. "Because of you, Peezhay."

She stilled. "Me?"

"Because you like big truck. I see you in it."

"In Boone's truck."

"Now my truck." He grinned. The sun glinted off a silver tooth. "Now maybe you like me too."

Oh no. PJ took a breath. "Boone and I are sorta . . . dating, Igor."

He said nothing, but his smile fell.

"You know what that means, right?"

He lifted a shoulder. "Maybe you want Russian man, like Connie."

PJ looked out the window, trying not to wince. Oh, boy.

They were through Kellogg and turning onto the highway. "Take 394 to Highway 100," she said.

They rode in silence. PJ stared out the window, wondering what she would say to Connie and if Jeremy would buy a truck for her, and hating that Boone wouldn't use his insurance money on new wheels so he could instead give her a house, and wishing she had her Dally wig so she could go back to pretending a life that at the moment seemed monumentally less complicated than hers.

She needed more sleep.

"Can we listen to some music?" PJ leaned forward and without thinking—probably thanks to the familiar make of the truck and her still-woozy mind—she hit the Play button on the CD player. "I Want to Hold Your Hand" came blaring out of the speakers.

"I love the Beatles," PJ said, leaning back.

"Me too," Igor said, drumming his fingers on the steering wheel.

The song ended and a Guns N' Roses song began.

Just like Boone's mix CD.

She glanced at Igor. "Where did you get this truck?"

"Casey sell to me."

"Casey . . . from Rusty's Real Deals sold it to you?"

"Give me a . . . deal. Very cheap."

Yeah, she bet very cheap. What if Boris's black eye and Igor's new wheels had something in common?

Like PJ and her overactive ability to jump to conclusions?

Yet her gut continued to tighten into a hard knot. "Igor, I think this is Boone's truck." But how could it be? Boone's truck had been stripped and totaled less than three days ago.

"No, my truck." He palmed his chest, looked at her, and smiled. "I have paper." He leaned over the seat and opened the glove compartment.

"Igor, look out!"

He swerved back into his lane and flicked out an envelope, handing it to her.

Inside were a bill of sale—he *did* get a deal—and a green title, signed over from Rusty's Real Deals to Igor Smurnoff.

"Sorry."

"My truck."

"It's just . . ." She forwarded the CD to the next song. Sure enough, a Nirvana tune. And the next would be back to the Beatles.

Igor followed PJ's directions into Dally's neighborhood, cutting down the alleyway.

Probably she should stop overreacting, seeing crime around every corner.

She was a professional, and a professional didn't jump to conclusions. A professional gathered evidence, scrutinized every angle, researched every lead. A professional looked past threats like Karla's or Missy's vengeance to the real perpetrators.

Like, for example, the burly-chested young man climbing into the back porch window of her . . . er, Dally's house.

Chapter *FOURTEEN*

PJ rarely backed down from a fight. That probably accounted for at least half of the trouble she'd landed in over the years—the words *double-dog dare* being among the most dangerous phrases in the English language. However, most fights didn't involve opponents with biceps the size of her thighs and a snarl that made her blood turn to icy shards.

Hence, when Igor rolled to a stop in the alleyway, his gaze on the young man entering her house (and after three days, she'd begun to feel proprietary), she hesitated before turning down his suggestion that he go in and perhaps extract some answers, Russian mafia–style.

She did, however, accept his offer to stick like glue in her shadow as she entered the house via the back door and crept into the living room.

And there stood Sammy, holding one of the chinchillas

in his massive hands, cooing to it in sweet, dulcet tones. He looked at PJ. "What are you doing here?"

She let Igor bump up behind her. "Seriously? You're going with that?" She clamped her hands on her hips, mostly to stop the shaking.

His glare dissipated to annoyance. "I was looking for the cat."

"You can do better than that." She pulled out her cell phone and opened it. "One more strike and you're—"

The cat appeared on the sofa, took one look at Sammy, and leaped for the open chinchilla cage.

"No!"

But PJ's shout couldn't compare to the screech of the chinchillas as the cage tumbled forward. PJ dove for it, managing to divert the landing, and the cage bounced against the sofa, scattering chinchillas across the room.

They scampered for cover, little spitting fluff balls.

"Catch them!"

PJ hit her knees, scurrying after one of the rats that had dashed under the sofa. When she stuck her hand under, teeth clamped down on her finger. "Ow!"

Out of the corner of her eye, she spied Igor, foot raised over a cowering chinchilla wedged into a corner. "*No!* Igor, don't kill it!"

"Iz a rat—"

"It's a pet—grab it!"

He gave her a dubious look, and she gestured to the animal with a don't-test-me expression.

He crouched, opened his hands, and advanced on the animal. She heard him howl as it found flesh, but her own quarry was making a run for the television console.

She bounded after it—and saw Sammy standing there, holding his animal, watching.

"The cat! Sammy, it's drooling!" She pointed at Simon crouched on top of the cage, pawing inside at two terrified chinchillas. The animals spit and screamed, dodging the paw.

Sammy picked Simon up by the scruff of its neck. Showing no partiality, the animal took a swipe at Sammy, then at Sammy's catch.

"Lock the troublemaker in the bathroom," PJ said to Sammy, meaning the cat, but maybe, yes, she could just hide with it. Indeed, hiding seemed entirely appropriate at the moment.

Igor righted the cage and plunked his chinchilla back inside. Sammy dropped his and now PJ rounded on her quarry. "C'mon, little chinchin, come to Mama—ow!"

"They bite," Igor offered.

She shot him a look and he lifted a shoulder.

Oh, Jeremy had better not be enjoying one second with Dally. . . . She lunged again and her hand closed around the animal. It screamed and squirmed and dug its needlelike claws into her hand as she dragged it toward her and closed her other hand around it. The animal gnawed at the inside of her hand, and she leaped a couch cushion on the floor and barely refrained from hurling the creature inside the cage. She slammed the door shut.

Her accomplices stared at her, as if they'd all survived a stampede of wild rhinoceroses. No one spoke for a long time. Then finally PJ mumbled, "Not a word to Dally." She pointed at Sammy. "And I'm not done with you yet." She leaned against the sofa, catching eyes with Igor.

Sammy seemed to measure the distance. Igor smiled, shiny silver tooth showing. Even to PJ it seemed more of a dare.

"Okay, fine. I'm looking for something that Dally has—something that belongs to me," Sammy said with a dour look.

"And it's buried in the chinchilla cage? By the way, if it is, it's staying there forever. Sorry."

"Maybe."

PJ swept up her phone from the floor and punched in a nine.

"Okay, I don't know where it is, but I asked Dally to hold on to something for me and, well, with her being gone, I started to worry, so I came over to get it back."

He certainly looked sincere. And sounded it, with the slightest edge of pleading in his voice. PJ closed the phone. "I'm waiting."

He didn't look at her. "It's a ring. An engagement ring. For . . . Morgan."

"Convince me—why exactly would you give Morgan's ring to Dally?"

Sammy went to the sofa, began piling the cushions back into place. "What happened here? This place is a mess."

"No, don't change the subject. Why was Dally holding Morgan's ring?"

Behind PJ, Igor had struck an appropriate henchman pose. He looked a lot like he might want to rip out Sammy's lying tongue. That, or cram him in with the chinchillas.

PJ glared at him in warning. "Down, boy."

Igor grunted.

Sammy shoved the last cushion into place. "Because I live

in a houseful of morons who are constantly having parties. My mother hates Morgan, and at my grandma's house things keep disappearing."

"Your mother seems to think Dally's behind that."

"She doesn't know Dally like I do." He headed for the kitchen and grabbed a broom.

PJ followed him, leaning one shoulder against the door-frame. "Like . . . ?"

"Like the fact that she goes over every morning to check on Grandma."

Okay, PJ appreciated that too.

"So where is Gabby's missing jewelry? Is your grandma losing her mind?" She winced with one eye to say it like that. But the Frank Sinatra comments, the costume room story . . . Evelyn's low-toned insinuation that she'd created an elaborate backstory from her lost dreams . . .

Sammy paused his sweeping, meeting her eyes with a tight-lipped expression. "I don't think so. . . . She's still pretty sharp."

"Then what's with your mom's accusations?"

"My mom wants the house pretty badly. She's deep in debt, thanks to all her plastic surgery. Thinks Grandma should be in an old folks' home." He stopped short of accusing his mother of fabricating the accusations, but there it lay, like the sugar dumped out onto the floor.

"Here's what I know for sure. Dally might look like a character in a teenage horror flick, but she didn't steal from my grandma." He swept the sugar into a dustpan and dumped it into the garbage can. He stopped then, looking like he might be ready to say more. Finally he sighed. "I trust Dally. She introduced me to Morgan. And I need to talk to her. Do you know when she'll be back? She's not answering her cell."

PJ picked up the Cap'n Crunch box, lamenting for a moment its lack of contents, then crushed it and stuffed it into the garbage. "I hope soon."

"I miss her."

PJ nearly believed him. Nearly bought into the texture of his voice, the one that begged her to trust him.

But despite Sammy's performance, she'd seen his familiarity with Dally's house. He knew his way around . . . probably even in the dark. Still, maybe the ring accounted for the cryptic, almost-frosty look he'd given her at the pizza shop.

Only, what if Evelyn had sent him over to sniff around, maybe do some pawing through Dally's vacant house to find the so-called missing jewelry?

Or—and PJ had to consider this also—maybe it was all an elaborate setup. What if he'd been the one stealing the jewelry and Dally had discovered the truth?

It wasn't beyond the scope of her suspicions to consider that he might also be the mysterious *R*. As in Sammy *Richland*. What if he'd been here looking for the note, hoping Dally didn't suddenly spoil things with Morgan?

Her stomach turned inside out at her final thought. Maybe Sammy, for any of the previous reasons, had gotten his hands on an old Impala—after all, he did work at a garage—with the intent of removing her from the equation. A guy who worked out as much as Sammy appeared to might have an old gym bag in the back of his car. He certainly had the biceps to wrestle a gal into the back of a vehicle.

PJ's head had begun to throb; she pressed a hand to her

queasy stomach. She wanted to throw her arms around Igor in gratitude that he still stood sentry behind her.

Sammy put the broom back in the corner and brushed past her. "Maybe the ring is in her room."

PJ connected a look with Igor, who moved to block the door, his obsidian eyes glittering.

Sammy stopped, bristling. "Move."

PJ laid a hand on Sammy's arm. "How about I try and get ahold of Dally?" Code for *back away quietly and no one will get hurt.*

Sammy looked at her, then back at Igor, as if measuring him.

PJ decided right then and there that the date with Igor and his big truck had been worth it.

Sammy turned toward the door. "Fine, but if it's disappeared . . ."

"Tell your grandma that I'll call her."

Sammy gave her a look that might have turned a lesser woman, or perhaps one without personal backup, to cinders.

The back door slammed behind Sammy.

"He doesn't like you." Igor closed the side window, his eyes on Sammy as he crossed the yard.

"Thanks, Igor," PJ said quietly.

He gave her a smile. "Now you like Russian man."

She couldn't deny a grin. *"Da."*

✳ ✳ ✳

Jeremy needed to pay her more if he expected housekeeping services. PJ closed the back door, listening to Igor talk in

Russian on his cell phone. He'd run her to the hardware store and helped her install new locks on Dally's house.

She sank down on the steps, aware that Sammy's Charger had stayed in front of Gabby's house all afternoon. As if, what—he might be standing guard over his grandmother?

She hated the turmoil inside that told her Sammy wasn't all he seemed. Or perhaps he was *exactly* as he seemed: intimidating.

But—she glanced at Igor, now pacing Dally's weedy backyard—she'd been known to misjudge people before. She would have never guessed Igor might spend the day helping her put Dally's house back together, including straightening her closet, mopping the kitchen floor, and even airing out the chinchillas.

She couldn't yet tell if anything was missing from Dally's possessions, not having taken an inventory prior to being shoved into the trunk. However, when she'd stared at Dally's bedroom, she felt it. Something . . . amiss.

Igor closed the phone, pacing back to her, his shadow long over her. "*Vso* okay?"

Yes, everything was okay. For now . . . She let him help her up from the stoop, feeling she owed him dinner at least. She was about to offer when he pulled out his keys.

"I have . . . business. I vill take you home."

Business. Right. She didn't want to ask.

Casting a long look at Gabby's as she climbed in to the truck, PJ thought she saw the curtain fall.

Twilight had begun to blanket Kellogg as Igor drove her through town, then pulled up at Connie's. A refreshing breeze stirred the fragrance of lilacs blooming in front of the house.

"Spaceeba," PJ said as she slid out.

Connie sat at the kitchen table reading a decorating magazine. The aroma of hamburgers grilling on the deck outside breathed into the house through the open windows. PJ
glimpsed Sergei on the deck in an apron, brandishing a pair
of tongs.

"Did you have fun with Igor?" Connie asked, not looking up.

"I should probably hurt you, but yes. He's a nice guy." PJ
slid onto the stool next to Connie, reaching for one of the
potato chips piled in a bowl on the counter.

"I know. I'm sorry. It was Vera's idea, and I—"

"I get it." PJ reached for another chip. She'd forgotten how
hungry she was. "It's just that . . . I have enough complications
in my life."

"Boone?"

PJ lifted a shoulder.

Connie closed the magazine, studied her. "Or that other
guy?"

PJ pulled the bowl into her embrace. "The other guy's
name is Jeremy, and no, he's not into me. It's just . . ." She
picked around the bowl for a chip with crispy ridges that could
crackle in her mouth. "Okay, the truth is, Boone asked me to
marry him."

"Really? Wow. Okay, I expected more excitement. Haven't
you always wanted this?"

"I don't know."

"Well, he's definitely pined for *you*."

"I doubt he was pining, Connie."

"Okay, so yes, he had that thing going with that reporter

woman, I can't remember her name, but we all knew he was holding out for you."

"Reporter woman?" PJ put the bowl back on the counter. "What reporter woman?"

"It doesn't matter anymore, does it? He loves you. And he asked you to marry him! That's wonderful! When's the wedding?" Connie got up and retrieved the pitcher of lemonade from the fridge, setting it on the counter.

"I haven't said yes."

Ice clinked into two glasses from the ice maker. Connie stared at her over her shoulder as cubes overflowed onto the floor. "What? Why not?"

"I don't know. Maybe it's what you said—too soon, too fast."

Connie scooped up the runaway cubes and tossed them into the sink. "Listen, Peej. You've always known you'd end up with Boone. He's your true love, isn't he?" Of course she had to put her hands over her heart, add a little swoon to her words.

PJ threw a chip at her.

"Seriously—why the hesitation?"

"Just because he was my first love doesn't mean he's my true love." The words fell from her mouth without a thought and lay there on the granite countertop, hard and unflinching. She stared at the marbleized surface, not sure where they'd come from.

But knowing, for sure, their truth.

"You don't love him?"

PJ reached for the pitcher and poured lemonade into her glass. "I didn't say that. I . . . I'm not sure he loves me."

"Of course he does."

"No, he loves the *past* me. The girl who too eagerly climbed on to the back of his motorcycle. The girl who was over the moon just because he walked into her life. But I'm not sure he really loves the current me. Or perhaps the me I want to be."

Connie leaned a hip against the counter. "And what 'me' is that, exactly?"

PJ stared at her glass, watching the ice cubes melt, and said nothing.

"I am not without my own PI resources, and don't forget that I'm part Russian now. Ve have vays of making you talk."

PJ allowed a soft smile. Then shrugged. "I just can't make another mistake. I seem to be tripping over my own bad decisions every direction I turn, and I can't trust my own instincts anymore. I can't seem to pull myself out of this spiral to get clear and hear my heart."

"You know what they say about the heart."

"Follow it?"

"I was thinking along the lines that it's fickle and lies to you. You might need to use your head on this one." She tapped PJ on the temple. "That, I trust."

PJ closed her eyes. "Why?"

"Let's see. You solved a murder, bonded the Russians with my son, and figured out a way to get Boris a job. Yep, you have a working noggin."

Davy's laughter drifted in from outside. PJ watched through the porch as Vera pushed him on the swing. They'd freed the goat to roam about the yard, and she stood watching Sergei work the grill, as if she might be a beef eater.

No, not *she*. The first goat had been a *she*. Until PJ had surreptitiously swapped it for a *he* goat under the unsuspecting noses of the Russians after the *she* goat had perished from hosta poisoning.

Aw, the entire thing knotted her brain. *She* worked just fine. After all, the goat did respond to the name Dora.

PJ touched her forehead to the cool granite counter. "Then read my mind. Tell me what to do."

"Have a hamburger."

PJ looked up to see Sergei stepping through the door with a plate of juicy burgers.

He put them down on the counter as Connie turned and grabbed plates from the cupboard. Behind them, the doorbell rang. PJ slid off the stool and padded to the door.

Boone stood there, dressed in his detective clothes and wearing a dark detective expression.

PJ hung her head. "Sorry I didn't call—"

"I'm here on official business, Peej. But yes, we've got a conversation waiting in the bull pen." He stepped into the house. "Is Sergei here?"

Sergei tossed his apron over a kitchen chair.

"Sorry to tell you this, Sergei, Connie, but . . . I arrested Boris tonight for car theft."

Chapter FIFTEEN

"I am entirely too familiar with the inside of the Kellogg police station." PJ sat on one of the orange molded chairs and rubbed her arms, trying to clear the gooseflesh. She didn't know if she should blame the arctic blast of the air-conditioning in the waiting room, the memory of her own not-too-distant night spent in a clammy cell in this very building, or perhaps Boone's icy tone as he drove her down to the station, followed by Connie, Sergei, and Vera in Connie's Lexus while Grandma Sugar watched Davy.

PJ hadn't had the courage to ask Boone where the Crown Vic might be. Not in his current state.

"Kidnapped, PJ?" His knuckles had whitened on the steering wheel and he'd looked over at her twice, something wretched written on his face. "You can't imagine what it might feel like to be me when I hear words like that associated with the girl I love."

Woman. Last time she looked, she was nearly twenty-nine. But she'd pillowed her head back on the seat, exhaustion rippling through her, saying nothing.

He'd abandoned her here in the lobby of the station, next to Sergei, who lasted roughly 2.3 seconds in the chair before he was up and pacing the floor. Vera shuffled away to visit Boris in an interrogation room. Connie silently fumed, shooting dark, lethal looks at PJ, occasionally shaking her head.

"I would agree with that statement," Boone said, following up on PJ's police station comment.

PJ opened one eye, stared at him hovering above her.

"Let's talk."

"Boone—"

"About Boris." He held out a hand as if to help her from the seat. She hesitated, then took it, relishing the warmth in his grip. He glued his other hand to the small of her back while he led her to his office. He closed the door behind her and gestured to a seat.

"You're sorta freaking me out."

"I'm sorta freaked out." He sat down at his desk, a space with a tidy pile of papers in an in-basket, a clear blotter, and pens lined up side by side. She felt as if she might be sitting in the principal's office. "Remember when I told you about Allison Miller? How she'd been working undercover for me?" He didn't look at her, his hands folded tight.

PJ rubbed her palms along her shorts, suddenly hot. "Yeah . . ."

"She was working to expose a group of car thieves. I . . . think Boris is working for them." He looked up then, as if to add bang to his accusation.

Boris, a car thief? "I doubt it, Boone. Boris is a good guy, and he was a cop back in his homeland. He's not going to flip that easily."

"I'm not sure he knew. He said he was ordered to repo the car, but Rusty denies that he sent Boris the order."

"Figures . . ."

"Which means it's Rusty's word against his."

"Consider the source."

"Consider the green card. Boris is a man on shaky ground here. At the least, we can revoke his visa and send him back over the pond to the motherland."

PJ ran her fingers across her eyes. Perfect. She'd turned her distant in-law into a carjacker. They should award prizes for her stunning ability to find trouble. "I swear to you that he hasn't been stealing cars."

"He claims he's been doing repo work for Rusty, and yes, Rusty has a number of cars he's repoed. Just not this one." He leaned over the desk. "Has Boris got a little private enterprise on the side?"

"What? No. I'm telling you, he was thrilled to get this job. . . . He wouldn't—"

"Listen, Peej, we don't want to put Sergei's dad in jail, but he's not talking and my hands are tied here."

"I think I found your truck, Boone." She sighed as she said it, feeling suddenly like a spy ratting out her contact. "I took a ride with Igor today. I found your . . . CD."

Boone leaned back, folding his hands over his chest. "My CD? My mix CD, the one I left in my truck? But it was stolen with the CD player. And the insurance agency hauled my truck away just a few days ago when they declared it totaled. How could it possibly be the same truck?"

"I know. And Igor has a legitimate paper trail—or what looked like it. He has proof of ownership. Bought it from—"

"Rusty's Real Deals."

"Bingo."

"So, I don't get it. How did it get to Rusty's?"

PJ lifted a shoulder. "Maybe Rusty bought it from the insurance company?"

"Without an engine? wheels?"

"I have an idea about that too."

Boone's eyes narrowed, pale blue lasers that seemed to be trying to pierce her brain. "Okay—I'm willing to listen for five quick minutes to your theories, but that's it."

She was too tired for this. But she *did* have a theory, at least a loose one, still taking shape. "You're not going to like it."

"Do I ever?"

"Boris just can't go to jail, Boone. Connie's already on shaky ground with her in-laws, and the last thing she needs is a convict in the family."

He hid a smirk.

"Stop. I was never convicted. In fact, I remember the charges being dropped."

"Did I speak? I don't remember speaking." He palmed the desk. "Just tell me."

"What if . . . Boris, unbeknownst to him, is repoing cars—only they're being listed as stolen. Like yours."

"But I didn't get mine from Rusty's Real Deals."

"Doesn't matter, just listen. Like I said, it's just a theory."

"Okay, so someone's been stealing the cars—like mine . . ."

"And they get stripped and then returned to the owner."

"Like mine . . ."

"And the insurance agency says it's totaled . . ."

"And sells it to a wrecking company."

"Then the thieves buy the car from the wrecking company as a legitimate sale, dirt cheap, maybe after a tip from an inside man."

Boone leaned forward in his chair, folded his hands atop his tidy desk. "Giving them a clean title. Then they put it back together with the same parts they stripped off it and resell it through Rusty's."

"At a profit. And yet, still at a discount."

"And it looks legit."

PJ pointed at him, the chill now gone from her skin. In fact, she could nearly feel the old, hot swirl of excitement, the one that started in her stomach and filled her heart, the kind that Boone used to be able to conjure up with just the rev of his motorcycle engine.

Boone smiled. "Okay, I'll bite. How do we prove it?"

"Well, we need to find out if any local insurance agencies have listed any stolen vehicles as totaled like yours, and then investigate their—what are they called, those numbers for each car—"

"The VIN number—vehicle identification."

"Right—check and see if the car was resold."

"Doesn't Jeremy investigate insurance claims?"

She could hardly believe her ears. *Jeremy* and *investigate* in the same sentence. From Boone's mouth. But . . . "Yes, actually, and I remember a number of open files investigating insurance fraud. What if the insurance investigations are linked to the car thefts?"

He gave her a familiar look, and she knew what was coming—the words to which she could never seem to say no.

"Boone . . ."

"Wanna go for a ride?"

✳ ✳ ✳

"I don't want to know how you learned to do this, do I?"

Boone perched on the top of Jeremy's office steps, the smell of musty carpet and moldy cement rising from the stairwell, holding a flashlight against the lock that PJ was currently picking.

"It's nof harr," PJ said.

Boone reached up and took the lock-pick wallet from her mouth. "What's that?"

"I said, it's not hard. Calm down. I learned it when I worked for a locksmith. You'd be surprised at what I can open."

"That's too much information for me. In fact, let's just forget that we're here having this conversation. I can't believe I'm an accessory to breaking and entering. Why didn't you tell me you didn't have a key?"

"You didn't ask."

He closed his eyes, ran a hand down his face. "What am I doing here?"

"Helping clear Boris's name and earning my family's undying gratitude."

"And yours?"

Maybe. It certainly helped that he'd taken her home,

allowed her to shower, fed her a sub sandwich, and then driven her in his Mustang, top down, to Jeremy's dark office in Dinkytown. And he'd done it all without mentioning the kidnapping once.

It only cemented the idea that he *didn't* want to know what happened. Just like he didn't want to know this side of her.

When the tumblers clicked, she turned the dead bolt back. "Yes." Then she moved to the doorknob.

"You know, I think you actually like this kind of thing." Boone had moved behind her, directing the light over her shoulder as she inserted the pick and the tensioner and went to work.

She said nothing. Twenty seconds later, the lock clicked.

"That was way too fast."

The door swung open. She crept inside and flicked on the light. "What can I say? I'm gifted."

He harrumphed behind her. "Does Jeremy know you can do that?"

"We're not that far into our relationship." She started a slow loop around the perimeter of his filing system, searching for anything that might point to an insurance company.

"Relationship?" Boone started on the other perimeter.

"Business relationship, Boone." But her words emerged sharper than she intended.

He stuck his hands in his pockets and sighed, took two more steps in silence, then: "Okay, I have to tell you something."

PJ glanced at him before kneeling beside a file folder, picking it up, and paging through it. A house fire investigation. She put it back. "If you're going to tell me that you don't want me working with—"

"I did a background check on Dally."

What? PJ turned toward him. He'd collapsed onto the sofa, his pale blue eyes on her. "And no, I don't like you working with Jeremy. Or impersonating this woman. Did you know that she has a rap sheet from her wild days in Chicago? It's long enough to wallpaper my apartment. Who knows what kind of enemies Dally has in her past."

"Boone—"

"Don't *Boone* me. I'm not dreaming all this up. I'm a cop; I've seen what kind of trouble a person like Dally attracts, and now you're in the thick of it with her. What if her past tracks *you* down instead and you get hurt, Peej? Or even . . ." A muscle flicked in his jaw.

She looked at him, at the worry on his face, and tried to put confidence into her words. "Nothing is going to happen to me, Boone." But her voice held the slightest tremor.

She moved over to the sofa and, kneeling again, put her hands on his knees. "I'm sorry I didn't call you last night. I dropped my phone or you would have been the first." This time, she meant it with everything inside her.

He leaned forward and took her face in his hands, running his fingers into her hair. "I don't recognize this girl I see, this one who scares me so much."

"Maybe that's the problem between us, Boone." She hooked her hands over his wrists. "I like this life, this job. I like helping people. People like Gabby, whose daughter wants to put her in an old folks' home just because she's misplaced some jewelry, even though I'm pretty sure Sammy's in on it, although I have to admit, it looks like he loves Morgan, but with all those muscles I think he's on steroids, which would give him motive—not to mention the fact that he also over-hauls cars, which maybe makes him a person of interest in your grand theft auto ring, although I admit maybe that's a stretch—"

"I'm confused."

"And then there are the Rockets, who need to win their next game, and since Morgan's out of the picture, I have to learn to really call the pitches instead of guess, which I'm pretty sure I can do. Thanks to Igor's help today, I was able to change the locks on Dally's house, so I should probably go back tonight—"

"Igor?"

"Yeah, poor Igor. I mean, the guy went out and bought a truck, probably your truck, just because he has a crush on me—"

"He has a crush on you?"

"Don't panic; he just thinks I need a Russian man."

"Do you want a Russian man?"

"And then there's Connie, who's overwhelmed with the Russians and needs Boris to find a job, mostly because of the goat and the potatoes in the backyard—"

Boone pressed his hand to his forehead.

"But Boris won't work at Walmart, and I can see why because of his past as a cop, and he's trying so hard to fit into this world, and he was so thrilled to get a job, but now he might be mixed up with car thieves too—"

"See, sometimes I don't even think we should talk, Peej. It just hurts me—my head and my chest too, because I might be having a heart attack. And frankly, although I see your lips moving, I'm not sure you're even speaking English." Boone put a hand over her lips. "Stop talking. Just . . . stop. You're in way, way over your head."

She moved his hand away. "That's not fair. Yes, I might sort of have issues with jumping to conclusions—"

"By that, do you mean seeing trouble where there's not any? Why do you have to find a mystery everywhere you turn?"

"Maybe I do. But I like who I'm becoming. I like helping people and learning what I can do. I like the me I see tomorrow. And . . . Boone, I need you to like her too." She took a breath and met his eyes. "Can you do that?"

He stared at her a long time, apparently out of words. Then he touched his forehead to hers. "Let me simplify all this for you. Gabby is losing her mind as well as her jewelry. Boris is a car thief, and one of Dally's exes is out to kill her. And Igor can't have you. Enough craziness. I want you to turn in your lock-pick case and that crazy wig, wash off your tattoo, come home, marry me, and be the girl I know and love." His voice softened. "Who I know loves me too."

Oh, Boone. She touched his hair, that cowlick above his right eye. Of course she loved him, like she loved the smells of summer over the lake or the taste of the wind on a late Saturday night. Boone was her history, the fabric of all her childhood dreams, and once upon a time, the voice that called her home.

"Please, PJ, say yes. Marry me."

She'd always found it sort of intoxicating—the way he looked at her as if she might be a mystery, one he couldn't help but want to solve. But tonight his expression seemed more desperate as he touched his lips to hers, cupped his hand around her neck.

Boone had always been easy in his affection, sweet and tender. Almost casual.

But all the casual had gone out of his touch as he took her mouth with his. He kissed her almost hungrily, with an urgency that she didn't recognize. It thrilled her, the not-so-dormant feelings of being in his arms so earnestly awakened. As he deepened his kiss, she curled into his embrace, let him pull her up to the sofa.

But when he tried to lean her back into the cushions, she put a hand on his chest. "Boone."

It took a second but he pulled away, his eyes in hers, his heart tattooing beneath her touch. He met her eyes, then lowered his head again.

"Boone." Her voice had more strength to it now, despite the burn in the middle of her chest. An honest part of her wanted to dive back into his arms and lose herself in the easy past.

Boone's arms were still tight around her. He stared into her eyes with a confused expression that made her want to cry. "Peej, I love you. . . ."

She nodded, even as she pushed again, away from him, untangling herself from his arms, from the danger of his affection. She trembled, her heart in her throat, bottlenecking her words. Her eyes burned as she clenched her jaw tight and shook her head. How easily she became a person she'd thought she'd escaped when caught in Boone's charisma. She pushed off the sofa.

He scooted back, his mouth a dark line, and held up his hands. "My fault. I know the rules."

She closed her eyes. Rules. That's all they were to him.

To her, it was more about pledging to live in a relationship not cluttered by guilt. About leading with her mind—even her heart, her faith that God had something better for her if she'd wait for it—and not her desires.

He'd risen and come to stand near her, and when she opened her eyes, he was reaching out to her. "I'm sorry."

She nodded. "It's not you, Boone. It's the fact that I want to be more than I was. It's about trusting God enough to wait—"

"Wait. Until marriage?" He knelt in front of her. "I love you. And I want to marry you. Isn't that enough?"

"But we're *not* married."

"Yet."

She didn't repeat his word, and after a moment he drew back, hurt in his eyes. "Peej, I understand wanting to wait until you love someone, but certainly that's okay with God. He is all about love." He touched his hands to her knees, a smile meant to charm on his face.

"God is about love—loving me and you, by the way, enough to ask us to wait for the best. Which is His way. But that's our problem, Boone—you don't want to do things His way. Not like I do."

"That's not fair. I believe in God. I just think you take this religious thing too seriously. Are you going to be a nun or something?" He added a chuckle on the end.

"C'mon, *that's* not fair."

His humor evaporated. "You certainly can't say that a Christian should be breaking and entering." He gestured to the door.

"Jeremy would understand."

"Why? Because he approves of your little PI crimes?"

"Because he's a Christian and he grapples with the gray areas too."

Boone stilled. Looked away.

She tried to soften her silence with a smile. "Boone, listen. The truth is, you're just too tempting. Always have been. And I can't think with you this close."

He considered her, running his eyes over her, sighing. "Apparently not tempting enough." Then he turned away, staring again at the files.

PJ whisked the moisture from her cheeks and resumed her hunt in silence.

What Boone couldn't know was how much she wanted to be with him. And how much she feared it. The closer she let him get, the harder it would be to say good-bye.

Good-bye. The word clanged in her head, then fell through her heart like an anvil. *Good-bye?*

He picked up another file and perused it. "Hey, I think I found something. Associated Insurance. They have three claims here that Jeremy investigated, all on late-model SUVs. All of them were stolen and came back stripped." He paged through it and lifted off a sticky note. "In fact, Jeremy's written a little note here to follow up."

She swallowed another rise of blistering tears and let a little bubble of pride swell inside for the Kane and Sugar investigative team.

Boone must've seen it because his lips pursed. "Boris is still in trouble, but I can admit that I'm biting. You might be onto something."

PJ found a smile. "See, I am a supersleuth."

"That's what I'm afraid of."

Chapter *SIXTEEN*

If she perished today, the last real day of Minnesota summer—aka Labor Day—she'd die a happy woman. PJ tunneled her toes into the balmy sand and lifted her face to the late-afternoon sun, letting it splash over her, caressing her face, loosening the knot in her brain. Behind her, a hot dog vendor tempted the beach bums with the aroma of dogs on the grill, and children laughing in the spray near the docks nearly coaxed her to dive off the end into the sparkling freshness of Lake Minnetonka.

Not that she particularly wanted to perish. In fact, with the dawn creeping into her room and the ribbon of sweet summer breeze tickling her awake this morning, and with nothing scribbled on her agenda for the day but a full plate of potato salad and a game of Frisbee with Davy, she had been reminded of how close she'd come to boiling to death in the trunk of a Chevy Impala less than forty-eight hours ago.

Which apparently didn't belong to Missy, according to

Jeremy and the FBI guy, Lee, who'd tracked her down for a face-to-face. How PJ wanted to have been in on that chat. If Missy's Impala was still in her possession, it wasn't the same vehicle now sitting in impound in a St. Paul lot, marinating old gym socks.

In other words, they were back to *nichevo* on the "bad guy who wanted to kill/harm/scare Dally" list. Although, PJ had started to drift in the direction of Sammy Richfield and his so-called ring alibi. Why had he *really* broken into Dally's house?

Oh, she shouldn't think this hard on a holiday.

Today all she wanted to think about was Davy and their Labor Day picnic and freedom. Freedom from worry about Gabby and what might be happening to her jewelry—or her mind, for that matter. Freedom from Dally and whatever she and Jeremy might be doing . . .

PJ sighed.

Freedom from the fear that she'd somehow land someone— perhaps Vera this time; she'd remained relatively unscathed by the PJ touch so far—in trouble, again. Although Boris's arrest wasn't technically PJ's fault, Connie blamed her and still wasn't talking to her; she was a walking iceberg of righteous anger. Probably the only reason PJ hadn't been kicked out of the house to take up residence in her Vic was because Boone had allowed Boris to walk out of the Kellogg City Jail a free man.

"Auntie PJ, come into the water with me!" Davy appeared, garbed in a pair of swim fins, a Speedo like Daddy, goggles, a snorkel, and a pair of water wings. Lake water dribbled off the saggy back end of his suit and onto her ankles.

"Oh, little man, I'd love to, but I can't. No swimming for

me today. But when you're done, you and I will make a sand castle, okay?" For the first time since letting Stacey paint Dally's tattoo down her arm, PJ wanted to scrub it away, go back to being just plain old PJ Sugar. But she hadn't heard from Jeremy, and until she got the all clear, she was still on the job. A sound night's sleep behind her, she planned on returning to her post right after today's picnic.

Davy stuck out his lip in an exaggerated pout but splashed back through the sand to the water's edge, where Baba Vera waited to swing him into the waves. And to think, only a few months ago, he'd been terrified of the water. Yes, she'd created a monster—the kid needed constant attention to keep him from floating away, but at least his Sugar genes had kicked in and he'd developed the appropriate passion for the beach.

"I'm glad to see you made it." The voice preceded the appearance of her mother, a thin shadow of elegance cast over PJ's sunbathing form. She held out a bottle of SPF 30. PJ hadn't tempted fate by wearing a swimsuit, lounging instead in a pair of shorts and a tank, but she still hoped to add another layer to her tan.

"Mom, you're in my sun."

"You'll get cancer. Don't you know that?"

PJ closed her eyes. "It's my one vice. Let me live large."

"If you want to be a wrinkled, dried-up apricot, not my—"

"Okay, fine." PJ sat up, grabbed the bottle, and began to work the lotion into her legs.

"I realize that a little skin cancer is hardly the danger you're used to . . ."

Something in her mother's tone made PJ look up with

a frown. Elizabeth wore her dark hair tucked into a wide-brimmed hat and now stared out at the water, her hands on her hips, her lips in a tight bud of emotion.

"Mom?"

"Boone told me you were kidnapped."

PJ's mouth opened, unable to figure out . . .

Oh. There he was, the rat, sitting at the picnic table with Boris, eating a hot dog. He didn't even look in her direction. Good thing, too.

"Did you invite him?" PJ looked back at her mother.

"Of course not. But he showed up, and despite my misgivings, it certainly wouldn't be polite to run him off."

Not like she had earlier in the summer, when PJ had appeared in Kellogg, and Boone had materialized on her doorstep like a homing pigeon. Or perhaps a hungry wolf.

But if the guy was on the hunt for allies, he wouldn't find one in Elizabeth Sugar. She disliked Boone only slightly more than she disliked PJ's newest job title.

"I didn't invite him either."

"Well, he certainly seems to be worried about you; I'll give him that much."

PJ finished slathering on the lotion, closed the top. "He's overreacting." Okay, even to her ears, that sounded weak. "I'm perfectly able to take care of myself."

Perhaps she should quit while she was ahead.

"He mentioned that he asked you to marry him." Elizabeth said it casually, clearly not wanting to start a fight. PJ had to give her credit for her groomed, nonchalant tone.

Like the woman didn't want to choke Boone on the spot with her silk scarf. But Boone, the Instigator and True Reason why PJ had spent the last ten years roaming the planet, must be pushed to the edge of desperation to confess to her mother that he wanted to marry PJ.

"I just hope you know what you're doing. You know what I think about Boone Buckam."

If her mother kept it up, PJ was just liable to say yes.

"Yes, Mom, he proposed. But don't panic. I haven't given him an answer . . . yet." She got up, wiping her hands on her shorts.

"Why on earth not? Is it so hard to figure out that he is only going to break your heart?"

"Uh . . ." PJ glanced again at Boone. He was laughing at something Sergei said. Like they were already brothers. She put a hand to her chest, sighing through the nettles. "Yes."

"Okay, I can admit that I've been hard on the man, but . . ." Elizabeth shook her head as if even she couldn't believe her own words. "Maybe he *has* changed. He's a cop now; I suppose that counts for something."

"He's a detective, Mom."

"Exactly. And . . . well, I guess he loves you, PJ. That's never been in debate." She looked away, out toward the lake, her face scrunching up as if she caught the wrong wind.

"Maybe that's not enough." PJ said it so quietly, it could have been a thought, but her mother glanced at her, the brim of her beach hat ruffling in the wind.

PJ had an image suddenly of Gabby, years earlier, wearing a movie-star smile. Beautiful Gabby, who had lived a life of glamour and fame . . . if only in her mind.

For a fraction of a second, something like a soft, empathetic smile surfaced on Elizabeth's face. "I suppose I should learn to trust you more." She wrapped her arms around her waist, cupping her elbows, and sighed.

The gesture appeared so frail, so resigned, that PJ reached out to touch her mother's arm. "Are you okay?"

"I'm fine, PJ. I just don't sleep well since your father passed."

Twelve years ago? Liar. Probably, more accurately, for the past two months since PJ came back to town. Since she started attracting international assassins or getting manhandled in the middle of the night. Since she started putting her nephew, and even her shirttail Russian relatives, in danger.

So much for the tangy breeze, the sounds of laughter, the day of freedom. PJ cupped her hand over her eyes, darkening the sun, her thoughts roiling. "Mom, listen. I know you're worried about me and Boone and my new job. But I really like my job. I'm pretty good at it. I think I even helped Boone find another clue to his carjacking ring. And . . . I wasn't on vacation. I was protecting this woman who is testifying against a drug dealer. I'm even trying to help her neighbor figure out who is stealing her jewelry." PJ turned back to her mother. "I want to do this. I want to help. I want to do some good."

Her mother looked at the ground, then up at PJ. Exhaled a long breath. "That's never been your problem. It's knowing when to stop 'doing good' that you have issues with."

Was this about Boone or her job or . . . "I have people depending on me, Mom."

Elizabeth considered her a long moment. Then, "Yes, you do, PJ. Yes, you do." She took the lotion from PJ's hands. "Where did you get that awful tattoo? Please don't tell me it's permanent."

"I don't think it's so bad. It's a magnolia—a symbol of something beautiful fighting to survive amid the trials of life. And don't panic. It's just paint. It'll wash off."

"I'll get the soap."

"Not yet; I need it for my job."

"I suppose it suits you. At least it's not as bad as a tattoo."

As in, a tattoo you couldn't wash away with a little Ivory and water. It followed you, branded you. PJ resisted the urge to put her hand over where *Boone* marked her, choosing instead to hear her mother's words: *"It suits you."*

Hmm.

"I think the hot dogs are ready," Elizabeth said as she turned away.

Boone looked up at PJ as her mother walked to the grill, where Connie rolled the dogs into a new position. He smiled, lifting a hand. He looked easy sitting there with Sergei, laughing, the wind twining through his hair, his legs and arms perfectly tanned. Oh, boy.

From the abyss of her bag, a canvas puddle in the sand at her feet, she heard her ring tone—Scooby-Doo. She grabbed at her bag, expecting to see Jeremy's number and instead reading *Caller Unknown.*

"Hello?"

She pressed a hand to her other ear, trying to cut off the voices from the beach, and finally heard sniffling or . . . strangled breath?

"PJ, is that you?"

"Gabby?"

"Oh, PJ, where are you? It's gone. Seb's necklace . . . it's been stolen."

* * *

"I promise I'll bring the Vic back, Boris." PJ stood outside Connie's house, the sprinkler across the yard hissing into the evening, Boone glowering behind her, swinging his key around his index finger as she went toe-to-toe with the Russians for her car.

"I need it for vork." His burly arms folded across his chest, Boris conjured up grainy Cold War–era images with an expression that suggested she might be trying to sneak out of the motherland with nuclear secrets, using *his* Crown Vic to do it.

"You're not going to work," PJ started.

"Like I said, I'll drive you, PJ," Boone interjected, a looming voice-over to the drama before her.

"I don't want your help, Boone."

"I need to vork—"

"Do you really have to go?"

PJ rounded and stalked past Boone to the Mustang, opening the door. "Just drive."

Boone wore a tight expression that italicized his martyrdom as he climbed in beside her. "Tell me again why you have to go rushing to the aid of this old lady?"

Boris waved, showing gold teeth as they pulled away.

"She's not just an old lady; she's my neighbor, and I think her grandson is stealing from her."

Boone said nothing, his chest rising and falling. "I wanted to take you for a drive tonight."

"I could have guessed that." And maybe she should be the slightest bit relieved that she'd avoided that scenario. Not that she didn't enjoy being tucked inside Boone's embrace, but it could be true that she liked it too much for her own good.

"Besides, the chinchillas need me. I need to get back."

"You're killing me here, Peej."

She gave him the smallest of smiles. "Thank you."

"Mmm-hmm."

She reached over and turned on the radio, humming to KQ92, then dialing over to the country station. A little Waylon should fit Boone's mood.

Boone let two songs roll by before turning down the volume. "I think I should stick around tonight. I don't like you being there alone."

"I have Gabby."

"Cute. I'm not kidding, PJ."

She turned toward him. "Okay, listen; calm down, hero. Jeremy is working with this FBI guy named Lee. Apparently he's watching Dally's house. He's the one who called Jeremy when I got nabbed. I will be perfectly safe. Plus—" she pulled out her cell phone—"you're on speed dial 1."

He angled her a look that suggested he wasn't impressed.

They pulled into her neighborhood and down the alley. "You can just let me off. I have to check the chinchillas, and then I'm going over to Gabby's."

"At least let me go in and sweep the house."

"Unless you're talking with a broom, I don't think that's necessary."

Boone grabbed her wrist as she moved to unlatch the door. "Speed dial 1?"

PJ leaned over and pressed a soft kiss to his lips. "And 2, just in case."

She waved as he drove away, then unlocked the back door, dumping her duffel inside. The chinchillas came to life with a screech of complaints as she lifted their cage door, checked their water, and dropped in more food.

She stood in the living room, listening to the house, the echoes that greeted her. Had someone been here while she was gone? Who watched her, and from where?

She approached the window, peering at Gabby's house.

The sun had begun to tuck in for the night, the shadows long across her groomed lawn. Gabby's front door light had flickered on but cast only a feeble spray of light, not enough to darken the front window. In fact, she could make out movement, and then . . . Wait. Something big. Or *someone* big. And the Big Someone had a little someone in his clutches, and he was . . .

PJ crept closer to the window and dug her fingers into the edge as she watched Gabby fall backward and disappear from view.

No.

No! Sammy was . . . killing his grandma?

Speed dial 1, speed dial 1 . . . only where had she put her phone? She'd just had it, and . . . oh, well.

She flew out the back door and toward Gabby's house, pounding open the fence, racing up the stairs and through the kitchen. Big band music blared on the console, and there in the family room stood Sammy, one arm around Gabby's waist as she hovered just above the floor.

She had one of her arms hooked around his shoulder, the other draped back as if in midswoon.

"Sammy!"

He jerked and nearly dropped his grandmother, who grabbed him with both hands around his neck as he pulled her upright.

"PJ!"

PJ leaped, piggybacking Sammy, clawing at his arms. "Run, Gabby! Run!"

Gabby stepped back. "Oh, my. PJ, what on earth?"

"He took your jewelry—or worse, he might even be high! Get out of here!"

Gabby looked from PJ to Sammy. "Is that right?"

"She's a crazy person, Grandma." He turned and in one easy move dumped PJ onto the sofa. She kicked out at him and he dodged, a frown on his face. "What is wrong with you?"

"PJ, calm down. I'm fine." Gabby sat down in the old recliner, eyes wide. "What has gotten into you?"

PJ's gaze connected with Sammy, who had stepped back and now crossed his arms over his beefcake chest and steely-eyed her.

"Uh . . . I, uh . . . you called me, remember?" She studied Gabby, suddenly wondering if the woman even remembered her frantic call to PJ only an hour—oops, two hours ago. "How did you get my number?"

"It was on my caller ID as a missed call."

Oh, that's right. She'd called Gabby yesterday. "You told me your necklace was stolen."

Gabby sagged, her eyes sad. "Yes, my necklace. I had it for church yesterday, but I can't remember where I last put it. I thought it was on the bureau, but maybe . . . I shouldn't have panicked. But you know, it was—"

"Yes, Seb gave it to you as an anniversary gift. I remember."

245

"Did I tell you that?"

PJ nodded.

"Oh, my." Gabby pressed soft, wrinkled hands to her forehead. "I just don't know what is wrong with me. I put things down and they simply vanish. Maybe I am losing my mind."

"You just misplaced it, Gran." Sammy knelt before her, swallowing her hands in his paws.

Yeah, sure. "Was Evelyn here in the past couple days?"

"No—not since you were here on Saturday."

"Then . . . I think you need to ask Sammy exactly where your jewelry is."

Sammy looked at PJ again, his expression incredulous. "Excuse me?"

"You know what I'm talking about." She gestured to his shoulders, his biceps, his entire body, and when he frowned, so conveniently confused, she flexed her arms.

Now Gabby also frowned at her. "What on earth are you doing?" Gabby glanced out the window as if worried the neighbors might see.

"Steroids, Gabby! He's taking steroids."

Sammy stood, shook his head. "Seriously? That's what you're going with?"

PJ glared at him, remembering her same words to him. "Ha-ha. Listen, Mr. Buff. I know the truth. Dally probably figured out the truth, and you were over there to . . . well, I don't know why—"

"I told you why." His voice was soft—deadly soft, or perhaps sorrowfully soft. "Granny knows."

PJ sat on the sofa. "Knows what?"

Gabby looked up at Sammy. "Are you sure?"

"I already told her."

Gabby turned to PJ. "Sammy is going to propose to Morgan."

"He told you that too? Gabby . . . what was he doing to you when I came in?"

Gabby directed her grin to Sammy. "I think you'll have to let her in on the secret or she's liable to do a citizen's arrest."

Or call Boone. Maybe. "What secret?"

Was that a blush on Sammy's face? One that made PJ cock her head and wonder exactly why she suddenly felt a curl of shame.

He swallowed, then ran a hand behind his fence-post neck. "Grandma is teaching me to dance."

PJ stared at him. "What?"

"I'm learning to dance, okay? Tango and two-step. And . . . Dally was my partner. Grandma was helping me learn the steps so I could dance at our wedding."

PJ tried to unlock the meaning behind those words. But what if Sammy was using his grandma, stealing her jewelry, handing it to Dally to fence . . .

Oh, brother. *"Why do you have to find a mystery everywhere you turn?"*

As if hearing Boone's voice in PJ's head, Gabby slid a soft hand over PJ's and squeezed. "Why did you think Sammy might want to hurt me?"

PJ closed her eyes. Pinched her nose. "I don't know. I just . . ."

"Oh, honey. I think it's sweet that you care about me. It's what makes you good at your job. But it's also a weakness. You can't just assume your instincts are correct—you have to use your head too."

PJ cradled her head in her hands. "What if I get it wrong? What if—"

"You're going to spend your life worried about every step you take?"

PJ couldn't look at her or Sammy.

"This is about Boone, isn't it?"

"No . . ."

"And even that little fiasco ten years ago?"

"I burned down a country club. Hardly a little fiasco."

"Oh, fiddle-dee-dee. You told me that you came back a different person, right? So, did you expect that it would all be easy? that you wouldn't make mistakes?"

"No, I . . ."

"You're so afraid that you're going to make a mistake—maybe miss something—that all you're doing is turning in circles. You're seeing things that aren't there and you don't know what to think."

PJ pushed her palms against her head. It was pounding. Most likely because Gabby was inside it.

Gabby touched her hand. "Sweetie. Of course you're going to make mistakes. But don't you know that God has a plan for each of them? The truth is, every time you fail, it's an opportunity for God to show you how much He loves you. You go read Psalm 18, verse 19. It says, 'He rescued me because he delighted in me.' *Delighted.* That means He likes you. He takes pleasure in you. He is, as Seb would have said, over the moon about you. And every time you do something that just makes you want to scream in frustration, you have two choices: to curl into a ball and hide or let God pick you up and dust you off and nudge you forward. Let go of your fear of being wrong and being judged, and draw with confidence to the throne of grace, because I promise you'll find mercy."

She patted PJ's knee. "That's a verse, too, by the way. Hebrews 4:16."

Mercy. Not getting what she deserved. Seemed to her she'd read that somewhere else recently. Yes, she needed mercy. And probably forgiveness. She closed her eyes and rubbed them. Why on earth would God delight in her . . . ?

Gabby handed her a tissue from the table. "I think it's sweet that you wanted to protect me. But Sammy is a good boy. He wouldn't hurt me. You have to have a little faith."

PJ glanced at Sammy, who slowly shook his head, clearly not as full of mercy as Gabby.

She grimaced.

"It's the truth," he said.

It did sound like the truth. In her head. In her heart.

"I'm sorry, Sammy. I'm just trying to figure out who might want to hurt Dally."

Sammy regarded her with cool eyes, but Gabby took her hand. "We know. Next time, I hope you'll trust people a little. Now get up and put on your dancing shoes. We need you, and it's time to tango."

Chapter *SEVENTEEN*

"He threw you into the trunk? Seriously?"

"Weren't you terrified?"

"Do you think they're still out there?"

PJ crouched at home plate, not sure which was harder to catch—Stacey's pitches or Morgan's barrage of questions.

She nabbed Stacey's fastball, moving her body in front of it, not rising when she threw it back.

"You're getting quicker," Morgan said. They'd been working for over an hour, the cool breeze of the evening playing with PJ's dark braids under her baseball cap. She had to admit to feeling a sort of normalcy when she resumed Dally's schedule. Breakfast with Gabby, who had spent the entire hour critiquing PJ's rather-iffy tango technique—hey, she was just filling in, right? Then her shift at the Scissor Shack—a full day of shampoos and sets under Linda's supervision, to Stacey's entertaining account of her Labor Day weekend.

"I wonder what Dally did," Stacey had said, curled up in one of the salon's black faux leather chairs, when they had a break between patrons.

"Me too," PJ responded, hating that her curiosity meter just wouldn't shut down. Yes, Jeremy had checked in with her yesterday before her return to Dally's, given her the report on Missy, but he'd been specifically cryptic about his whereabouts and activities.

She hated how her imagination took over. Or that she even cared.

Good thing Morgan dropped in to shanghai her for softball practice after work. It was only four days until their next game, and tomorrow night she had a tango lesson with Gabby and Sammy. It kept her brain off who might be stalking . . . well, *her*, what Boris might be doing, and who might really be stealing from Gabby.

And of course, her rather-pitiful attempts at the tango. PJ hoped to keep from knocking over any more priceless antiques next time. Last night, despite moving back the furniture in Gabby's little family room, she'd managed to take out a vase full of plastic gardenias. Meanwhile Sammy had crushed her toes under his freighter-size feet more times than she wanted to count. If she heard, "Well, you're sure not Dally" from him one more time, she'd start stomping on the tops of *his* feet.

Now her stomach growled, and her brain, not to mention her thighs, burned with Morgan's list of fast-pitch instructions. *"The catcher is the leader on the field. Only the catcher can see all the plays at once—and her job is to read the batter, read the field, and keep the batters from getting on base and especially from scoring runs."*

No pressure there. She'd listened to Morgan explain Dally's

list of pitches: fastball, changeup, drop ball, rise ball, screwball, curveball, and knuckleball.

"Remember, when the batter comes to the plate, you're not only considering her stance and how she hits, but the game situation, the condition of the pitcher, and even the weather. You have to constantly think strategy."

"I need ice cream," PJ said as Morgan hobbled up to the plate and pretended another hitter stance.

"I'm in the back of the box. You have a runner on first. Pitcher is fresh."

"I don't know—fastball?"

Morgan lowered the bat. "Drop ball, inside. You want to make them bunt."

PJ lifted her mask, sighing. "I can't do this, Morgan."

Stacey came in from the mound. "What's the holdup?"

"PJ's crumbling."

"I'm not! I'm just . . ." She tumbled back in the dirt, stretching her cramped legs. "Confused."

Stacey collapsed on the edge of the grass and picked at it.

Morgan leaned on the bat. On the field next to them, a group of six-year-old T-ballers scrambled around the bases.

"Let's play that," PJ said.

Stacey smirked.

"I think the kids are so cute. Their parents stand on the sidelines and tell them which way to run." Morgan giggled.

PJ sat up. "Oh, that's perfect. I have an idea." She looked at Morgan. "*You* call the pitches. You know what you're doing, and I can catch and throw. So you sit on the sidelines and do the heavy thinking. We'll make up some new signals; I'll glance at you, grab them, and translate them to Karla."

"That's a great idea! Do you think we can pull it off?"

"You don't know this, but I was born to sneak around."

Stacey grinned. "You put that on your résumé?"

"Maybe."

"I think it will work," Morgan said, straightening. "Let's do it."

PJ pulled off her catcher's mask, holding her wig in place as she did. It was more of a formality. She had no illusions that she might be fooling anyone watching. "I would hug you, but I smell pretty bad. I promise, you don't want to get near me."

Morgan eased her way down to the dirt. "Apparently, I don't even need to smell bad to repel someone. Sammy's been ignoring me for the better part of a week."

PJ eased off her glove, flexing her hand. "What? I saw him chase away the adoring fans the other night. He's crazy about you."

"Not anymore. He used to be so . . . attentive. He'd show up to all our games, come over after work; we'd go running together. Now every night he's busy, and sometimes I only get his voice mail. I think . . . maybe he's seeing someone else."

"Uh . . ."

"And now Reggie—you met him at the pizza parlor— he asked me out, and I'm wondering . . . well, I don't know. I love Sammy, but maybe I'm setting myself up to get hurt."

"Oh, Morgan . . . maybe you should talk to Sammy." PJ glanced at Stacey, who was regarding PJ with a strange expression.

"I did. He told me he was working. Even yesterday. But I know the shop was closed. When I swung by there, it was dark. He lied to me."

A cheer went up from the next field.

"Give him a chance, Morgan. Don't cut him off too . . ." PJ glanced at Stacey, who was frowning. "What?"

"Nothing. Only . . . you sounded a lot like Dally just then."

Maybe because she and Dally were keeping the same secret? PJ managed a feeble smile.

Morgan reached over and tugged on PJ's braid. "You do remind me a lot of Dally. Someone I can count on. A true friend."

A true friend. That was a description of Dally, wasn't it? She wasn't the kind of person who stole boyfriends or got into fistfights or clipped old ladies' jewelry. In fact, over the past week, PJ had to agree that Dally and she were a lot alike, like Jeremy had predicted. Just a couple of women trying to figure out how to live with themselves and their mistakes.

"Thanks, Morgan."

"I'm just glad that you're okay. But who do you think is after Dally?"

PJ shook her head. "Maybe Karla?"

"With the big game coming up this weekend? No. She knows I'm out of commission." Morgan lifted her bandaged ankle.

"I was really thinking it might be Missy. I was thrown into an Impala. But according to the FBI, she still has hers."

Stacey was leaning over her legs, stretching. "No, she doesn't. I saw Missy yesterday, hanging out at Rick's softball game. She has a hot new convertible MINI Cooper. I remember because I wondered how she could afford it on her nursing assistant salary."

She had a new car? "But then what happened to the Impala?" Had Jeremy or Lee gotten it wrong?

Stacey angled her a dark look. "Maybe she 'lost' it in a parking lot on the Wisconsin border."

"Why do you have to find a mystery everywhere you turn?"

PJ stood, brushed off her uniform. "I don't know who kidnapped me. Unless, of course, it's Dally's mysterious Mr. R."

"Mr. R.?" Morgan rose, swung the bat over her shoulder.

"Yeah, I found a note in Dally's stuff. A Dear John rebuttal. A 'You'll regret letting me go' kind of note signed only by the initial *R*. I got to thinking that whoever the *R* was, maybe it was someone who might have something to lose if that note ever got out into the open."

"Mr. R.?" Morgan repeated, now staring hard at PJ.

PJ could practically see Morgan's thoughts written in her expression. As in Sammy *Richland*?

PJ quickly said, "I think it's a first name, not a last."

Morgan said nothing.

"Don't panic, Morgan. Sammy's still into you."

Morgan made a face at her.

PJ made one back.

❋ ❋ ❋

Night had shifted over the neighborhood by the time PJ returned to Dally's house. She walked up the sidewalk, swinging her mask and glove, aware of how she'd acclimated to the neighbors—the rottweiler next door was already barking, seeing her even from a half block away. The gardener across the street lifted his spade in hello.

She noted that Sammy's Charger, usually lounging at the curb in front of Gabby's house, was conspicuously absent, but across the street, farther down, she noticed a black Ford Focus. Had she seen it before? It suddenly appeared in her memory.

As she passed Gabby's house and turned in to Dally's walk, the car door opened.

She froze, one hand on her mask, quickly reviewing her self-defense techniques. At the least, she could lob him upside the head, flee to Gabby's. Where Gabby could clock him with one of her porcelain vases . . . ?

Out stepped Mr. FBI. Or at least who she assumed to be the man Jeremy had assigned to watchdog her. He appeared every inch an FBI man in his dark blue suit, shorn hair, and all-business look as he crossed the street.

"Hello," he said, extending a hand when he got closer. PJ considered it only a moment before she took it. He was taller up close, with wide shoulders that pulled at his suit coat, betraying a regular date with a gym. His brown eyes barely scraped over her before lingering on the house. "I'm Lee Simmons."

"You're the one who called Jeremy the other night."

Lee glanced back at her. "You okay?"

PJ nodded. "Thanks."

"I just wanted to let you know I'm out here. You let me know if you need anything."

"How about a large pepperoni pizza with mushrooms . . ." Oops. No sense of humor. "Thanks."

He nodded and turned back to his vehicle. It occurred to PJ that if he was trying to maintain a sense of distance, perhaps attempt to catch the perpetrator, he might, you know, be a little less conspicuous? When Jeremy wanted to fly under the radar, he'd motored around in an old VW Rabbit masquerading as a pizza delivery guy.

But maybe that was the point. Lee wanted to stand out. As a deterrent to whoever wanted to throw her into the back of vehicles. He'd get no arguments from this iffy softball player who needed a shower.

Unlocking the front door, she pulled it closed behind her, resetting the dead bolt.

She ran a bath and soaked for an hour before emerging a prune. Then, cozy in her Superman pants and a clean tee, she fed the chinchillas—she knew better than to let them out—raided the cupboard only to surface with Cheese Nips (scary how much she relied on Gabby to feed her), and stood at the entrance to Dally's room a long time trying to put her finger on what might be missing. Her gaze traveled over the bed, the closet, the dresser . . . *the dresser*. The picture of Mount Rushmore was missing. She went over to the dresser, looked behind it, under it. No picture.

If only she could remember the face in the picture. She stood for a long moment, trying to re-create the memory, and finally gave up. She probably could confirm with some surety that it hadn't been Sammy. . . . She would recognize a man of his bulk.

Still, it irked her as she finally curled onto the sofa with the remote. Scanning through the channels, she landed on AMC. *Roman Holiday*. Gregory Peck and beautiful Audrey Hepburn, runaway princess, hiding her identity.

Runaway . . .

Princess. She heard Jeremy's voice, low and soft in her mind. *Princess*. She probably shouldn't like it, shouldn't like the way it made her feel pretty. Even royal. Shouldn't like the smile that slid up his face when he said it.

She turned off the television and sat in the darkness, eating Cheese Nips. Okay, she could admit it—she missed Jeremy. For some reason, when he'd suggested she work for him, she'd believed it might be, well, together. Surveillance . . . together. Breaking into country clubs . . . together. Saving small countries . . . together.

But no. Dally was with Jeremy. And she was here with the chinchillas.

Not that it mattered. She closed the box and lay back, closing her eyes.

"Poppy? Patsy? Phoebe? You will tell me if I get it, right?"

They sat on the front steps. Even with his face lost in the shadows, she could trace it without looking—dark eyes, square jaw with a scrape of whiskers.

"You may call me Anya."

He smiled at her. "Thank you . . . Anya."

Wait, was her name Anya? No . . . Danya? Dalya?

No . . . Trouble . . . Boone called her Trouble.

"You're not what I'd call trouble."

I'm not?

The phone rang and she jostled awake, blinking into the flickering darkness, watching . . . Hey, how had the television turned on? Sure enough, Gregory Peck had invaded her subconscious, not only "not calling her trouble," but now talking on the telephone.

She reached below her hip, pulled out the remote where she had lain on it, and watched as Gregory Peck conspired to trick poor Audrey.

From inside the tomb of her bag, she heard her cell phone tone. She dug it out, not looking at the caller ID. "What, Boone?"

Silence.

"I'm sorry. Did I interrupt something?" Jeremy's voice emerged deep and smoky, quiet.

She clicked down the volume on Gregory and propped her feet on the coffee table. "Hi." Her tone came out shorter than she intended.

"What's the matter?"

"Nothing." Just . . . "Nothing."

"Well, I wanted to check on you. Where are you?"

"Dally's. I met your friend Lee outside."

"Good."

He sounded tired, his voice roughened by lack of sleep. It turned something inside her and made her ask, "You okay?"

"Yeah. It's just . . . I hate not knowing where you are and if you're okay."

Really? Oh, her heart shouldn't leap so wildly at that. So what? She was his employee; of course he wanted her to be safe.

"And I hate babysitting. Dally's in the other room. Probably sulking because I won't let her go out to the Rockets game this weekend."

See—it wasn't about her. He was bored. "There're only six days left. Dally testifies on Monday."

"You're doing a great job."

PJ pressed her hand to her face. "No, I'm not. Yesterday I blamed Sammy for breaking into Dally's house and accused him of stealing from his grandma. And unless Morgan and I come up with some new signals and learn them right so she can call the pitches, the Rockets are going to lose the final game of the regular season. And then there's Connie, who isn't speaking to me because I got Boris a job as a car thief."

"Calm down, Princess, and start at the beginning." Jeremy sounded as if he were trying not to laugh.

"It's not funny, Jeremy." But his use of the forbidden nickname made her turn off the television. Lie down on the sofa, imagine him sitting across from her—and while it was her dream, maybe she'd add a foot massage. In her mind, he sat there, the moon on his face, his smile rakish, those eyes watching her with something akin to amusement.

"1-800-Trouble-Solver at your service."

"I don't even know where to start."

"You just have to face the facts, Princess. It's never going to happen."

"What?"

"You being perfect. I mean, you have to have a few flaws for us commoners to relate to you."

"Funny."

He went quiet on the other end. Then, "PJ, you're a woman who, let's say, seizes opportunity. But you have to stop trying so hard. You're already a good PI."

"I am?"

"Well, you will be." His voice softened. "Stop trying so hard to prove yourself."

Had he been talking to Gabby?

"I should probably start with confessing my crimes, then."

"What, did you steal home?"

"Oh, you're a funny man."

"Just a little softball humor."

"How about this, smart guy. I broke in to the office and hunted down an insurance fraud, right there in your files."

"You broke in to the office?"

"Well, see, like I said, Boris got arrested for carjacking, and I think it's an insurance scam, and I remembered that you did some investigation—"

"I found a number of insurance agencies that had listed stripped vehicles as totaled and sold them to a local wrecking company in town."

PJ smiled. "You're pretty good."

He gave a low chuckle that rumbled through the phone line. "I thought so. Most of them were high-end SUVs or trucks. It bothered me."

"Well, Boone's on the case now."

"Boone?" Something sharp edged into his tone. "You were with Boone?"

Of *course* she was with Boone, and a defensive tone nearly found her lips as she said, "Boone was trying to help me." But she tempered it, because, well, was she *with* Boone? "He was going to hold Boris unless I threw him a bone, so we did some investigating together. . . ."

"Oh." Only it sounded like . . . *oh*. Or, *no*. Whatever it was, however, he covered it up with a fast "He'll take care of the case? There's no reason for me to be worried, right?"

Worried? He worried about the case . . . or her? She wasn't sure she wanted to know. "Yeah, he's looking into it."

"Good." Jeremy paused. "So . . . you told Boone yes, then."

The way he said it, suddenly all business, created an ache

right in the center of PJ's chest. "No, actually." She barely breathed the words, as if testing them.

"You told him no?"

Was there a little rise to his tone? As if fueled with hope? surprise?

"I . . . well, not exactly. I haven't answered him."

The silence on the other end stretched out so long, PJ checked her phone to see if they were still connected.

Finally, again, "Oh."

That was it? She wasn't sure why she pressed her lips together, why her throat tightened. It wasn't like he was the one standing between her and Boone. No, it was more the old PJ in her path, while the new one hovered like a specter, haunting their future. . . .

Still, his single nonword was a punch, like the one delivered back at the gym.

"PJ, are you still there?"

She closed her eyes. "Umm-hmm."

"So, what were you doing before I called?"

She flicked the television back on. Muted it as Gregory Peck followed Audrey Hepburn through Rome. "I was watching an old movie. You probably don't know it—it's called *Roman Holiday*."

"*Roman Holiday*. Gregory Peck and Audrey Hepburn, about the princess who tours Rome for a day and falls in love with a newspaperman. Great flick."

She wanted to see his face. He had a way of lifting one side of his mouth, his eyes full of mischief, when he teased her. "I don't believe you."

"Please. I'm a huge Audrey Hepburn fan. Some guys hang

out at the bar; I go to old movies in the park. And this is my favorite. The princess running around Rome, thinking that the reporter guy has no clue who she really is, and all along, he not only knows but is trying to protect her—"

"He's not trying to protect her! He's using her to get a scoop!"

"But then he falls in love with her. Because everyone else sees her the way they expect to, but he sees her for who she really is. A woman with spunk and laughter. A woman he wants to be with but can't."

PJ opened her mouth and nothing came out.

"A woman he wants to be with but can't."

Why couldn't he?

Just as the question was finding its way from her heart to her mouth, Jeremy gave a low laugh. "I love the part where they're sightseeing, scooting around Rome on that moped. Having fun together."

"What—*what* are you talking about? The entire time he's deceiving her, taking pictures of her, leading her on."

"Yeah, but it's not like he minded having a good-looking princess on the back of his bike. A part of him had to be falling for her right then."

PJ pulled out the Cheese Nips. "Oh, please."

"If you'll remember, he did tell the judge they were going to the church to get married. Can you say *Freudian slip?*"

"She assured him she wouldn't hold him to it, and he didn't argue."

"Some guys have a hard time saying what they feel. Maybe he wasn't ready to propose or anything, but some part of him wanted to communicate that he liked her. A lot. That he liked spending time with her. That she was fun and interesting and made him laugh, despite her crazy driving."

The Nips became sandpaper in her throat. She got up and maneuvered by the glow of the television light to the kitchen, where she drew some water from the tap.

"You know my favorite part in the entire movie?" Jeremy asked when she didn't say anything, when she couldn't think of anything to say. "The wall of wishes. All those plaques of people who wished for something, stuck them on the wall, and then saw their dreams come true. Wouldn't it be great to . . . wish big, then know that it would happen?"

PJ sputtered, coughed.

"Are you okay?"

She slapped her chest. "Yes. Yes. Just went down the wrong pipe."

"I'll bet you loved that scene where he fought the Secret Service and saved her."

No, no, Jeremy, go back. What would you wish for?

But maybe she didn't want to know. Not yet. So, "Hey, she did her own saving! She smashed a guitar over a guy's head."

"Sorta like throwing donuts, I s'pose."

"Whatever gets the job done, pal." But she smiled at his tone as she wandered back to the television. And wouldn't you know it, there was the kiss, Hepburn and Peck, right there on the screen. "She was pretty, wasn't she?"

"Sure. But I'm partial to redheads. Like Lucille Ball."

She could practically see Jeremy's smile. "Very funny. You want to know what my favorite line is? Well, besides when he tells her that she should always wear his clothes?"

"She should."

"What's with guys wanting girls to wear their clothes?"

"I think it's the girls wanting to wear the guys' clothes."

"You've never let a girl wear your jacket?"

Silence. Uh-oh.

"Never had a girl I wanted to wear my jacket."

"Never?"

"I haven't had much time for, well, jacket wearing. Tell me your favorite line."

"Fine. It's when they're standing there, after their adventure, realizing what they feel for each other, and Joe, the reporter, says, 'Life isn't always what one likes, is it?' And the princess says, 'No, it isn't.' It's their way of declaring their love for each other."

"No, it's not. That's their *wish*. They want the world to be different. A world in which they could be together. And that's why they never declare their love—because they don't want to break the magic."

"You know this movie scarily well."

"Told you. I love Audrey Hepburn."

"Methinks you're a romantic, Jeremy Kane."

"If you're talking poetry and roses, probably not. But, maybe . . . if I found the right escaping princess, I might be that guy." He gave a sigh, long and loud and theatrical. "She'd probably leave me and break my heart, just like Audrey."

Break his heart?

"You told Boone yes, then."

"In the meantime," Jeremy continued, "if you want, we can do lines from *My Fair Lady*. Another great story about a woman who's transformed by a man."

PJ simply couldn't keep up. Didn't know if she even should.

"Oh, is that what *Roman Holiday* is about? I thought it was she who did the transforming—or perhaps redeeming—of Joe. Turned him into a nice guy."

"I guess you could say they redeemed each other."

The chinchillas had begun to settle, their screaming dialed down to an occasional squeal. On the screen, the credits began to roll.

Finally Jeremy broke the silence. "You going to be okay over there?"

"I'm okay, Jeremy. Just alone."

"Sorry about that, Princess. But if it makes you feel any better, I'm alone too."

No, actually . . . it didn't make her feel any better at all.

Chapter *EIGHTEEN*

"It's not that I don't love you, but when does the next train leave?"

PJ stood on the back step of Gabby's house, her hand raised to knock, listening through the screen door. She knew she was early for her dancing lesson with Sammy—frankly she wanted a few pointers on how to stay ahead of his feet. The last two nights had been an exercise in pain. If the guy hoped to tango Morgan around the dance floor, he'd have to learn to count first. Dally must have worn her steel-toed industrial boots when dancing with him.

Not that PJ was any Ginger Rogers. But at least she knew which foot to lead with.

"Are you out of your mind, sending him off alone? Are you sure you've thought this out?"

Sending who off alone? PJ recognized Gabby's voice, but who was she talking to? PJ eased open the door, sticking her head inside.

"Oh, I don't know you as well as I did when you were a child. But you were one of the dumbest children I ever met!"

What? PJ came through the kitchen and found Gabby standing with her back to the door, wearing a red hairnet, white gloves, an elegant black coat, pajama bottoms, and heels.

Playing to her audience through the front picture window. "Gabby?"

The woman spun, eyes wide, her hand to her chest. "Oh . . . Alfred! I'm glad to see you. Which of these two fabrics do you like best?" She picked up two pillows from her sofa.

PJ looked from the pillows to Gabby, who wore an expectant expression. "Uh, the blue one?"

Gabby gave a little shake of her head. "You *probably* hate them both."

"I do?"

"So do I." She tossed them aside, lowered her voice. "Why don't you skip garbage disposals and have a drink with me?" She smiled at PJ, raising a suggestive eyebrow.

"Uh . . ."

Gabby angled her head forward. "Line?"

Line? PJ held out her hands in surrender.

Gabby rolled her eyes, put a hand to the side of her mouth, and stage-whispered, "Haven't you heard? I'm no longer a part of the cocktail party set. I'm the lady in Houghton with a rich, full life."

"I'm the lady with the rich, full life?" PJ studied her for sweat across her brow, maybe glassy eyes. "Okay, Gabby, what's the deal? Stop it."

"Why . . . am I bothering you?"

"Really, you're sorta scaring me."

Gabby smiled wickedly and laughed, reverting back into some role with her sultry voice and the way she batted her eyes. "You're a liar."

What? "I'm not a liar." Okay, so maybe she was a little liar, but it was for a good reason, and . . .

Gabby sashayed over to her, swinging her hips. PJ was pretty sure even she couldn't move like that. The elderly woman trickled her fingers down PJ's arm. "I bet I just make you nervous, that's all."

"Yes. That's a safe bet." PJ peered out the front window. *Please, Sammy, show up soon.* All Gabby's words about not losing her mind now pinged in PJ's.

"You can relax now. I'm leaving. I have a performance to give." Gabby danced out of the room, back into the kitchen, leaving PJ standing in the front room, baffled. Maybe Evelyn was right. Maybe . . .

"Oh, PJ—*Please Don't Eat the Daisies!*" Gabby's head poked around the corner. She'd lost the hairnet. "I'm pretty good, aren't I? I remember when Doris got that role. Oh, she was so thrilled."

"*Please Don't Eat the Daisies?*"

Gabby came in, took PJ's arm, drew her into the kitchen. "How about some tea?"

The coat and gloves hung over the back of a kitchen chair, the heels tossed beneath the table. "Of course, I do *Calamity Jane* much better." She broke into song, holding her hand to her chest, dancing. "'Once I had a secret love that lived within the heart of me . . .'"

"Gabby, are you okay?"

"'All too soon my secret love became impatient to be free. . . .'"

"Gabby, you're freaking me out!"

She stopped singing and sighed. "Oh, fiddle-dee-dee. Haven't you ever wanted to disappear inside a movie?"

The teakettle on the stove began to whistle.

PJ pulled out a chair as Gabby turned off the kettle and pulled two teacups from the cupboard. "Have you eaten supper yet?"

"I had yogurt and a bowl of microwave popcorn."

Gabby shook her head. "And you say *I* frighten *you*." She poured water into the cups. "Sugar?"

"Yes?"

"Okay." She turned and dumped a spoonful into PJ's cup.

Oh . . . not . . . oh, well. PJ examined her for any more craziness as Gabby set her tea on the table and shook her head. "Now, tell me, how do you like dancing?"

Dancing? So she remembered their lessons. And she *had* called her PJ. . . . "I think the tops of my feet are purple."

Gabby laughed. "Sammy'll get it. And so will you. Let him lead a little more. He's not very confident, and he needs someone to trust him."

"Hence the bruised feet."

"Well, no one gets it right off. That's why it's called practice. Why, Fred used to be in the studios for hours and hours. And you know how good he was." She smiled at a vision somewhere beyond PJ's right shoulder. "The key is to stop looking at your feet. You'll only trip over them."

Gabby's gaze came back to PJ's as she dipped her spoon into a saucer of strawberry jam, then ladled it into her tea and stirred. "Oh, by the way, I saw him."

PJ had her gaze on the jam now dissolving into the tea. Did Gabby know that wasn't sugar?

Her worry must have shown on her face because Gabby laughed. "We drank it like this during the war when sugar was rationed."

"Uh, who did you see, Gabby?"

"Roy. Or Guy. Or something like that. I can't remember his name." She flicked her wrist. "He was outside, twice now."

"Roy?" The mysterious *R*?

"Dally's boyfriend. I saw him in his car—once watching the house, once driving by."

A shiver tickled down PJ's spine. "When was this?"

Gabby closed her eyes. "It sometimes gets so cloudy. I'm pretty sure yesterday or the day before . . . No, it was . . . Oh, I don't know. I remember you had your softball equipment with you."

The night she'd been kidnapped? "What did he look like?"

"Oh, the same. Tall, dark hair. I never liked his eyes." She took a sip of her tea, leaned forward, cutting her voice low. "Always seemed like he was hiding something." She leaned back and gave PJ a knowing nod.

"Do you think he'd ever want to hurt Dally?"

The cat jumped up on the table. "Oh, Simon, why do you do that?"

PJ reached out a hand and ran it down the cat's body. He let out a rumble.

"I don't know. Dally broke his heart. You know men."

Not really. But she did have a clue how it might feel to break a man's heart.

The cat's gaze was on the spoon. Before PJ could catch him,

he swept his paw across the table and the spoon clattered to the floor. Simon peered over the edge. Let out a mew.

"He's always pushing things off the table. Shoo." Gabby waved her hand and Simon jumped down.

Outside, PJ heard the Charger pull up, a thunderous roar that could probably be heard in Tibet.

"I'll tell Sammy to take it easy on you, Dally. I know your big game is coming up this weekend."

PJ expected a wink, something, but Gabby just patted her hand and got up to greet Sammy at the front door.

* * *

"I think I can actually feel my feet." PJ closed the screen door and stood on the back steps of Gabby's house after her Friday night dance practice, letting the night fall over her. The brisk smell of a fall storm ladened the air, a few scattered leaves running for cover in the wind. Gooseflesh pimpled on her forearms.

"Very funny, PJ. I'm getting better." Sammy hiked one foot onto the stoop, swinging the keys to his Charger on his finger. "If you'd just let me lead, that would help."

"Hey, I've never been good at following." However, she smiled at Sammy. Despite his bulk, he had begun to move like a dancer, with more confidence in his step as he twirled her around the room or sent her out in a turn. "You're great at the waltz, but I think I like swing dancing the best."

"Just wait until I toss you in the air."

How had she missed Sammy's boyish charm? or worse, ever believed he could have meant his grandmother harm?

"Oh, I think you'll have to reserve that move for Morgan."

Inside, Gabby was preparing a cup of tea. PJ glanced toward the house, then lowered her voice. "I hate to ask this, but . . . have you ever seen your grandma . . . act out a movie?"

Sammy grinned. "Like, for example, anything starring Doris Day?"

"Yes!" PJ nearly crumpled with the relief coursing through her "Yes. I caught her the other day acting out *Please Don't Eat the Daisies*. She wanted me to participate!"

"Be glad she didn't put a top hat on you and make you sing 'Singin' in the Rain.'"

"I was afraid that she'd . . ." PJ shrugged, not wanting to put form to her fears. "Do you know if she ever found her necklace—the one she called me about on Sunday?" She added a chagrined smile. "Sorry about that again."

"You're forgiven again. She hasn't found it yet. She's awfully sensitive about it because Grandpa gave it to her. This isn't the first time it's gone missing, although the last time, we did find it behind the bedside table. I think she takes it off in her sleep. We're always finding her jewelry in the cushions of the sofa or under her bed."

"But jewelry is missing, right? Your mother practically accused me of stealing."

The wind stirred the leaves, unhinging a few more early victims and tossing them into the yard. "Yeah, I think so. Jewelry and maybe some other things. Keys. A watch I'd left here. Things *are* disappearing. . . ."

"Maybe she's taking them off and then forgetting she's doing it."

What seemed like panic entered Sammy's eyes. "Do you

think she's getting Alzheimer's?" He shot a glance at the kitchen, where Gabby moved against the outline of the curtain.

"I don't know. We just need to keep an eye on her, I guess. But I'm glad to know I'm not the only one enlisted as a silver screen stand-in."

Sammy pocketed his keys. "Thanks, by the way." He held out his arm, and she shoved hers through it. "You make a great Ginger Rogers."

They rounded the corner of the house. "And you're getting there, Fred."

A car parked in front of Sammy's Charger pulled away from the curb, tearing down the street.

PJ stilled. "I wonder who that was." Her eyes scanned the road for Lee, her heart thumping like Doppler in her throat.

"You okay?" Sammy stopped, looked at her. "You're shaking."

PJ untangled herself from his arm. "I'm fine . . . just remembering my adventure in a trunk."

"Let me walk you home."

"All the way next door?"

"Hey, those steroids need to be good for something, right?"

"Hah." But she let him walk her around the fence and up the front walk, let him wait until she closed and latched the door. And double-checked the latch.

She kept the lights off as he walked away and finally got into his car. Lightning crinkled the dark sky, and far away, thunder shook the night.

PJ blew out a shaky breath. She had to admit that she'd be glad when this assignment ended. For a moment, she debated calling Jeremy.

Jeremy. Not Boone.

She crossed her arms and leaned her head against the doorjamb.

"If it makes you feel any better, I'm alone too."

His parting words wouldn't leave her. Those, and his comment about breaking the magic of their relationship. Okay, so he'd been talking about the characters in the movie. Technically. But she didn't have to be a supersleuth to recognize the parallel. They did have something between them, a friendship that made her feel alive and new.

"I guess you could say they redeemed each other."

Maybe. Because in Jeremy's eyes, she saw a different woman than the one reflected in Boone's. Around Jeremy, the baggage of her past didn't press into her, and she could taste the beginnings of something new, not unlike the fragrance of fall, the hint of change in the tang of the breeze.

After another cascade of thunder, rain began to ping on the roof. PJ moved to a window, watching lightning fracture the sky.

In the split-second flicker of light, she saw a figure standing in Gabby's backyard. Hunched over, knees to the ground.

Gabby.

PJ ran through the house, her pulse beating her to the door as she flung it open, tore down the steps slicked by the rain. She splashed across the backyard, hooking her hand on the rail, rounding it. Mud splattered her legs as she ran up the alley. "Gabby!"

The woman looked up at PJ, her face barely visible under the clouds that manacled the sky. Rain poured down her face in rivulets, her pink housecoat like parchment as it pasted to her body. She pushed her hands through the mud. "Where is it?"

PJ dropped to her knees, grabbing Gabby's arms. "Gabby, what are you doing?"

"I dropped it—I dropped Seb's necklace!" Gabby's face was wretched with smeared mascara and pasty red lipstick smudged beyond the outline of her lips. "I came out after Simon—that stupid cat—and slipped. My necklace must have fallen . . ." She pressed her hand to her throat, leaving behind a muddy print.

PJ took her hands. "Gabby, you weren't wearing your necklace today. Remember? You lost it a few days ago. You haven't found it yet."

Gabby stared at her. "I haven't?"

"I don't think so." PJ put her arm around the older woman's thin shoulders. Under the driving rain, Gabby seemed to melt away to nothing more than bones. "We need to get out of the rain."

Gabby's breath caught and she shook her head. "What if it's true, Dally?" She put her grimy hands to her face, her eyes round with something that resembled fear. "What if I am losing my mind? I know I had that necklace. Just today." She sat back in the mud with a plunk, drawing her knees up. Staring out into the darkness, the rain hollowing her face, she aged by decades. Her hands were gnarled and dirty, her hair flattened and slate gray, her feet bony and misshapen. "What if Evelyn is right?"

PJ sank down beside her, put an arm around her again. "We need to go inside, Gabby."

"What if I'm making it all up?"

"Making up what?"

"My life!" Gabby turned in PJ's arms and grabbed her shirtsleeve. "What if I did dream it all—Fred and Doris and Marlon—?"

Marlon? As in Brando? PJ held her breath.

"What if I imagined it all, trying to be a woman I'm not? a woman I never was? What if I am crazy? What if I concocted everything—why would I do that?" She pinned PJ with a wild look.

"I don't know. I . . ."

"Did I want it too badly? Was it not enough that I had a good life? a wonderful husband?"

PJ held Gabby tightly, running her hand down the bones in her back. "You're not crazy, Gabby." *Please, God, don't let her be crazy.* Because it wasn't crazy to want to be more, was it? to believe that you were a star?

Gabby shuddered for a long moment, until finally she leaned back, her hands taking PJ's. "I don't want to be crazy, PJ," she said, letting the rain drench her and scrub the makeup, the mud from her face. Lightning strobed again, but Gabby didn't move, just tightened her hold. Firm, despite the frail bones, her grip pressed into PJ's, the mud like cement as it filled the cracks in PJ's hands. "I don't want to be crazy."

Thunder argued in the distance, a retreating voice even as the driving rain began to ease. Down the alley, a car splashed through soggy craters. Water poured off the gutters, spitting out the debris of the storm.

"Me neither," PJ said softly. "Me neither."

Chapter NINETEEN

Focus on the game. Focus. On the GAME!

Karla's pitch came sailing into her glove with a resounding and sharp whack!

"Sturrrike one!"

Ow.

But PJ didn't flinch, didn't even grunt as she pulled the softball out of the pocket and flung it back to Karla, a perfect shot over her right shoulder.

She glanced at Morgan, sitting on the far edge of the dugout, as the batter gave a couple practice swings. Morgan adjusted her cap. Curveball.

The batter crouched over, and even PJ could see that a high ball would be her weakness. But knowing which pitch to call still baffled her. Thankfully, Karla was playing along, although she still hadn't exactly warmed to PJ.

"You'd better not lose this game for us or you're going to lose

something else." Karla's voice edged into PJ's head as she relayed the signal. If it weren't for Morgan calling the shots, PJ had no doubt she'd be tussling with Karla in the dirt again, no amount of waxing on or off saving her as Karla loosened the teeth in her jaw.

No wonder Dally had to be so tough.

Karla glared at her and threw the ball hard over the plate. PJ watched it curve in and nabbed it as the bat whooshed over her head.

"Strike two!"

PJ arrowed it back to Karla, her arm feeling hot, the old adrenaline rippling through her. How she longed to be out at shortstop, in Stacey's position. She loved scooping the ball from the dirt, throwing it on the run, hearing the satisfying whack of the ball connecting with the first baseman's glove.

Morgan gave the signal for a changeup, and PJ shot it to Karla.

"Strike three!" the ump called when the batter whiffed again.

PJ threw the ball back, standing up to stretch as the next batter came to the plate. One out, top of the last inning, the Rockets were one run ahead, and the Sting had a runner on second base. They just had to hold them. Behind her, the stands were full, even for a Saturday afternoon, with possibly the entire population of south Minneapolis milling about the three fields. She'd scanned the seats once for Jeremy, but no, he'd kept Dally from attending, as promised.

Probably a good idea. What if Dally's stalker was in the crowd? Sure, she'd all but ruled out Sammy, but there was still Missy Gainer to consider—a very angry Missy, who played shortstop for the Sting and now glared at her from second base. Wow, that *was* purple hair. Bold, striking purple, it matched the run of tattoos down both muscled arms. And the snarl on Missy's face every time she looked at "Dally." At least PJ had kept her cover.

"Batter up!"

The batter stepped up to the plate. Lanky and stiff, she stood as if she might be afraid of the ball or even Karla.

Yeah, well, Karla inspired fear on and off the field.

PJ knelt behind the plate and, confirming with Morgan, signaled for a fastball, low and outside.

It would help her concentration if she didn't keep glancing at Missy scraping the dirt with her feet like a bull.

Or keep reliving Boone's barely cordial tone during yesterday's phone call. Yes, he was still investigating the auto ring, but no, he wasn't going to share information, and mostly he called to see if she might be willing to come to her senses, hang up her PI badge—which she officially hadn't earned yet—and come home.

PJ had spent most of the night listening to the chinchillas, thinking about Jeremy alone with Dally, considering Boone's proposal, worrying about crazy or not-crazy Gabby falling and hurting herself alone in her house, and even bemoaning little Davy playing on the beach with his new grandma, who might be deported thanks to PJ.

PJ should come with a warning label: *Close proximity to PJ Sugar just might cause lifelong damage.*

She kept her focus through two strikes, but as she reached for Karla's pitch, the ball nicked off her glove, skidding into the dirt.

In an explosion of energy, the batter tossed her bat and took off for first base.

Shoot! PJ lunged for the ball, missed, and scooped it up again, only to hear the umpire yell, "Safe!"

When she turned, Missy had advanced to third. And as the skinny girl on first base gripped her knees, hauling in breaths, PJ had a blinding vision of Karla grinding her bones into dust.

"Sorry!" she hollered as she threw it back.

Karla plucked it out of the sky and narrowed her eyes. "C'mon, Catch! Look alive!"

PJ shot a glance into the gallery, her heart jump-starting. But no, not Jeremy. And not Dally.

"Keep your eye on the ball!"

Keep your eye on the ball. Right.

PJ hit her mitt a couple times, grabbed Morgan's call for the plate crowder, and sent it off to Karla.

The ball came flying in, inside, and the batter whiffed it.

PJ grabbed it, bobbling it just a second. Threw it back.

Morgan signaled for an inside drop ball.

PJ watched Karla receive it, nod slightly, and size up the batter.

The ball smacked into her glove. "Ball!"

Karla's glare landed—thankfully—on the umpire. PJ returned the ball, biting back words of encouragement, like "In the pocket now, Karla."

She looked to Morgan and saw that Sammy had appeared, leaning against the side of the dugout chatting up Morgan. Apparently he didn't realize his girlfriend was secretly playing catcher this game.

C'mon, Morgan, give me the signal.

Karla was staring at her, waiting. But even as PJ watched, Morgan turned and looked at PJ, mouth open. Then something that seemed dangerously like accusation entered her eyes.

Behind her, Sammy was talking fast, using his hands, but Morgan just stared at PJ.

What now? PJ waited.

Morgan cocked her head but gave no signal.

Fine. She could probably call the pitch. PJ signaled for a fastball.

Karla shook her head just slightly.

PJ signaled again.

Karla stepped back and fired it into the pocket.

"Ball two!"

"Ball?" PJ stood. "It was right there."

"It was inside, Catch. Just play the game." The ump seemed unfazed by PJ's dark look. Or perhaps she just wasn't as good at it as Karla.

"She's crowding the plate. Of course it looks inside. But it was right on the money."

"You want to play or get thrown out of the game?"

Was he giving her choices? Because what PJ really wanted was to rewind to about two weeks ago to the parking lot outside the Windy Oaks Motel and send *Jeremy* out for donuts. Apparently, she belonged in her cute little Bug—and how she missed it now—watching life from a safe distance.

PJ threw the ball to Karla. Crouched again. Shot a look at Morgan, who seemed to be trying to incinerate her with a glare.

Signaling for a screwball, PJ held her breath until it dropped beautifully into her glove.

"Strike two!"

PJ returned the ball, seeing movement at first base. Skinny wanted to steal—PJ could see it in her eyes. But her gaze shifted to Morgan, who now turned and slapped Sammy across the face.

He barely flinched before he connected his gaze with PJ's. Oh no.

But she didn't have time to put the pieces together, to name her instincts, because the batter moved, sliding back into the box.

If PJ signaled another screwball, the batter would connect and send it into the next field and the sixth-grade Little Leaguers. . . .

PJ kept her gaze off Morgan and guessed wildly. How about an outside curve?

Karla pursed her lips.

PJ held her breath. *C'mon, Karla, show a little trust.*

The ball sailed in, a beautiful outside curve that would be a strike regardless of how blind the umpire might be.

The batter grazed the ball and it popped up.

PJ expected it and snatched it on the way down. She was already on her feet, already throwing to second. "Get down!"

Karla ducked as the ball shot to second base, where the second baseman grabbed it and tagged Skinny just as she hit the dirt.

"PJ, look out!"

She didn't have time to figure out the voice or who might be blowing her cover, just to react as she turned and saw Missy charging her. She smacked into her, full body contact. PJ flew back, slammed against the wire cage, and slumped to the dirt.

"Out! Out! No run!"

Ow.

The stands erupted. Stacey came barreling across the field, whooping. "You did it!"

Everything hurt as PJ groped for her lost breath.

Karla reached her first. "Good throw!" She may have even been wearing a hint of a smile.

PJ was checking for broken bones as she met Karla's grip. The brawler hauled her to her feet.

"You okay?" Karla said, but her words were barely out before Stacey took PJ down again in an enthusiastic jump.

"Two outs! You saved the game!"

"Ow!"

Stacey thumped her twice on her catcher's padding. "Now that's my Dally!" She winked, grinning.

"Good job, Dally." The voice came from behind the crowd, which parted for Missy, who stood over her, shaking her head. "I see you still have your skills on the field—I hope you still got it for my cut and color next week." She whipped off her hat, shaking out all that purple hair like ribbons off a package. "I'm counting on you to do what you promised and turn my mess bloodred." She held out her hand to high-five PJ, who met it with a smack, trying to keep up.

She remembered the run-in between Missy and Dally that Morgan had recounted. Maybe Morgan *had* heard the word *die*. Only, not so much *die* as . . . *dye*. Missy certainly didn't look like she wanted to take Dally out into the back alley and finish the job she started a week ago. Or today, at home plate.

Cross Missy off her list of Dally-napping suspects.

"Good game, Catch."

The low voice parted the jubilation and found her heartbeat. Boone.

He suddenly appeared above her, a shadow of concern and pride, holding a half sack of popcorn. As he extended his hand to pull her to her feet, something sweet and warm filled her chest.

Boone? Here? The question came out before she could censor her tone. "What are you doing here?"

His smile fell, as if she'd accused him of stalking.

"Is this your boyfriend?" Stacey came up behind her, stuck her hand out to Boone, who looked at PJ as if she'd slapped him. "Hi, I'm Stacey."

"That's not Dally's boyfriend. He's a cop. And he's got dark hair." Missy winked, nudging her. "Unless you got someone new, Dally?"

A cop. How did she know Boone was a cop?

Wait. *"That's not Dally's boyfriend."* Which meant she was talking about Dally's real boyfriend. A cop. A *cop*?

"Yep, she's definitely moved on." Morgan pushed past Missy and Stacey, murder in her eyes. "'Give him a chance, Morgan . . . ,'" she mimicked. "What was that?"

PJ looked at her, past her to Sammy, standing with his hands in his pockets. He gave a small shake of his head.

Oh, Sammy, just tell her the truth. "I don't know what you're talking about, Morgan."

"You've been seeing him, haven't you?"

Around them, the jubilation ceased. Eyes bored into her, accusing. "N-no, Morgan, of course not!"

"I'm not stupid. I saw someone walking out of his grandma's backyard just last night arm in arm with Sammy."

PJ shot a glance at Sammy as her mind replayed the stroll to the street, the car screeching away from the curb. Sammy shook his head, panic on his face.

"But the fact is, it was you, wasn't it?" Morgan continued. "Yet, according to Sammy, he hasn't even laid eyes on you. Which makes me wonder—what are you two hiding?"

Uh-oh.

PJ's mouth opened. Sammy's eyes widened as if trying to laser some message into her brain. She shot a look to a frowning Stacey and avoided Karla and her back-alley expression. PJ didn't have the courage to glance at Boone. "That's not true, Morgan. I—Sammy—we . . . can explain."

"*We?* I knew it. I should have never trusted you." Morgan raised her hands as if to strangle . . . PJ, herself, Sammy? PJ didn't know, but she stood there, tripping over the explanations, horrified at the deceit that choked off her voice. "What was all that 'oh, Morgan, give him a chance' noise? I'm such an idiot."

"Morgan—" PJ reached out to her but Morgan stepped away, something feral in her eyes.

"Stay away from me." She turned and broke through the crowd.

"Um, maybe you shouldn't come out for pizza with us," Stacey said softly. "Good throw, though."

"Stacey—"

Stacey waved halfheartedly. "Later . . . Dally."

Oh, perfect. PJ hazarded a glance at Boone. He'd crumpled his popcorn bag, his lips a tight line. She grabbed his forearm as he turned away. "It's not true."

"Is this why you're so surprised to see me?"

"No! I . . . just meant I didn't know you were going to come to the game."

He didn't smile. "I can leave."

She wasn't making this better. And it scared her suddenly, how much she didn't want him to leave. How relieved she'd been to see him. How delighted. "No . . . I didn't mean it like that."

His smile returned slowly, but it unknotted the fist in her chest.

"You don't believe her, do you?" PJ shot a glance at Morgan, now trying to keep Sammy from helping her hobble to the car. From this vantage point, he appeared to be attempting, vainly, to dig himself out of trouble.

Boone slid an arm around her shoulders. "Give me more credit than that."

Sometimes Boone was so easy to love.

"Need some pizza . . . uh, Dally?"

She smiled at him, at the twinkle in his eye. "You know me too well."

His hand slipped into hers. "Please don't forget that."

Chapter TWENTY

"That was some play. You still got it, Sugar," Boone said as he opened the door to his Mustang. He tugged on her hat as she climbed in. "And you're kinda cute with the long black braids. You might need to keep the wig when this gig is over."

"For more undercover gigs?"

He slid into the driver's side. "Forget I said that."

"Ah, but you did. Which means you're starting to accept the truth."

She still couldn't believe that Boone had shown up to watch her game. And the fact that he'd seen her winning throw . . . Whatever he said, he still rooted for her.

"*Accept* is such a wide term. Let's say, *realize*. I wouldn't even stretch it to *tolerate*."

"Using your charm again, huh?"

"As much as I can spare." He pulled away from the ballpark. "Want to change clothes?"

"No—I have an idea. Let's pick up a pizza from Hal's, take it over to Connie's. I need a peace offering."

"You might need more than pizza, Sugar. Connie's still fuming about everything that happened with Boris."

PJ toed off her shoes, leaned back, and put her feet up on the dash. "That's an understatement. But at the moment I'm more concerned about Gabby. Last night she came out into the rain sort of confused. She seemed to get me mixed up with Dally."

"Isn't that the point?"

"She knows who I really am. And it's more than confusion. I caught her acting out a scene from *Please Don't Eat the Daisies* earlier this week, almost as if she believed it."

"*Please Don't Eat the Daisies?*"

"It's a Doris Day movie. Who, by the way, Gabby says she knew." PJ sighed. "I'm worried that all this time she *has* been losing her mind. Maybe just a little. And right now she could be lighting something on fire, maybe wandering around, getting lost. The first time we met, she must have been outside—otherwise, how could she have heard me screaming? It's always bugged me."

"She *is* pretty old. What is she, a hundred?"

"No one could ever accuse you of being politically correct, could they?"

"Sorry."

"The woman is more spry than I could ever hope to be. She's over eighty, though."

"Then it's time for her mind to give out. It happens."

She glanced at him, wondering if he was thinking about his mother. Only his mother's mind had fractured long before even her fifties and had more to do with her daily dose of vodka martinis than her age.

"Evelyn, Gabby's daughter, is looking for a reason to put her in a home. And I hate to be the one who gives it to her." PJ took off her cap, longing to take off the wig too. Soon.

Boone reached over, patted her knee. "That's the one thing we can count on. Your good intentions."

"What do they say about the road to hell . . . ?" PJ covered her face with her hands. "Not only that, but I blamed Missy and Sammy for kidnapping me, and now I don't think it's either of them. I suppose it could be this Roy fella that Gabby saw, although if she's losing her mind, who knows what she saw? Besides, apparently, he's a *cop*."

"A *cop* is after you?"

"Besides you, I mean."

"I'm not after you. Or at least . . . whatever. You're not going back to Dally's tonight. Maybe never."

Great. She said nothing as they merged onto 394 toward Kellogg. Finally, "Why did you come out to the game, anyway?"

Again, he didn't speak. Instead he drummed his fingers on the steering wheel.

She watched his chest rise and fall, and hers tightened. "Is it Boris?"

He shook his head. Pursed his lips. Sighed.

"You're freaking me out."

"It's us, Peej. It's me." He tapped his brakes as they exited at the Kellogg sign.

The noise in the car cut in half, and she could nearly hear her own heart beating. *Us? Me?*

"Maybe I am accepting some truths. Like . . . you're not

ready." He glanced at her. "And I'm afraid of pushing you away."

PJ met his eyes and nodded. "It's not that I don't love you, Boone."

"Feels that way." His jaw tightened. "Frankly, I'm not sure you even want me in your world."

"That's not true. You can't believe that. Really?" She reached over and wove her fingers through his.

"When I came up to you at the game, I thought maybe you were expecting someone else."

He let her fill in the blank, but by his expression, it wasn't hard for her to guess whom he assumed she'd expected. "No, Boone, I was just surprised. . . . I didn't think you knew about my game."

He sighed. "I think . . . What if I took off the pressure? What if I . . . withdrew my proposal?"

She yanked her hand away. "You can't do that."

"I can't?" He glanced at her. "I think I can."

"No, you can't. It's like . . . taking back a Christmas gift."

"One that you haven't opened yet."

"Yes, but you put it under the tree with my name on it—you can't just take it back. It's unethical." She narrowed her eyes at him. "Is it even legal?"

Although she couldn't see his eyes behind his dark glasses, she could imagine them going wide. He managed to keep his smirk from turning into a smile. "Yes. I think it's legal."

PJ folded her arms. "It shouldn't be. You give a girl a proposal, she has the right to answer it before you yank it away."

"Then answer me," he said softly.

PJ closed her eyes.

He turned in to Hal's and got out. "I'll pick up a couple of take-and-bakes."

"And a couple two-liters, please," she mumbled.

He disappeared into Hal's.

"Then answer me."

"Answer me."

She stared at the sky, still pale blue like Boone's eyes, no cloud in sight. Wasn't this what she wanted? Her guy showing up at her softball games, cheering her on, buying her pizza? wanting to spend the rest of his life with her?

He deserved an answer.

Or maybe she didn't deserve his proposal.

He returned, holding the two-liters under one arm, balancing two pizzas with the other.

She reached for the pizzas, set them on the backseat, then grabbed the sodas and cradled them in her lap.

They didn't speak as they drove to Connie's.

Boone pulled up. Stopped the car. "I need an answer or I'm taking it back."

"Which is sort of an answer too."

"No. I put out the question. But I can't live waiting for an answer. It . . . hurts too much."

She looked at the floorboards. "I never wanted to hurt you."

"I know, Peej. Maybe it's just too soon. Maybe we need more time."

Yes, maybe. Although, deep inside, in a place she didn't want to acknowledge, a dark truth lingered. Time might not be enough. She was never going back to the person she had been.

She swallowed and got out of the car. "Are you coming in?"

He ground his jaw tight. "Do you want me to?"

She stared at him, saw everything she'd always dreamed of in his beautiful blue eyes—love, longing, even regret.

Oh, it wasn't supposed to be like this. She was supposed to return to Kellogg, fling herself into Boone's open arms, and feel a sort of completion, as if she'd come full circle. But even as he looked away, his eyes closing, as the summer heat beaded on the back of her neck, she tasted the chill building between them, like the trudge from autumn to winter, subtle but turning their relationship from something sweet and heady to crisp and icy.

She opened her mouth, but it stuck there, her pleading for him to understand. To believe in her. To look forward instead of behind.

She didn't look at him as she turned and walked up the stairs, every step tearing her heart from her chest.

Connie's front door was unlocked, and PJ shoved one two-liter under her arm as she pushed it open.

An angry voice spilled out. "—following me, Boris. I saw you."

PJ stilled just inside the door. Casey Whitlow, his outline blocking a view of Boris, stood in the kitchen, his back to her. Sweat dribbled down the back of his white T-shirt, and he held out his hand as if he held—

"I should just shoot you now."

A gasp, and PJ's gaze turned toward Vera, clutching Davy to her, hands over his chest, her own eyes wide. Clearly they'd just come in from the backyard, what with Vera's gardening shirt covered in dirt and Davy in a swimsuit, dripping wet from the sprinkler.

Where was Connie? and Sergei?

Casey let out a word that should have made Vera cover Davy's ears; then he motioned them closer with his gun.

PJ shook her head when Vera glanced at her. Thankfully, Casey didn't turn as Vera shuffled over to Boris. PJ crept inside, sidling over to the stairs, heart in her throat.

Outside, she heard Boone's car pull away. *No!* Why hadn't she insisted he come in?

"Did you think I wouldn't see you sneaking around my lot, Boris? following me? What did you think you saw?"

She wasn't sure where to move. Or how. And from this position, PJ spied Casey's weapon—a gun that looked a lot like Boone's Glock.

"Nichevo," Boris said, but his eyes didn't look like they'd seen nothing. No, they looked like twenty years of Russian law enforcement, hard and dark as Boris moved in front of his wife, his grandchild. He didn't even seem to be breathing hard.

"Speak English."

"I no see anyzing," Boris said quietly. He held his hands up, but he wore a flinty look that made PJ realize that only Casey's gun gave the younger man an advantage.

Until Davy caught sight of her from the corner of his eye.

"Auntie PJ!" Davy ripped free from Vera's hold and lunged toward her before Boris or even Casey could stop him.

Casey turned, his dark eyes narrowing on PJ even as she caught Davy with one arm and turned him away. "Run upstairs and play, little man," she said softly.

Davy looked at her for a moment, then to her shock, ran upstairs. She heard a door slam, shaking the house.

And then only the thunder of her own heartbeat.

"Welcome home, PJ," Casey said in an oily tone.

PJ surrendered when he motioned her into the kitchen with his gun. She had set down one bottle of soda but still clutched the second in a death grip.

"What are you doing, Casey?"

Sweat dribbled down from the edge of his cap, a trickle of stress, dragging with it the sludge of grease. He was a hostage taker on edge, the kind she'd seen in movies or on *Law & Order*—she probably watched that too often—who ended up shooting his victims before turning the gun on himself. What was the first rule of hostage negotiation? Oh no— she hadn't gotten that far in her field manual. She was still on "How to Lose a Tail."

Or maybe, how to lose a man. If only she'd had an answer for Boone, he'd be right here. . . .

"I'm trying to figure out why your Russian here is following me."

"Maybe he likes you. . . . Nah, that can't be it." Oh, she couldn't help it! Why did she have such a stupid mouth?

Or worse, why hadn't she listened to her instincts about Casey and Allison and blabbed them to Boone? She was so good at doing it for every other crazy thought.

"They found her body last night in the Kellogg harbor."

Probably now wasn't the time to accuse Casey of Allison Miller's death. But she put it all into her eyes as she obeyed and sidled up to Vera.

"I saw him following me—in his flashy black Vic."

Her Crown Vic? It wasn't flashy. Just . . . large.

Boris didn't move. Not a muscle in his face or his body.

Casey lifted the gun, pressing it against Boris's forehead. "Who are you working for?"

Everything inside PJ coiled tight.

Vera gasped.

Boris's jaw twitched.

Oh, why hadn't she asked Boone to come in? Why . . . ? Except . . .

"She was working for me—sort of an informant on an investigation."

Her breath caught. *Boone had sent Boris to track down his car thieves.* Just like he'd used Allison as a source of information.

Boris was working for *Boone.*

"No vone."

Boris said it so softly, nonplussed, that PJ had no doubt he had a past buried somewhere in Russia that said he knew exactly how to stare down death.

Vera put a hand over her heart.

"Then I'll start with her." Casey turned the gun on Vera and, with the smallest of breaths in, pulled the trigger.

Except, PJ had seen his breath, and right before the shot cracked the air, she swung her soda bottle. Up and around like a fast pitch, it came down across Casey's arm, just like Jeremy had taught her.

Granite chipped off the counter in a spray of needle-thin shards.

Vera screamed.

Boris leaped. He slammed Casey onto the tile floor, cracking his head against the surface. He finished off with a swing across Casey's jaw that made PJ wince.

And right then Boone flew in from wherever he'd been

hiding and yanked the gun from Casey's hand. Boris landed another punch before he let Boone haul him off.

Vera leaped into Boris's arms as Boone tucked the gun into his belt. "Don't move, Casey. For your own good. I have a feeling he's not quite done yet."

Casey wiped the blood from the corner of his mouth but didn't move.

"What are you doing here?" PJ sputtered. "I thought—"

Boone gave her an enigmatic look. "You left the pizza in my car." He lifted a shoulder. "You may not love me, but I didn't want you to hate me."

Her mouth opened. "Boone, I don't—"

"What is going *on*?" Connie stood in the doorway, clutching a bag of groceries.

Sergei bumped up behind her, looking suddenly ferocious as he stared first at his mother weeping in his father's arms, then at Casey lying on the floor.

Boone hauled Casey to his feet. "It's all over, Connie," he said, his voice turning professional.

Connie dropped her groceries right there on the floor. "Where's Davy?"

"He's upstairs," PJ said, although she stayed right where she was. Connie had a nearly rabid look on her face as she took the stairs two at a time.

Sergei debated half a second, then charged into the kitchen. "Who iz zis?"

Boris answered in Russian, which, from the wide-eyed, then furious look on Sergei's face, PJ assumed must be vibrantly colorful. She did pick up a few words. Like *gun*. And *shpeon* was easily translatable to "spy."

Even Boone seemed to be getting the gist of the conversation, because he glanced at PJ with a tight-lipped look. "I had no idea he'd take it this far."

"Who, Boris or Casey? Because even I remember Ally's dead body, Boone. Did you think that if Casey found out about Boris, he wouldn't come after him? and *my family*?" She heard sirens in the distance.

Boone's jaw tightened. "I'm sorry."

"Not half as sorry as I am." As if to punctuate her words, Connie thumped down the stairs, or rather tripped, nearly falling as she wrestled an armload of PJ's belongings, spewing clothes on her descent. Connie careened toward the door and banged it open, and then, with all the force in her size-four body, flung the pile out into the yard.

As if magnetized to her possessions, PJ drifted toward the door, her breath trapped inside her chest as Connie whirled, shoved past her, and ran again up the stairs.

She nearly took out Davy, who stood on the landing, one whitened hand clutching the railing.

The family behind PJ had gone silent. So had Boone.

"Connie?" PJ started, not sure what she should go after first—her laundry strewn over the front steps and across the rosebushes, or Connie, who thumped around upstairs, probably in PJ's bedroom.

PJ had just turned toward the stairs when Connie reappeared, this time holding one of her expensive 500-thread-count sheets by the corners, the rest of PJ's clothing, toiletries, and shoes shoved inside. She didn't even glance PJ's way as she linebackered past her and, in an outstanding athletic move that rivaled an Olympic discus thrower, flung the remainder of PJ's existence out the door.

PJ tried to breathe, her eyes blurring.

Connie whirled, her chest rising and falling, her long hair wild around her head, her skin blotchy and red. She opened her mouth, and for a long, painful moment, nothing emerged.

PJ lunged for the opening. "Connie, I—"

"Don't, PJ. Don't. Speak." She lifted her gaze to Davy and fixed it there as she said quietly, *too* quietly—so much that it felt like a scalpel, clean and neat and slicing PJ to the bone— "Get out."

✳ ✳ ✳

At least she had a sheet. And her Chuck Taylor sneakers. And at least two pairs of jeans. She might have left a T-shirt in the garden, wedged behind the roses, but by the time she'd fished out all her visible clothing, the sky overhead was glazing dark, only a few stars emerging to watch as she crammed her possessions into the trunk of her Vic.

She still wore her softball uniform and had unearthed a change of clothes before climbing into the backseat, where, under the cover of the creeping darkness, she put on a pair of worn jeans, her flip-flops, and a tank. Virtually the same attire she'd worn when she had slunk back into Kellogg. And probably the same outfit she would wear as she crept out again, hopefully without sirens and red lights neoning in her rearview mirror.

Boone had worn the look of a felon, barely casting an eye at PJ picking up her skivvies from the lawn as he'd toted Casey down the steps and into a waiting cruiser he'd called to take him to the station. Where Casey would be charged with the murder of Allison Miller, former girlfriend, as well as the attempted murder of Boris and very possibly Davy and Vera.

PJ didn't blame Connie for kicking her out of the house. Not really. She had practically tempted trouble to Connie's door, not once but twice in the same summer. She adjusted the front seat, her nose curling at the telltale odor of Boris's stakeout hours in her car. Nice. She dried her cheeks with the palm of her hand, then motored out into the night, away from the lights leering from Connie's Craftsman home.

She couldn't help but look. Nope. No one silhouetted in the door to wave good-bye.

She should just keep driving. Head west, back to California, or maybe east this time, start over in New York City. She couldn't return to Dally's—not with a real-life stalker waiting to hunt her down, now that Missy and Sammy were no longer suspects.

Truly, now she would have to sleep in the Vic. Talk about foresight.

She crawled down Main Street, braking as she passed the beach and then suddenly turning in.

Parking and getting out, she kicked off her flip-flops and barefooted her way across the cool, forgiving sand. Under the moonlight, the sailboats sliced the night like cutlery, the gentle lap of the lake licking against their hulls. Her stomach leaped at the bewitching smells from Hal's Pizzeria and the hickory off the grills down at Sunsets. But food would only dull her pain.

Going to the play area, she sat on the merry-go-round, pushing it with one foot.

Round and round.

Always ending in the same place.

In the distance across the grassy park, she spied movement and after a while recognized the hobo of Kellogg, a bum who lived under the Maximilian Bay Bridge down the road. He peered in garbage cans, searching for morsels. PJ dug into her pocket. She had a couple bucks left from the twenty Jeremy had given her for donuts nearly two weeks ago. One homeless person should look out for the next.

How did one become homeless, exactly?

Perhaps in her case it was easy to pinpoint—she'd become homeless because she'd alienated everyone in her world. Connie and her mother. Boone, whose heart she'd handled with all the sensitivity of a bulldozer, not realizing how easily it might crumble in her grip. Maybe it had always been that fragile. She had just never realized her own power.

Even Jeremy hadn't called her in nearly three days.

She stopped the merry-go-round—her stomach had taken on the disposition of a beached lake trout—and pushed off, slinking down into the soft sand. She scooped up a handful, let it run between her fingers, wincing at the memory of Davy's wide eyes as Casey held a gun on him.

Dear Lord, what have I done?

She buried her face in her arms folded across her updrawn knees and closed her eyes, seeing Boone's wounded expression as she'd left the car. As she'd told him no, even without words.

In the lot behind her, a car pulled in. For a wild moment, she hoped it might be Boone coming to look for her. But the car circled and drove away, ignoring the sobbing of the woman marooned on the Kellogg city beach.

"Are you okay, ma'am?"

She turned at the voice, gentler than she'd expect from someone with his attire—a pair of ragged jeans and an Army jacket.

The Kellogg hobo stared at her, concern in his eyes. "You're bleeding." He pointed to her forehead.

Huh? She lifted her hand to her head. Rubbed it. Sure enough, it came away red. Only . . . "No, it's just paint." Her tears had moistened the skin on her arm and smeared her body art bloodred. She stared at it, dark and oily on her hand. What had Stacey said about Dally's motto? *"Every day the choices you make tell you who and what you are."*

Her choices had told her that she was a troublemaker. A woman who lived from one mistake to the next. Who messed up the lives of the people she loved. So much for being a new, different person, one who didn't litter mistakes in her wake. Maybe Boone was right: she'd always be the girl from the past.

"You sure you're okay?" The hobo was still standing over her. He appeared younger than she'd thought—maybe in his early sixties, although his eyes seemed ancient.

"I . . . uh, yeah." She dug into her pocket, held out the cash. "This is for you."

He frowned at her.

"Please. I wish I had more."

He nodded, and for a second she thought his gaze glistened in the moonlight.

"Thank you." He took the money, considering her for a long moment. Then he pulled out a wadded handkerchief from his pocket. He barely looked at her as he handed it over. "To wash off the blood."

She took it, feeling a sort of pity—she wasn't sure for whom—as he shuffled away.

Maybe she didn't want to wash it off. Maybe she wanted the reminder, just like Dally, of her mistakes. She stared at the painted mess on her arm. Another beautiful thing she'd destroyed.

"But it isn't without struggle, hence the blood, despite the beauty."

She shook her head, laying her head again into her hands, not caring that, thanks to the red and green paint, she'd probably end up looking bruised.

At least her outside would match her inside.

The wind shivered through the trees and prickled her skin as the lake turned inky.

Why was it so hard to get it right? Why did she have to end every day staring at the ceiling, cataloging her failures? Why did she always feel . . . less?

In her pocket, her cell phone vibrated. She fished it out and debated a long moment before she opened it. Her voice sounded more tired than she meant. "Hi, Jeremy."

"Where are you?" His tone came out brisk, worried.

"Watching ducks waddle across the beach."

Silence. "Lee called. Said you hadn't been at the house for a while. He was worried."

Lee was worried. At least someone cared if she ended up in the trunk of a car. She watched as the family of ducks meandered near, picking at the debris of the beach. They crossed into the limelight, then slipped into the watery trail of luminescence. The moon hovered just above the horizon, a brilliant orange ball shooting out a trail of light like a golden carpet, undeterred by the hiccups and ripples of the black terrain.

Beckoning.

"You okay, Sugar?"

"I don't think I can do this, Jeremy."

She closed her eyes, not sure how the words had edged out, but now that they had, feeling with them a sort of release. A comfortableness. Failure had become so safe, honed over years of quitting and moving on.

"What are you talking about?"

She drew a finger across the sand. "I think I need to leave."

"PJ—"

"No, listen, Jeremy. Two more days and Dally will testify. Even if someone figures out she's gone, they won't find you. *I* don't even know where you are."

"That's not the point."

"I can't do this job. I make mistakes everywhere I turn, accusing people, getting people into trouble. Boone's right. I'm nothing but trouble."

She heard him swallow on the other end. "Don't do it, Princess."

"Don't call me that."

"Why not? That's how I see you. I don't know why you can't accept it."

"Because you don't know me."

"I don't know the donut-throwing, karate-wannabe, former-accused-arsonist you? What you can't accept is that I *do* know you. And I like you not *anyway* but *because* of the crazy you. And I believe in you, Sugar."

She wiped her cheeks, probably smearing red paint down her face. "You don't mean that."

"Yes, yes I do."

"You shouldn't."

Silence. "Tell me what happened."

She stared out into the darkness, at the waves clawing the shore. It reminded her of the dream she'd had—had it been over a week ago? How she'd been at the helm of the car, gunning after herself.

"Boris worked undercover for Boone, trying to solve that car-theft ring, and Casey found out and came after him, and he held up my family. Davy, at the end of a gun, again."

Jeremy made a little noise that matched the pain in her heart.

"So Connie threw me out."

"Oh, PJ, I'm sorry. Why didn't you call me?"

She wrapped her hand around her ankle like the rope in the dream tethering her from her escape. "I was embarrassed. Not only that, but I'm pretty sure that Missy or Sammy didn't kidnap me, which means there's someone else after Dally—in fact, it might even be her boyfriend, a guy named Roy or Guy. Gabby said she saw him a couple days ago. But . . . well, who knows, really, because Gabby could be dreaming the whole thing."

"Dreaming it? What, is there something wrong with Gabby?"

"I think so. She thinks she lives in a movie."

"Depends on which movie."

"Jeremy . . ."

"Okay, so we're sticking with depression. No humor for you."

"Depression's all I got. Why can't I get this right? What is wrong with me?"

"Nothing. And everything. You're human. And if you didn't make a few mistakes, you wouldn't need God, would you?"

She'd forgotten that Jeremy shared more than her profession and penchant for trouble. He also knew about forgiveness and what it felt like to be a person changed by grace, longing to live every moment for Christ. "Jeremy, how long have you been a Christian?"

"Long enough to know that whenever I think I've got it right, then I need to watch out. That's usually a couple steps before I fall on my face."

"And . . . then what?" Off in the distance, she made out the form of the hobo digging through the Dumpster next to Sunsets.

"Then you crawl on your knees to the throne of grace, because God loves you and wants to save you."

She caught her breath. "Gabby said almost the same thing to me. 'Draw with confidence to the throne of grace, because I promise you'll find mercy.' Only . . . why would God keep on bailing me out? Over and over and over. He's got to be tired of me by now."

Jeremy drew in a long breath. "God is totally *other*, PJ. He's different from anything we have ever known. Which means you can't base God's actions on how you see yourself. You're living as if you're still chained to the past. Don't you know you're free? It's time to lift your eyes off your failures and put them on the truth."

She heard Gabby's voice again: *"Stop looking at your feet. You'll only trip over them."*

His voice softened. "'Draw with confidence' means with wild boldness. Like God is going to catch you."

The image of Davy leaping from the top step sluiced into PJ's mind.

"That's grace, Princess. It's being caught by God. Because He wants to."

"I wish I could believe that. . . ."

In the silence, the waves lapped the shore. A wrapper tumbled by, pushed by the wind.

Finally, "Oh, PJ, I wish you could see what I see."

"I wish I could see it too." She winced even as she said it, wishing the wind might snatch the words away.

"Don't leave. I know it's the easy thing. I know it's the familiar thing. But you don't want to . . . and I don't want you to."

She didn't even have a quip for him, something about fetching coffee or buying donuts.

"You still there?"

"For now."

"Just be careful, okay? And don't run away on me. I . . . need you, Princess."

He hung up before she could—before she wanted to—protest. She closed the phone. Tapped it against her knee.

The throne of grace.

"I'm sorry I just keep messing up, Lord." She drew in a breath, smelling the fresh water, the night scent as it combed the trees. "I'm so sorry."

"Draw with confidence . . ."

She heard the words like the wind, softly, and closed her eyes, "Help me to jump . . . like Davy, into Your arms."

Tracing the moonlight across the dark plain of the water, PJ slowly realized that as she'd sat, it had stretched out like a spotlight and puddled her in the middle.

Chapter TWENTY-ONE

PJ veered off Highway 35 south, away from a new beginning and onto the exit that led her, hopefully surreptitiously, back to Dally's neighborhood.

"Don't run away on me. I . . . need you, Princess."

A streetlamp poured light down on the empty parking spot in front of Gabby's that the Charger normally occupied. She drifted up to the curb, parked, and got out. Only a glow in the back of Gabby's house—the kitchen lights, probably— suggested someone was home.

Dally's place collected shadows, emanating danger as it sat in darkness, the streetlamp just barely illuminating the porch. PJ paused at the entrance to the walk and took a second to search for Lee. Sure enough, she spotted his car, three down and across the street, out of the hover of the lamplight. She peered toward it but couldn't make out his outline.

Next door, the rottweiler lounged on the porch. He lifted

his head and let out one bark as she advanced up Dally's walk. Apparently she wasn't worth the energy of a full-out alert anymore.

Movement on the porch stilled her. She froze, halfway up the walk. A form stood in the darkness, someone by the front door. "Hello?"

Where was her two-liter when she needed it? She gripped her phone like a Mace bottle. "Who's there?"

The figure stepped off the porch and into the light. Lee.

Relief whooshed through her, shaking her limbs. "You scared me."

"Where've you been?" He looked tired, despite his clean-shaven chin. In this light—and in his suit coat and tie, with the badge at his belt, the bulk of his shoulder holster—he reminded her a little of Boone in his full detective regalia. His cool eyes scraped over her. "Are you okay?"

She came onto the porch, brushing passed him. "I'm fine." She stopped and looked at him, even as she pulled out her key. "You haven't seen any . . . strange guys around here, have you?"

"Why?"

She lifted a shoulder, eyeing again the rottweiler, who watched them with lazy, unconcerned eyes. Funny that he wasn't clawing at the fence to take out a piece of Lee's backside.

"I'll bet you're getting tired of this gig, huh? All for a woman who won't even appreciate it," Lee said.

"I think Dally appreciates it," PJ said.

"Why? Have you talked to her?"

"No, but Jeremy has."

"Really? Where is Jeremy?"

She put her key into the lock. "He won't tell me."

"Yeah," Lee said quietly. "He won't tell me either."

She opened the door, then flicked on the light. "That's how PIs are—secretive."

She was about to close the door behind her, but Lee stepped into the frame. "I think you should call him."

"No, Lee. He's busy. Besides, you're here."

He shut the door slowly, turning and closing in on her space.

That's when she smelled it, a mentholated odor that . . . seemed . . . No, it couldn't be . . .

She looked at him as her heart thudded.

"Apparently he's a cop." Her own voice thundered in her head even as the missing photograph of Dally and her boyfriend in South Dakota swept into her mind. It had gone missing right after the second break-in.

She stared at dark, tall Lee, who looked like a . . . *cop*, who had been here . . . too many times, because once was enough for Gabby to recognize him. Lee, from Chicago, who had helped Dally relocate, who knew her whereabouts . . . as if he were keeping . . . tabs on her. . . .

"She thinks that one of Finch's contacts is after her. . . ."

"Another witness got killed . . ."

Lee, who said he'd *seen* PJ get shoved into the trunk of a car but, although he was a trained FBI agent, had lost her whereabouts. Thankfully, he'd called Jeremy twice.

Lee, who wanted to know where Jeremy was so . . . what? He could track down Dally . . . who would get killed while in Jeremy's custody? They'd blame Jeremy. Or at least never suspect Lee. . . .

Or . . . Leroy. As in Leroy Simmons.

Roy.

Why, oh why, couldn't her instincts kick in one minute, even one *millisecond*, sooner? PJ backed away. "What do you want, *Roy*?"

The name registered on his face in a look that sent a chill through her. "So, you figured it out." He pulled the gun from his holster as PJ edged toward the living room. "Now listen. No screaming or anything unprofessional. I just need your help." He gestured at her phone. "Call your boyfriend."

"Boone?"

"Funny." He nodded at her. "Jeremy won't show up for anyone but you."

"You're the one who kidnapped me so that Jeremy would show up and you could track down Dally! Did you steal Missy's car too?"

His mouth tightened to a hard knot.

She took another step toward the chinchilla cage. They began to stir. "I'm not calling Jeremy. Sorry."

"Oh, I think you are." He pointed the gun at her feet. "It'll be hard to wear flip-flops without toes."

Her eyes widened. "Now, listen . . ." She bumped up against the chinchilla cage. One of the fuzzy rats let out a scream. Leroy pointed his gun at it.

"What are you doing? You can't kill a chinchilla!"

He stared at her as if she'd joined PETA. "Yes, I can. They're bred for their fur."

"That's a horrible thing to say." Behind her, she gave the cage a tiny jiggle. The others began to scream. The house filled with sounds of mayhem and terror.

Lee gave her a dark look. "Funny. Make them shut up or I'll shoot them one at a time."

"What am I going to do—sing them a lullaby?"

"Fine." He aimed the gun at the cage.

"No!" PJ turned and shoved the cage over. The door broke open as it spilled onto the floor. The chinchillas streamed from the cage, escaping into the room, screaming, spitting, hiding.

"Oh, my!"

PJ froze, wide-eyed, horrified at the newcomer's voice.

Gabby stood in the kitchen, dressed in fuzzy pink slippers, a housecoat, and pink flannel pajamas, her hair in a hand-kerchief. "The powder puffs are out!"

Lee turned toward her. "What is she doing here?"

Gabby shuffled into the living room. "Oh, I lost him, Dally. I lost Simon. Is he here?" She lifted her feet as chinchillas ran toward her. "Make them stay away!" She stared at PJ, fear on her face.

"It's okay, Gabby," PJ said, casting a glance at Lee, who pursed his lips at her. He'd pulled his gun to the side, out of sight. "Simon isn't here. It's time to go home." She stood and nudged Gabby toward the door. "Go home, Gabby."

Gabby looked at PJ, then to Lee. "I'm a good girl, I am."

Oh no, more movie lines. PJ touched her shoulders. "Go home to Simon. I'll be over later."

But Gabby stopped at the door, peering at her. "Simon isn't there. Just Marlon."

"Right. Brando. Tell him hi." She noticed the kitchen door hung open, the locks, but apparently not the latches, fixed. She watched Gabby pad down the steps.

"Don't even think it, PJ. I'll go after you both."

She turned back to Leroy. "She's crazy, you know. She didn't even see you."

"I know." He motioned her to the sofa. "She's been crazy for a long time. Now dial."

PJ sat down, shoving her hands between her knees. "No."

He sat on the coffee table in front of her, holding the gun loosely. "Yes."

She swallowed, studied him for a long moment. "How can you do this? Dally trusted you. She probably loved you. And you lied to her."

"No, I didn't. I loved her. But she couldn't get it through her head not to testify. If she'd just listened, then none of this would have been necessary. Instead she told me to stay out of her life. . . . She did this. It's her fault. She just couldn't see that she should leave it alone. Otherwise people were going to start getting hurt. Like my family back in Chicago."

PJ clenched her jaw. Swallowed. She stared at Lee but saw Boone, saw his desperation, heard him as he pleaded with her to stop. But she could no sooner stop being a PI than she could stop breathing.

And she needed a man who watched her back. Not blocked her way.

"If you love her, then why didn't you just let her go? Why hurt her?"

"Listen, I was hired to do a job."

"Hired by who?"

"Finch. He just wanted to keep her quiet. But she wouldn't, so it came down to her or me. That other witness—only a reminder to all of us that Billy Finch is still in charge."

Not anymore. PJ stared at her phone.

"Call him."

"No."

"Call him."

She shook her head.

"You are so stupid. Really? Is it worth this?" He leaned forward as if to press the gun to her foot.

She brought down her hammer fist, hitting his arm hard. It swung wide, and he jerked forward.

She grabbed him around the neck and slammed his head down onto her knee. Blood spurted from his nose. Kicking him in the gut, she scrambled over the back of the sofa, landing hard on the floor.

A chinchilla cowering in the corner screamed.

Lee let out a word that put her teeth on edge. "You're not going anywhere!" He leaped before she could find her feet and took her down, scrubbing her chin onto the wooden floor. "You're going to regret that—"

"So will you, dude!"

PJ felt, more than saw, Sammy's presence, as he yanked Lee off her. She winced at the sound of fist against jaw. Lee slammed into the wall, shaking the house, his gun long gone. Sammy clamped a paw over his neck, then twisted Lee around in an arm bar, his face pancaked against the wall. "Don't move."

"That's right!" Morgan hobbled around the sofa, wielding a bat. And behind her, Karla looked like she might want a piece of Lee herself. Stacey appeared in the doorway, carrying a tire iron.

The Rockets to the rescue.

"Oh, for crying in the sink, you already got him!" Gabby appeared in the door behind Stacey, holding her cast-iron skillet.

"Gabby!" PJ sprang to her feet. "Are you okay?"

Gabby smiled. "I still got it. Hollywood didn't know what they were missing."

"No, they didn't, did they?" PJ grinned at her. "You deserve an Oscar, Gabby."

"Sweetie, I may be eccentric, but all the reels are rolling up here."

PJ glanced at Sammy, still looking like a prizefighter as he manhandled Lee.

He gave her a sheepish smile "Grandma called me and said she thought you were in trouble. I was down on one knee . . . pleading my case to Morgan. I asked her to marry me."

She had to give him points for perseverance. PJ turned to Morgan. "And?"

"He told me you two were learning how to dance. Is that true?" Morgan still held the bat.

"Gabby was teaching us," PJ said, suppressing the urge to ease the weapon from Morgan's hand. Thankfully, she lowered it as sirens wailed in the distance. Obviously someone had also called 911.

"Well, fiddle-dee-dee, what's your answer?" Gabby said, her eyes shining.

Morgan dropped the bat. "Yes. My answer is yes." She stepped close to Sammy as if to kiss him.

"Don't you move, mister," Gabby said to Lee, still plastered to the wall. She waggled her skillet at him just in case he might have missed that.

Morgan saw it and instead ran her hand down Sammy's cheek. "Maybe your grandma could teach me to dance too. After all, she has great dance moves. I saw her in that movie with Doris Day, *Romance on the High Seas*—I even have the DVD."

"Oh, pshaw. I was only an extra." But Gabby smiled, tilted her head, batted her eyes.

Only an extra. Hardly.

"Why was he trying to hurt you, PJ?" Near the door Karla radiated a prison-yard menace. She glared at Lee.

The fact that her team had come running when Gabby called nudged something deep inside PJ. She could hardly breathe, cutting her gaze from Karla to Gabby, at the friends rising to her rescue.

"I wish you could see what I see."

"Because my partner is protecting Dally, and L*eroy* here is working for Billy Finch."

PJ got the appropriate response of anger from Gabby. "I knew he wasn't good for Dally."

"All this time he was supposed to be keeping her safe, but he was hired to keep tabs on her, to keep her from talking, and if need be, to kill her before the trial. He was probably thrilled when she put herself into my partner's custody—what better way to deflect attention away from himself when she wound up dead? Maybe he even used her fears to plant the idea that Finch was after her—which he was, of course, but she didn't know how close. But first Lee had to cover up his relationship with Dally. He remembered that she had a picture of him in her bedroom. Which is why he broke in twice. Why he ransacked the house. Even why he threw me into the trunk of a car: so he could follow Jeremy back to Dally and finish her—and maybe us—off.

"Only, why didn't you?" PJ gave Sammy the go-ahead and he added some muscle incentive to her question.

"Because he saw me, and we spent the afternoon tracking down Missy Gainer," Leroy growled.

Oh. Jeremy had believed her.

Gabby squealed as a chinchilla ran over her foot. She reached down and grabbed it. "I think we better get these powder puffs back in their cage before Dally shows up."

As if lured by the prey, Simon bounded out of Dally's bedroom and jumped on top of the television. He let out a mew.

"Mother!"

PJ made a face even as Gabby's countenance fell.

Evelyn.

She stormed into the house, looking like she had been pulled away from a bridge game, and froze, her gaze first landing on Lee, then Sammy, over to PJ, and finally melting into a look of horror at her mother and her cast-iron armament. "What are you doing?"

Gabby glanced at the skillet, lowered it. "Saving PJ."

"Who is PJ?"

PJ raised her hand.

Evelyn stared at her with a sort of openmouthed confusion. "That's Dally, Mother. I'm sorry, but that's the last straw. You are moving, as fast as possible. First you call the house and hang up on me, and now I find you in your pajamas— Sammy, what are you doing to that man? Let him go."

"He's trying to kill . . . ?" Sammy glanced at PJ, as if asking, *Which name?*

"Me," she filled in.

"Mother, you're staying the night with me." Evelyn advanced on her mother. "And away from—" her expression found the word before she did—"this riffraff."

"Hey!" Stacey said, finally coming to life. "PJ—or Dally . . . both!—aren't riffraff."

"Don't start with me, missy," Evelyn said, her finger in Stacey's face. "Whoever that is there has been stealing from my mother—"

"That's not true!" PJ said, more for Dally than herself.

"Are you saying that my mother is losing her mind?" Evelyn rounded on PJ, cocking her head to the side.

Losing her mind? No more than any of the rest of them, probably. But PJ could recognize a trap when she saw it: either Dally was a thief or Gabby was losing her mind. She opened her mouth, not sure what words should come out.

Behind her, something fell to the floor with a clatter. PJ jerked around, catching Simon in the act as he leaped from the television, having swatted the remote control onto the floor.

"You're a scoundrel," Gabby said, scooping him up.

Suddenly PJ looked from Evelyn to Gabby and back. And smiled. "And a thief too, I think."

Evelyn frowned.

PJ ran a hand down Simon's body. "I'll bet if you look behind the television console, and perhaps even the bookshelf, and try behind the bureau, you'll find Gabby's jewelry displaced by Simon the scoundrel here."

Gabby looked at the cat, then at PJ, and beamed.

"PJ!"

The voice echoed into the room a second before Jeremy

appeared in the doorway. Karla took one look at him and moved aside. He thundered past Morgan, past Sammy strong-arming Lee, straight to PJ.

PJ's adrenaline had reset, but Jeremy was still in the red zone, his breath coming fast, as if he'd run all the way from wherever he'd stashed Dally to get to her front door.

Leaving Dally for her.

She smiled, expecting a hug. Or even an "Are you okay?"

Not "What is your problem?" He skidded to a stop, nearly shaking, his eyes ferocious. Snagging her arm, he pulled her into Dally's bedroom, kicking the door shut.

"You're scaring me a little."

Raking a hand through his thinning hair, he rounded on her, saw her smeared arm. "Is that blood?" If it were possible, he looked even more horrified.

She shook her head. "Paint—it's body paint. I'm not hur—"

He reached out and pulled her hard against his chest, both hands curling around her back as he bent down and pressed his lips to the top of her head. She didn't even have time for a breath. She just hung on, wrapping her arms around his waist, feeling his chest rise and fall with relief.

She let herself breathe him in. His strength. The mystery that surrounded him. Even a hint of desperation.

Too soon he moved her away from him. "I swear, you are going to give me a heart attack." He cradled her face in his hands, searching her eyes with his. The hungry look had returned, ravaged his expression, and he didn't even bother to hide it. He shook his head, swallowed, then said almost under his breath, "Oh no, PJ. I'm not ready for this."

Then he leaned down and kissed her.

There was nothing gentle about it, yet she felt the essence of him in his touch—deliberate, protecting, despite the over-powering sense of fear as his mouth moved against hers. Claiming. Devouring.

And she kissed him back, something that surprised her most of all. As if she'd slipped into another persona or maybe one she'd become. She slid her arms up to curl around Jeremy's amazing shoulders. A feeling rushed through her as if she'd been stirred. Although there might have been some screaming way in the back of her head, a tone that sounded like panic or even betrayal, for this moment she ignored it and let herself kiss him.

Jeremy.

Jeremy!

She caught her breath as he broke away from her, his eyes hard in hers. A beat passed between them.

"Oh no," he said again, even as he pressed his forehead against hers.

Oh no? She certainly didn't feel an *oh no*, but then again her world still seemed to be careening . . .

She took a breath and leaned toward him.

"PJ?"

Another voice jerked her away. Boone. For a second she froze, seeing herself caught in Jeremy's embrace.

The whirring inside her stopped as the door slammed open and Boone filled the doorframe. His face went pale as he scanned between PJ and Jeremy. And back. "PJ?"

Jeremy let her go.

And then it was only her, standing alone, and the rest of her life staring at her from both sides of the room.

CHICAGO DRUG DEALER SENTENCED TO 50 YEARS

MINNEAPOLIS (AP)—Billy Finch, notorious drug dealer and gang leader, was sentenced today to fifty years for possession of fifty kilos of cocaine, accessory to first-degree murder, and the attempted murder of his former girlfriend, who agreed to testify against him at his trial.

"I knew Billy wanted to hurt me. I never dreamed he'd use an inside man to do it," key witness Dallas Morrison stated outside the courthouse after the sentencing, referring to FBI agent Leroy Simmons, also charged with the attempted murder of both Dallas Morrison and a Kellogg resident. Agent Simmons had served as Ms. Morrison's relocation agent.

"I guess you just don't know who you can trust," Morrison said as she left with her teammates from a local softball league.

✳ ✳ ✳

"Ball!"

PJ clapped her hands. "C'mon, Karla; she's a whiffer! Give her a knuckleball!"

"What's the score?" Jeremy stepped into the dugout and settled next to PJ on the bench, plopping a white bag onto her lap. "One of those is for me."

"Six to two, top of the fourth. No outs. Dally is in rare form. Last inning she tagged out a runner who popped up a ball and tried to make it to first."

"Aw, but she doesn't have your bullet throw to second," he said, not looking at her as he took a sip of coffee.

She glanced at him. *Wait—what?* "You saw the game?"

He nodded toward Morgan behind the plate. "How's her ankle?"

PJ gestured to her own uniform. "She can catch, but I'm her pinch hitter."

"And a bridesmaid, according to Stacey. She filled me in at the trial. You're going to look fabulous in peach."

"Please." She opened the bag and couldn't suppress a grin. Two fat bismarks lay side by side. "If I eat this now, I'm liable to hurl as I run to first base."

"A lovely visual, as usual, Sugar. And on such a beautiful morning."

She reached into the bag just as he snatched it from her lap. Glaze gooed her fingers, and she licked them one by one. "How'd you know I was playing?"

"I'm a PI. The sofa in the office was empty before noon on a Saturday morning. And I LoJacked your new wheels. In that order."

"You LoJacked me?"

"How else am I going to keep track of you?" Jeremy took a bismark from the bag, holding it in a napkin as he took a bite. He held the pastry out to her without looking. "Although there probably aren't that many vintage baby blue 1967 Volkswagen Beetles running around Minneapolis."

She took a bite, the custard filling the nooks and crannies of her stomach after a sparse breakfast of an old granola bar she'd found in her bag. She wiped her chin. "I know. She's a beauty, isn't she? I couldn't believe it when Gabby opened her garage and gave me her hidden treasure. Recently restored by Sammy, no less. I tried not to take it, but oh, it makes me feel normal again."

She grabbed Jeremy's wrist and took another bite of the bismark before he could take it away.

"So, I was wondering if I could borrow the Vic. I have some surveillance to do."

"You're on a case without me?"

"Your life is pretty busy—I mean, you're a Rocket now. You don't have time for me anymore."

"I'm never too busy for a case!"

He took another bite. "No, no. The Rockets need you."

"Listen, it's just fun to be a part of something bigger than myself again." PJ watched as Morgan delivered the signal to Karla.

"You still are. Kane and Sugar Investigations."

She turned to him, missing Karla's strike. "Really? Kane and Sugar?"

He grinned at her. "No."

"Funny. Thanks a lot."

He nudged her with his shoulder. "But maybe someday."

Maybe someday . . .

He'd said exactly nothing about their kiss two weeks ago, while she in the meantime untangled herself from Boone.

Not that she'd ever be completely untangled from Boone. Not when he knew her so well, understood her fears, her mistakes. But as she'd stood there in Dally's house, seeing her past and her future on two sides of the room, the truth hit her like one of Karla's in-the-pocket pitches.

She'd never be who she longed to be with Boone always reminding her of who she'd been and who he didn't want her to be.

"We're not done yet, Peej. I know you can't live without me." That painful conversation, out on the front lawn of Dally's house roughly an hour after he'd discovered her in Jeremy's embrace, still burned like an ember in her chest.

He'd shown up on her doorstep hoping to do some damage control after their fight. Instead, he'd discovered his future in pieces.

But couldn't he understand that she'd never look at him without seeing the PJ who so easily, so carelessly, jumped on the back of his motorcycle and rode off with her hands locked around his waist, right into trouble. And while Jeremy might embody his own brand of trouble, at least she didn't see her mistakes in his eyes when he looked at her.

Like now. Something deliciously mischievous swirled in Jeremy's eyes as he took another bite of bismark.

"Maybe someday?" she finally said.

He lifted a muscled shoulder. "You keep working on your PI license, and we'll see."

"So you haven't given up on me, even with the mess I made of . . . well, Dally and Gabby and even Boris."

"You did save Gabby from the old folks' home."

PJ held up a finger. "And located her jewelry. There was brilliance there."

But the real brilliance had been in the teary look in Gabby's eyes when they'd pushed aside the furniture and revealed Simon's stash of jewelry, including the emerald necklace. *"Thank you for believing in me, PJ."*

Jeremy finished off his bismark. "Mmm-hmm."

"And I helped Sammy propose."

"You're seriously taking credit for that?"

She cheered as Karla knocked off another strike.

He took another sip of coffee. "I will admit that the Boris thing turned out. Which brings me back to the Vic. Suppose he's going to get his own wheels soon? I'd sure like to borrow it."

"Give him a call. But if I find out you took him on a stakeout . . ."

"No worries there, Sugar. Hey, how are you and Connie doing?"

"Why, do you need your couch back?" She didn't exactly know where he'd gone to roost after she'd commandeered the office for her temporary lodgings. But yes, she had to find someplace else to stay, and soon.

"Nope."

Nothing else but a smile. He kept his eyes on the game.

"She's still mad. But the fact that Boris suddenly found a little of his old self again—the investigator—has her softening. He's applied for a couple security positions that Boone's lined up. And I got to take Davy to the beach last Saturday. Under guard, of course."

"Sergei?"

"My mother."

He grinned. "Right."

Karla struck out another hitter. PJ leaned back against the cool cement wall, settling her hand on the cage next to her. The animal inside let out a squeal.

Jeremy searched for the source, made a face. "You have got to be kidding me."

"It's a gift from Dally."

"It's a punishment."

"The fact that Dally would part with a chinchilla says a lot."

"Yeah. Like, 'I'll get you, my pretty'?"

The chinchilla spit at him.

"That's right, Puffy; you tell him."

"Puffy?"

"We're trying out names."

He shook his head and took another sip of coffee, watching as the next batter stepped up to the plate and smacked the ball hard to the shortstop. Stacey snatched it out of the air and peeled it off to first base.

The crowd behind them lit up with a cheer—Sammy and Gabby sitting on the bottom row, Missy and Rick on the end, Missy with a bold new red hue to her hair. PJ hadn't bothered to wave, to fill her in, to introduce herself. Some identities just couldn't be explained.

Like this new one, a woman jumping boldly into the arms of her heavenly Father, believing big in His mercy and grace. At least for now, that's what PJ was trying, one breathtaking day at a time.

Jeremy leaned forward, bracing his elbows on his knees, watching the game. "Listen, I've been meaning to apologize.

I should have listened to you about Dally's boyfriend. When you mentioned that Gabby had seen him recently—and when I heard the desperation in your voice—I knew I needed to press Dally about it. I wanted to kill her the moment Leroy's name left her mouth."

He stared at his cup, running his thumb along the edge. "I thought I was going to lose you," he said softly.

PJ didn't look at him, couldn't look at him. Not with the tangle of emotions in her chest, ones she couldn't—wasn't sure she *wanted* to—name nearly suffocating her. "Oh no, I was born to be a PI. You can't shake me that easily."

"That's right. The panther. I forgot."

"Better not," PJ said, grinning.

The team ran in from the field, flowing into the dugout. Dally settled beside PJ. "Hey there, boss," she said.

Jeremy lifted his coffee to her.

Karla stepped up to bat. She hit a beautiful line drive into center field on the first pitch.

Stacey took a couple practice swings and stepped into the batter's box.

"Sugar, you're on deck."

"Don't eat my donut," PJ said to Jeremy, rising.

"Only if you promise to knock it out of the park."

She stepped out of the dugout and looked back at him, with his baseball hat on backward, dark eyes brimming with something untamed even as he grinned at her.

"Oh," she said, trouble in her tone, "I promise."

Author's Note

A few years ago, I brought the wrong child to camp. It wouldn't have been a big deal except camp is six hours from my house (one way), and I'd made a big production of packing and making sure my son was all ready. Instead, my daughter should have been the one with the clean sleeping bag and the fresh socks. Somehow (through the graciousness of a good friend), she made it to camp, but the story lives in infamy in our family as an example of Mom's tendency to overcommit.

And it wouldn't be as funny if it didn't happen all the time. Yes, in my head I think I *can* write four books a year, redecorate my house, run the children's church program, write and produce a children's musical, run a story-crafting service, teach at conferences, speak at women's retreats, help my hubby with his business, and be the kind of mom who throws huge prom parties. It's just that they *all* sound like great ideas! And I like being at the center of the fun!

However, it doesn't get pretty when I miss events or perhaps lose my temper or wind up in bed with a migraine or a cold. Worse, I'm my own accuser—why can't I get it right? I hate my own mistakes, my own tendencies to get in over my head. I hate looking backward with a wince.

I brought this frustration to the page in *Double Trouble*—in PJ's desire to be the Greatest PI on Earth and her tendency to both overcommit and see trouble wherever she turns. I wanted her to fall, to scrub her chin on the ground, and to taste failure. Because only then could I tell her what I long to hear myself—that God doesn't expect us to be perfect or not to make mistakes. He longs to forgive us . . . and then to empower us.

"Draw with confidence to the throne of grace, because I promise you'll find mercy." I love that message, because it's when I am most distraught that I must remember God is the best friend I can have. He's not going to love me less after He saves me than before! He longs to reach out and pull me close, despite my perceived ugliness, because He is crazy about me, as hard as that is for me to believe sometimes. *"Draw with confidence. . . ."*

The PJ Sugar series is all about discovering that God has great plans for even messy girls—like PJ, like me. He likes them! He made them this way, and He doesn't expect them to be perfect. I hope you'll continue PJ's journey with me in the next book, tentatively titled *Licensed for Trouble*, due out later this year. Thank you for reading. Draw with confidence, friend!

IN HIS GRACE,
Susan May Warren

About the Author

Susan May Warren is a former missionary to Russia, the mother of four children, and the wife of a guy who wooed her onto the back of his motorcycle for the adventure of a lifetime. The award-winning author of over twenty books, Susan loves to write and teach writing. She speaks at women's events around the country about God's amazing grace in our lives. Susan is active in her church and small community and makes her home on the north shore of Minnesota, where her husband runs a hotel.

Visit her Web site at **www.susanmaywarren.com**.

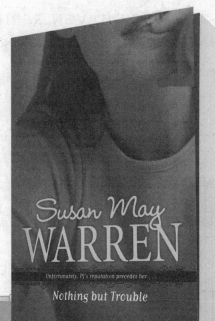

More great fiction from

SUSAN MAY WARREN

THE DEEP HAVEN SERIES

Romance, suspense, and adventure on Minnesota's North Shore . . .

THE TEAM HOPE SERIES

Meet Team Hope—members of an elite search-and-rescue team who run to the edge of danger to bring others back. Unfortunately, they can't seem to stay out of trouble. . . .

THE NOBLE LEGACY SERIES

After their father dies, three siblings reunite on the family ranch to try to preserve the Noble legacy. If only family secrets—and unsuspected enemies—didn't threaten to destroy everything they've worked so hard to build.

A CHRISTMAS NOVELLA

A story about family, traditions, and rediscovering the *real* magic of Christmas.